P9-CQU-988

"Delightful romances involving colorful and yet realistic characters make these two stories by Maureen Child a veritable feast for the eyes. The large Italian family of the Candellanos is very convincing and the characterizations are so mature and honest that the author is to be applauded for such skillful crafting and accurate portrayal . . . the heartfelt emotions leap from the pages, and the delicately blended humor and pathos render these stories memorable . . . after the exhilarating first story, readers will feel compelled to read the other one too, and neither disappoints. Maureen Child is an author to watch out for."

—*The Road to Romance*

"A fresh tale of family, conflict, and love . . . the characters are endearing."

—*Old Book Barn Gazette*

"Both of these novels are engaging contemporary romances with a warm ensemble that feels like the kitchen of many readers. The story lines will hook readers because the characters seem genuine and friendly."

—*Harriet's Book Review*

"Fall in love with this delightful family with these two tales, and prepare yourself for the next installment."

—TheRomanceReader.com

St. Martin's Paperbacks Titles
by Maureen Child

And Then Came You:

Sam's Story

MAUREEN CHILD

St. Martin's Paperbacks

AND THEN CAME YOU: SAM'S STORY

Copyright © 2004 by Maureen Child.

ISBN: 0-312-99752-3
EAN: 80312-99752-6

Printed in the United States of America

St. Martin's Paperbacks edition / July 2004

St. Martin's Paperbacks are published by St. Martin's Press, 175 Fifth Avenue, New York, NY 10010.

10 9 8 7 6 5 4 3 2 1

For Mark
Always

Chapter One

The summer of hell was just getting started.

And Samantha Marconi was already dreading it.

"You'd think I could at least have some coffee," she muttered grimly as she glared into her pitiful substitute for a morning beverage. Tea. What was the point? Without *real* caffeine, how could she be expected to face what was coming?

Outside the cluttered but clean kitchen of the Marconi family home, a summer storm raged. Tiny fists of rain battered the windows and raced down the gutters. Sam shivered.

Symbols of foreboding crouched in every corner of the room like medieval gargoyles waiting for the opportunity to pounce. Anyone with half a brain could see that the cards had been stacked against them. The wrath of the gods was about to fall. The boom was lowering.

As if nature were determined to prove her right, the trees were whipped by a wind that drove in off the ocean and slapped a loose shutter against the side of the house.

Have to fix that. She jotted it down on the mental list of notes she was constantly updating. Of course, she'd made the same mental note during the last storm, but that wasn't really important at the moment. What was important was that she was the only member of the Marconi Construction Company who'd bothered to show up for the meeting.

She took another swig of tea, and made a face at the taste just as the back door flew open.

Sam jumped as the doorknob slammed into the permanent notch in the wall that had been carved by years of Marconi girls flinging that door open with enthusiasm. A tall woman dressed in a fire-engine-red rain slicker stood framed in the open doorway. Her blue eyes danced and a smile curved her wide mouth. Rain rushed in around her as if it had been perched on the porch waiting for a chance to sneak inside.

"Shut the door." Sam inched her chair away from the fingers of wetness reaching for her.

"Hi to you, too."

Under the big table, Papa's huge golden retriever, Bear, whined and thumped his tail against the floor in greeting. Sam was feeling less enthusiastic.

She tossed a quick look over at her younger sister and snarled. "Don't push me, Mike. I haven't had coffee. Where were you?"

Michaela Marconi grinned and lifted a cardboard tray high, as if she were offering up her firstborn child to the gods. "Getting supplies. Crap, you're still miserable in the morning."

Sam's gaze fixed on that tray and the three tall cups nestled within. Her nose twitched, blood pumped, and something close to awareness skittered inside. "If that's coffee, I'll consider letting you live."

"Better than coffee." Mike's blond eyebrows lifted for emphasis. "Lattes. From Stevie's."

"There is a God and She loves me." Sam sighed dreamily. Stevie Ryan Candellano, the mistress of the coffee bean, made perhaps the best latte in central California. Here in Chandler, Stevie's shop, The Leaf and Bean, was a gathering place for the locals and a mecca for customers willing to drive in from Carmel and Monterey just for a taste of one of her cinnamon rolls. The woman was a wizard in the kitchen, give her an espresso machine and Stevie could light up your world like nobody else.

"Muffins, too?" Sam shoved her hated cup of tea aside and made a grab for the closest coffee cup just as soon as Mike set it on the table.

"Of course." Mike shucked the rain slicker, shook it once, flinging droplets of icy water in every conceivable direction, then hung it on a hook by the door. Her blond hair was braided and lay in a single thick rope across her right shoulder. Her black T-shirt was stamped MARCONI CONSTRUCTION and the letters were faded. Her jeans were worn and faded, too, and her work boots looked as though she'd been kicking ass for generations. Plopping one hand on her hip, she said, "Cinnamon streusel and those blueberry ones with the crunchies on top. And," she added, reaching into the bag, "a plain biscotti for Bear." She tossed it under the table and grinned at the eager crunching sounds.

"You may live," Sam muttered, taking her first sip and letting the magic slide deep inside her.

"Gee, thanks." Taking a seat in her traditional spot at the wide kitchen table, Mike grabbed her own cup of coffee and shook her head. "I'm so glad you moved back in just to make my life a carnival."

Sam was the first to admit that it felt a little weird to

be living in her father's house again. After all, she'd
been out on her own for five years. But while her new
house was being tented for termites and having its
scarred floor sanded and varnished, here she sat. Still,
it could have been worse. At least the Marconi "mansion" was here, as always, just waiting to be *home*
again.

The pale lemon-yellow walls of the kitchen were determinedly cheerful and most of the appliances were as
old as Sam was. Despite its ragged-around-the-edges
appearance though, it was an inviting house. A place
that welcomed you in, then surrounded you with the
good kind of vibes that attached themselves to homes
where love lived. She'd grown up here. The middle
daughter of three. She'd fought with her sisters,
sneaked out of her room to go to parties and been
grounded when she was caught. She'd laughed and
cried and always known that this place . . . this one
spot in the universe . . . was where she would always
be welcomed.

Temporarily living at home wasn't too bad. Of
course, living with Mike again was a different story.

"Quiet," Sam said. "I'll need a minute, here." She
closed her eyes and took another sip, feeling every cell
in her body slowly shudder and wake itself. Okay,
maybe hell wouldn't be so bad after all. She mentally
sent all the little forebodings of disaster into hiberna-
tion and tried to focus on her little sister.

Mike continued to mutter to herself, but otherwise
kept quiet. It was a comfortable thing, Sam thought.
The crashing storm outside, the familiar warmth of the
old kitchen surrounding her, and a hot cup of coffee

cupped between her palms. What more could anyone want?

"Good." Another voice growled from the doorway leading to the living room. "You're both here."

Sam sighed. *Solitude would be good.*

"You're the late one," Mike pointed out, already tearing the crunchy top off one of the blueberry muffins.

Josefina Marconi tossed her head, sending a dark brown ponytail swinging back over her shoulder. Her T-shirt was bright red, also stamped MARCONI CON-STRUCTION, but naturally, on Jo's shirt, the lettering was crisp and neat. As were her jeans. Dark blue denim that somehow or other Jo managed to keep clean despite the amount of work she did. Her work boots looked as though they'd been polished—and probably had been. Jo was the organized one. The one to whom lists were foreplay and a good filing system was damn near a sexual experience.

Sam shook her head. She herself fell somewhere between the two women—and not just in the birth order. Not as neat as Jo, nor as disorganized as Mike, Sam was the happy medium. At twenty-seven, she was the peacemaker, the one who jumped into the middle of any raging Marconi storm and spilled oil on churning water.

The Marconi girls never changed. And, Sam told herself as she half-listened to Mike giving Jo a hard time, there was a familiar comfort in that.

This was her place in the universe. The house where she was raised, here, in Chandler, California, would always be home. Chandler was small enough to be cozy but big enough to avoid the claustrophobic atmosphere some small towns had that choked the life out of their citizens.

Chandler sat smack in the middle of California. Bordered on one side by the ocean and on the other by a stand of trees thick enough to actually be called a forest, it had the best of both worlds. The sea breeze drifted through town, easing the hottest days of summer, and the smell of the pines at Christmastime gave you the feeling of being trapped in a Currier & Ives lithograph.

Chandler was Mayberryesque. Heaven knew she'd heard enough of the tourists muttering just that to be aware of it. But it was more than that, too. The town had started generations ago as a cluster of houses springing up along the coast road.

People had lived here and gone to work at the canneries, on the fishing boats, or at the wineries that dotted the California landscape. A lot of those first settlers had been Italian, drawn to the climate which was so much like that of the country they missed so desperately. And little by little, over the years, Chandler had grown and blossomed until it was a small city in its own right and had no need to depend on outside jobs to support it.

Sam'd grown up here. She'd gone away to college and come home to mourn when things hadn't gone just as she'd planned. She'd mourned again when they'd lost their mother nine years ago, but together the Marconis had come out the other side of pain stronger than when they'd gone in.

"Earth to Sam!" Jo huffed out a breath, stepped into the room, snatched up the last cup of coffee, and sat down in the chair that had been hers since she'd left a highchair behind. "I'm late because I was on the phone."

"With who?"

Mike asked the question. Sam didn't really care who Jo'd been talking to. Not yet, anyway. She'd need a few more sips of latte to get from merely awake to interested.

"Our former secretary," Jo snapped and rustled one hand into the bag from the Leaf and Bean before pulling out a cinnamon-streusel-topped muffin. Practically growling, she took a bite as though she wished it were someone's head.

"Former?" Mike asked.

"That's what I said." Jo sat up straighter in her chair and shook her head fiercely, until her hair whipped from side to side like a happy dog's tail. "*Former.* Tina just quit."

"I knew it," Sam muttered, finally feeling as though she were fortified enough to join the conversation. "I could feel it in the air. Bad stuff coming."

"God," Mike said on a snort. "You sound like Nana."

Jo laughed shortly and reached down to pet Bear's big head.

Sam was not amused. She lifted her right hand, pointed her index finger and pinky in the age-old ward-off-the-evil-eye hand sign, and said, "Whatever works."

"Well hell, why not go outside and clack two sticks together?" Mike rolled her blue eyes and blew out a breath that ruffled her bangs.

"Everyone knows you do that to cut a storm, not to

ward off doom," Sam said with a half-smile. Seriously, coffee could improve your outlook until even the har- bingers of disaster could look like fluffy kittens.

"Back to reality, if you don't mind?" Jo waved one hand until she had their attention. "We are now short one secretary just when the Big Job is set to start."

"You don't have to say 'big job' in capital letters."

"That's what you think." Jo flicked Mike a quick look, then dismissed her. "This is as Big as it gets and we all know it."

Oh boy, did Sam know it.

Every summer, without fail, the city of Chandler's very own local wacko brought in a construction team to work on her house. Sounded simple, of course. And that's where the trap lay. Because there was *nothing* simple about Grace Van Horn and her never-ending quest to drive carpenters, contractors, and all of their teams insane.

A widow, Grace had more money than she knew what to do with and enough free time to make her dangerous. The major construction firms in the area took turns deal- ing with her. And this summer . . . the Marconis were up to bat. From July through September, they'd be working with Grace. It made Sam tired just to think about it.

So she didn't.

"Maybe it won't be so bad this year," Mike said wistfully.

"Oh, please," Jo said. "Last year, Grace changed her mind about the Italian tile for the foyer so often, Mr. Donovan had to take a 'rest' afterward."

Sam rolled her eyes. "It wasn't that bad. I mean, he had that ulcer before Grace."

"Yeah, but it wasn't *bleeding* until she got to him."

"Good point," Sam said. "And the year before that, there was the fiasco with Baker Construction. I don't think Mr. Baker *planned* on retiring that early."

"His own fault," Mike put in. "He never should have gone along with Grace about that astronomical tower on the roof. No way were the beams strong enough to support that mess."

"That's the point," Jo snapped. "Grace has a way of talking you into doing things you'd *never* consider otherwise."

"Okay, fine," Sam acknowledged. "It's going to be misery and we all know it." Just thinking about a summer of Grace made that happy coffee glow slide away and Sam wished to hell Mike had brought back a gallon of the stuff.

"But well-paid misery, and isn't that the important part?" Mike lifted her coffee cup in silent salute as she tossed Bear a piece of her muffin.

Yeah, Sam thought. But wasn't there a steep price when you traded your soul for gold? "God, it's going to be a long summer," she moaned.

"Is *no one* going to ask why Tina quit her job?" Disgusted, Jo looked from one to the other of her sisters.

"Fine." Sam straightened up, willing to talk about absolutely anything besides Grace Van Horn and the coming headaches. "I'll bite. Why'd she quit?"

"Cash Hunter."

"Him again?" Mike squirmed in her chair, planted her forearms on the table and leaned toward her sister. "He got to another one?"

Cash Hunter, mysterious carpenter, man of all work, and apparently the champion Woman Whisperer of all time. One night with this guy and women were lining up to go off and be Dr. Schweitzer, Madame Curie, and Mother Teresa all rolled into one. He'd been in town only a little over six months and already he'd become a legend.

"Tina told me she was leaving town. Going back home to Georgia to work for Habitat for Humanity."

Sam winced. "Well, you can't fault her for wanting to do a good thing."

"I didn't say that," Jo snapped, throwing her hands wide. "Sure, it's nice. But what is it about this guy that can make women take sharp right turns with their lives? I mean, before this, the closest Tina's ever come to altruistic was *not* asking for change when she handed the Salvation Army Santa five dollars last Christmas."

"What happened to Lisa?" Sam wondered aloud, as she flipped through her mental list, trying to recall the other women Cash had charmed into sainthood.

"She moved to L.A.," Mike said around a mouthful of muffin. "She's working with the Literacy Foundation. Really loving it."

Jo nodded, waved one hand at her. "And Paula?"

"Oh, I know this one," Sam said, perking right up. "Paula's living in Chechnya now. Working for a foundation that arranges adoption for war orphans."

"Cash Hunter must be stopped," Jo muttered darkly. "This guy is like a master hypnotist or something. Is he drugging them?"

"Oh," Mike said. "That's good. Now he's an evil scientist."

"Well, he's *something*. I don't get it. Just don't get how a man can make a woman come all unglued."

Mike snorted. "Apparently you have *not* been meeting the right men."

"Funny." Jo shifted a look at Sam. "Seriously though, what is this guy up to? What is he doing that's so fabulous it makes women want to turn their lives around?"

"I volunteer to find out," Mike said, grinning.

"You stay the hell away from him," Jo said, offering some of her muffin to Bear.

Sam laughed and shook her head. "No wonder that dog's getting fat. And stop taking Cash so personal, Jo."

"The dog's not fat. And the Cash thing is just weird."

"Fine," Mike offered. "You want me to stay away from him, *you* go sleep with him. But report back to us before you run off to join a convent."

"You just get funnier and funnier."

"I try hard."

"Not hard enough," Jo muttered, then ignored Mike to shoot a look at Sam. "We're gonna need a new secretary."

A curl of worry unwound in the pit of Sam's stomach. "Don't look at me."

"Why not? You'd be great."

Sam glared at Mike. "Thanks, I don't think so."

"Come on, you're perfect for it. You'll be dealing with Grace anyway and—"

The imaginary gargoyles Sam had entertained earlier perched on her shoulder and howled. "Why'm I going to be dealing with her?"

Jo and Mike exchanged a quick, secretive look that told Sam that this had already been discussed and she'd been chosen. She choked on a gulp of coffee and coughed hard enough that she was pretty sure her eyeballs were going to pop out of her head and roll across the table. And still she managed to croak, "No way."

"She likes you," Jo said.

"Because I almost never argue with her like *some-one*"—she glanced at Mike—"I could mention."

"Hey, I have opinions."

"Too many." Jo glared her youngest sister into silence, momentarily. "You worked well with her last time, Sam."

"That was three years ago."

"And it's our turn again," Jo said. "We all know it. We all deal with it. *You* get to handle it." She took another bite of muffin and, now that the matter seemed settled, acted as if she were really enjoying herself.

"I don't get a vote in this?" Sam was sputtering now and she knew it.

"Sure you get a vote," Mike put in. "But you're one vote, we're two. Majority wins. Congrats."

"Ain't democracy grand?" Jo asked no one in particular.

"My own family turning on me."

"Damn straight." Mike grinned and took a long drink of her coffee. *"And,"* she added, "let's not forget the Home Show in July."

The Home Show.

This just kept getting better.

Every year, the San Jose Convention Center hosted the Home Show, giving local contractors, designers, and suppliers a chance to show their wares to the thousands of people who lined up to see the latest in home improvement. And like everyone else in the county, the Marconis would have their own booth where they'd demonstrate home repairs, painting techniques, and solicit new clients for the business.

It was three solid days of making nice and answering dumb questions—with the added fun of keeping Mike from losing her temper while answering those dumb questions.

Sam shuddered. "Can't I please forget?"

"Not a chance," Mike said, laughing. "But Jo's taking care of the booth setup since you're gonna be dealing with Grace."

"And what's *your* job this summer, then?" Jo said, gaze narrowed.

"Watching you guys." Mike shot a look at each of her sisters and gave them a slow grin.

Jo wadded up a napkin and threw it across the table at her.

Sam groaned.

Trapped like a rat.

No way out.

The summer of hell was just getting started and already she felt the flames licking at the soles of her feet.

"Hey," Jo said, "could be worse."

Rain blustered against the windows and the wind howled. That loose shutter slammed into the house with the rhythm of a heartbeat and the light in the kitchen dimmed, then brightened as the power flickered. As signs went, not that dramatic.

"Never say that," Sam warned. "It's a direct challenge to the gods."

"Really, Sam." Mike shook her head slowly. "*Way* too much like Nana."

Maybe, she thought. But it didn't hurt to cover your bases. Besides, Sam'd noticed over the years that once things started going downhill, more often than not, they just picked up speed.

• • •

By afternoon, the sun was shining and water was dripping off the trees in the front yard. In fact, she'd just about convinced herself that maybe they'd survive the summer of hell after all.

Until the doorbell rang.

With a fresh fight brewing between her sisters, and Bear snoring under the table, Sam gratefully escaped the kitchen where they'd been working for hours, and headed through the living room. She hardly glanced at the big, square room with its overstuffed sofas, magazine-littered coffee table, and rose-colored walls decorated with years' worth of framed family photos.

She grabbed the brass knob, turned it, and yanked the door open. Good thing she still had a grip on the doorknob. It gave her something to hold on to while her world rocked.

He was taller than she remembered.

It had been nine years since she'd seen him. Since he broke her heart. And he hadn't even had the decency to get bald and fat.

"Hi, Sam," the voice from the past said. "Been a while."

Chapter Two

"Oh, my God."

She'd expected the UPS guy, delivering her new paintbrushes. The one person in the world she *hadn't* expected was Jeff Hendricks. Her lying, treacherous, backstabbing, no-good, son of a bitch ex-husband.

Now maybe people will listen to me when I talk about signs of foreboding.

For one wild, weird moment, Sam was eighteen again. Pain glanced through her body like sunlight bouncing off a mirror. His ink-black hair was still just a little too long, grazing the top of his shirt collar. His deep blue eyes were fixed on her and the mouth that had once done some amazing things to her body was nothing more than a grim slash across his features.

He didn't look any happier to see her than she was to see him. Small comfort.

So why was he here?

"A while?" she echoed finally. "Not long enough."

"Good to see you, too," he said tightly.

She still hadn't let go of the doorknob and she thought about giving it a hard push, slamming the door in his face, and pretending she'd never opened it. As if he could read her mind, he spoke up again quickly.

"We have to talk."

Sam laughed shortly. Couldn't help it, really. It blew out of her throat and scraped the air. "Oh, that's a good one, coming from you."

When she'd tried to talk to him nine years before, he hadn't even bothered to answer her letters. *Now* he wanted to talk? She didn't think so.

He sighed, then swept the edges of his brown sport coat back and shoved both hands into the pockets of his slacks. If he started jingling the coins in his pockets, she just might hit him.

"I don't like this any more than you do," he said.

"Sam?" Jo's voice, coming from the kitchen. "Who is it?"

She stiffened. Her sisters wouldn't be real pleased to see the man still referred to in the Marconi household as the Bastard standing on the porch. Best to just get rid of him before a bloodbath could erupt.

Man, how could a day go from crappy to downright rotten in the time it took to open a door?

"Nobody," she called back and wished it were true. Instead, her day was still racing downhill and the speed was blinding.

Stepping out onto the porch, Sam pushed past him, pulling the door closed behind her. It was as if the morning rain had never happened. The sky was a blue so clear it almost hurt to look at it and the wind carried the fresh scent of the sea. From down the street came the sounds of kids playing at the park and she caught a whiff of smoke in the air, telling her that Mr. Bozeman was firing up his back-yard grill.

Everything was as it should be.

Normal.

Except for the fact that a man from her past was suddenly crowding her present. Dammit, a woman shouldn't be distracted when trying to deal with someone like Jeff. She needed all cylinders firing. All thrusters up and moving.

All bullets primed and pointed.

Sam walked across the porch and stomped down the five steps to the brick walkway leading to the street. She didn't bother to look behind her. She knew Jeff was following her. Not only could she hear his footsteps on the worn brick, she *felt* him.

And how weird was that?

He reached out, grabbed her arm, and pulled her around to face him. A bolt of something hot and completely inappropriate sliced through her like lightning spearing through storm clouds. For one heart-stopping second, she was eighteen again and feeling that electric charge that only happened when Jeff touched her.

It had always been that way between them. Right from the first. And in that eternity-filled second, she remembered everything she had spent nine years trying to forget. Heat poured through her, boiling her blood and clouding her brain.

Instinctively, Sam yanked free of his grasp and took a step back. "Do *not* touch me."

"Sorry." He lifted both hands in mock surrender and nodded agreement to her terms. "It's just—" He stopped, glanced around, then shifted his gaze back to her. "This is harder than I thought it would be."

Something cold and tight squeezed Sam's heart, but she steeled herself against it. She'd wasted too many nights crying into her pillow over him. She'd buried her dreams, surrendered her innocence, and she wouldn't go back. Not now. Not ever. Whatever he had to say to her didn't matter. He wasn't a part of her life anymore. He was just . . . a life lesson learned. "Say what you came to say and then leave."

She hadn't changed.

Somehow, Jeff had expected . . . hell, he wasn't even sure of that. But he *hadn't* counted on taking one look at her and getting slammed in the chest with what felt like a hammer blow. He should have known this wouldn't be easy. Nothing about Sam had ever been easy. That was part of her attraction all those years ago.

Until Sam, no woman had ever refused him. Sounded cocky as hell to admit, but it was the simple truth. Some of those women had been more interested in his bank balance than him, but still. He'd never struck out with a woman until the first time Sam had said no to an invitation to dinner. And damned if her resistance hadn't made her all the more appealing. They'd come together in a rush of heat and want and need and they'd convinced themselves it was love. But if it had been, it wouldn't have burned out like it had, right?

Yet here he was again, standing next to her, looking down into those same, pale blue eyes and feeling too damn much.

Nine years was a long time. And God knew he had plenty of reason to resent Samantha Marconi—although he had one very good reason to be glad they'd been together, no matter how briefly. She stood there glaring at him, and damned if a part of him didn't enjoy it. Her blue eyes flashed with sparks and the demented part of him found it both annoying and arousing.

Her long, reddish-brown hair fell down her back from a clip at the nape of her neck. It looked as soft as ever and he was half-tempted to reach out and touch those tumbling curls, just to see. But he figured she'd take his hand off at the elbow in the attempt, so he let that one go.

She wore curve-hugging jeans that were faded and decorated by splotches of dried paint in a rainbow of colors. Her dark blue T-shirt, proclaiming MARCONI CONSTRUCTION in faded white letters, fit her way too well and the toe of her heavy work boot tapped against the bricks like a clock ticking off the last remaining seconds before a bomb blast.

Her blue eyes were wary and the jut of her chin told him that she hadn't mellowed any over the years. Fine. Just as well.

"Sam, there's a problem."

"A big one as far as I'm concerned," she said, folding her arms over her chest. "You're here."

"Just as sweet as ever, I see."

"Why would I change?"

"Dammit, do you always have to immediately go on the defensive?"

"Hello? When being attacked, defending yourself is pretty much standard operating procedure."

"Who's attacking?"

"You."

"I haven't said anything yet." Stupid. He knew it was stupid and he still couldn't stop himself. They were sliding right back into the same kind of arguments they used to have. The circular kind. Where

there was no beginning and no end. It just was. Like
mold on bread. It was a fact of life that defied descrip-
tion.

"You're here, aren't you?"

"To tell you something."

"Write me a letter." She started past him for the
house and he had to risk losing a hand by grabbing her
arm again.

"Dammit, Sam—"

Her gaze fixed on his hand for a long minute, then
she lifted it and looked directly into his eyes. "Move
that hand or lose it."

He was desperate, not foolish. He released her. "We
have to talk."

"We have nothing to say to each other."

"Wanna bet?" He was following her, his long legs
keeping pace with her quicker steps.

"We're divorced," she reminded him.

"Wanna bet?" he asked.

She stopped dead.

At least he had her attention. He hadn't planned on
blurting out the truth like this, but trust Sam to make
any conversation the beginning of World War III. "Finally. A breakthrough."

"What're you talking about?" Her voice was hoarse
and now that he was looking a little closer he could see
that the gleam in her eye was more of a glassy look.

"Are you sick?" he asked.

"Getting sicker by the minute," she shot back.
"Now, are you going to explain the whole 'divorce'
statement or not?"

He pushed one hand through his hair, then shoved
that hand in his pants pocket again. Old habits kicked

in and he started to jingle his keys nervously until he saw her left eye twitch. Then he remembered how she'd always hated that habit of his and decided he didn't need to infuriate her even further, so he stopped. "The divorce never went through," he said bluntly, figuring there was no easy way to say it. "We're still married."

Her mouth opened and closed a time or two. She blinked, then stumbled backward and plopped down hard onto the third step. Tipping her head back, she inhaled sharply, blew it out again and said, "What?"

"You heard me. Dammit, I can't believe it, either, but it's true. The county clerk who handled the paperwork? He never filed the papers."

"He never—" She pushed herself up from the step, walked a few paces, then whirled around to stare at him. "What do you mean, he didn't do it? It was his *job*."

"Apparently, he didn't much like his job."

"So he just didn't do it?"

"Right." He watched her face, noted each emotion as it played over her features and understood completely. Since he'd gotten the call from the county seat a week ago, he'd been going through the same thing. "No consolation, but we're not the only ones."

"Huh?" She shook her head as if trying to clear her vision while she looked at him.

"There are fifty other couples out there, still married when they thought they weren't."

She held up one hand. "Color me selfish, but all I'm thinking about at the moment is *us*. We're really still—"

"Married. Yeah."

"Oh, my God."

"That about covers it."

Behind her, the front door opened. Jeff shot a look at the woman stepping outside. "Hi, Mike."

"Oh crap," Sam muttered, and he thought that summed up the situation pretty well.

Mike didn't smile, just called out over her shoulder, "Hey, Jo. The Bastard's here."

"Great," Jeff muttered.

"Shut up, Mike." Sam shot her sister a warning look that Mike paid no attention to at all.

"What's *he* doing here?" Jo demanded, pushing past her younger sister to come down the steps and stand beside Sam.

"Hi, Jo," he said, despite the frigid atmosphere suddenly swirling around him.

There was a time when the Marconi girls had actually liked him, Jeff remembered. Now, he'd be lucky if he left here with all his limbs attached. They weren't happy to see him? Well, tough shit. It's not like he'd been looking forward to this little reunion, either.

"I thought we weren't speaking to him." Jo's voice, soft.

"We're not." Mike walked to the edge of the porch and picked up one of the hammers out of an open toolbox. Slowly, she slapped the heavy metal hammer head into her palm as she kept her gaze on Jeff.

He could take a hint. Besides, he'd done what he came here to do. And it was plain he and Sam wouldn't be talking any further right now. Not with her sisters ready to rip his lips off. He was only surprised that Hank Marconi, his genial ex—or not so ex—father-in-law wasn't out here, demanding his head.

"You need to go, Jeff." Sam's gaze, still locked with his.

"I'm going."

"And don't come back." Mike walked down the steps, too, flanking the other side of Sam.

The sisters were more different than alike; the only feature they shared were the pale blue eyes they'd inherited from their father. Yet no one seeing them now could ever doubt their connection. The three of them stood there, not even touching, yet linked together into a single unit to stand against all invaders. And even though it frustrated the hell out of him to be facing it, a part of him wondered what solidarity like that felt like.

"Good advice," Jo pointed out.

"Okay, look." Deliberately ignoring the other two women, Jeff stared only at Sam. "I'm staying at the Coast Inn. When you're ready to talk, call me."

"Yeah," Jo snorted. "That'll happen."

"Get out of town, weasel-dog."

He shot a glance at Sam's sisters. "Really good to know the Marconi girls haven't changed any."

Jo and Mike looked ready to rumble, but it was Sam who answered him. "No, we haven't. But you haven't changed, either, Jeff. Still giving orders, expecting them to be followed."

"I'm not—"

"Mike's right. Go away."

Frustration simmered inside him, but there was no help for it. He wasn't going to get anywhere with her now, and besides, he had to get back to the inn anyway. He'd already been gone longer than he'd planned.

Nodding, he turned and headed for his car, parked at the curb. With every step, he felt the icy stares of three sets of eyes boring into his back—and he was grateful the Marconis weren't armed with more than a hammer.

Two hours later, the Marconi sisters were still arguing in circles.

"It's a good thing Papa's not here," Mike grumbled. "He'd have a stroke."

"Thanks," Sam said. "That's helpful."

Mike jumped up off the overstuffed sofa and stalked around the living room. "You want helpful? How about I go over to the Coast Inn and hit him with a hammer until he doesn't move anymore?"

"For God's sake, Mike, sit down." Jo sounded more resigned than angry and Sam thought that, at least, was a step in the right direction.

"How can you and Jo both be so calm?"

"This is *not* calm," Sam told her younger sister. She didn't feel calm. She felt . . . as if she were standing between two boats, with a foot in each, while trying to keep her balance during storm surf. Sooner or later, she was going to get wet. The question was, would she drown? "This is . . . hell, I don't know what it is." She lifted her gaze to Jo. "Can you believe this?"

"No." Jo scowled thoughtfully into her Diet Coke. "What's he want from you, anyway?"

"A divorce, apparently." Sam shook her head and leaned back into the sofa cushion. Snatching up a pale pink throw pillow, she clutched it to her middle like a shield. "But Mike started swinging her hammer before he could tell me."

"Should have hit him with it," Mike said, still radiating fury.

"Not until we know what's going on." Jo's voice was calm, cool, but her eyes flashed with indignation. "I'm guessing he's got more divorce papers for you to sign."

"More divorce papers. For God's sake, I'm *married.*" Sam still couldn't believe it. For nine years, she'd lived her life as a divorcée. The very first divorced woman in the history of the Marconi family—as Nana had continually reminded her for the first year or so of her humiliation. The taunts had finally stopped when Sam had offered to sew a big red *D* on her clothes.

But now what? She'd dated. She'd had sex. Okay, not a lot of sex, but *some.* Did that make her an adulterer? Great. So now the scarlet letter on her clothes would have to be the *real* scarlet letter? "This is great," she said, "just perfect. It's a wonder women aren't lining up outside the house just to take their turn at having my life. It's just so damned entertaining."

"So long as you've got your sense of humor," Jo said.

Sam sneered at her.

"So what're you gonna do?" Mike stopped pacing and dropped onto the sofa, sinking into the old, faded cushions. She propped her booted feet on the battered coffee table, scattering magazines to the floor.

"Go talk to him, I guess."

"I vote a big no to that," Mike said hotly.

"You don't get a vote." Sam threw the pillow at her.

"You shouldn't go alone," Jo said.

"It's not like he's some psycho stalker or something," Sam argued.

"Nope," Mike muttered again, "just a bastard."

"You're not helping," Jo told her.

"And you are?"

While Jo and Mike argued without her, Sam's brain raced with too many thoughts to keep track of. She'd been doing so well. She'd put Jeff and everything he represented into a small corner of her mind and only took it out three or four times a year to torture herself. She'd moved on. Built a life that had nothing to do with the girl she'd once been and her long-forgotten dreams. But now she was faced with him in the flesh. Right here in Chandler.

The past was suddenly way too close.

And Sam knew there'd be no letting go of it again until all the *t*s were crossed and all the *i*s dotted.

"I have to tell him."

"Are you *insane*?" Mike's voice hitched high enough to crack glass.

"That might not be a good idea," Jo said.

"Ya think?" Mike choked out a laugh as she jumped off the couch to stalk around the perimeter of the room.

Sam shook her head. "He has a right to know. And I have to tell him."

Jo took a drink of her soda, then bent to set the glass on the table in front of her. "He didn't want to know nine years ago, remember?"

"Do you really think I could forget?" Sam jumped up from the couch and stared at her sisters. They'd been there for her through all of it. But they hadn't actually *lived* any of it. They couldn't know. Couldn't possibly understand what it had been like to survive when you thought your heart was breaking.

She did, though.

Sam had made it through and now, nine years later, she had to do what she thought was best. Despite what her family thought. Despite the fact that Jeff wouldn't want to hear it.

"Yes, I remember," she said, and heard the soft catch in her own voice but couldn't do a thing to stop it. "I remember all of it."

Mike frowned and grabbed up a throw pillow, hugging it close to her chest. Jo stood up and, after shooting a glare at Mike, faced Sam. "It's probably not a good idea."

"Maybe not."

"It won't change anything."

"I know that, too."

"And you're still determined to tell him?"

Sam inhaled sharply, deeply, then let the air slide from her lungs. "Jo, the man's got a right to know he has a daughter out there somewhere."

"Yeah?" Mike asked, stepping up to stand beside them. "And when you tell him you put your baby up for adoption? Then what?"

A small ribbon of pain wrapped itself around Sam's heart and gave a twist. "Then I'll sign the divorce papers. Again. And we'll go back to our own lives."

And right now, even the looming chore of having to deal with the summer of hell was looking pretty good to Sam. Anything, to get back on an even footing. To get back to the world as she knew it. A world where she and Jeff Hendricks were simply casual strangers who happened to have made a baby while sharing an all-too-brief marriage.

"Sooner the better, you ask me," Mike said, glowering at no one in particular.

"Who asked you?" Jo challenged.

"You should have," Mike retorted, "but nobody listens to the youngest."

"Ask yourself why," Sam said.

"Jealousy, pure and simple." Mike laughed and held out her right hand.

"Whatever helps you sleep nights." Jo slapped her right hand on top of Mike's, then the two of them waited for Sam to complete the triad.

When she did and the three of them stood joined together, as they had since they were children, Jo spoke softly. "Your call, Sam. But whatever you decide to do, we're with you."

Chapter Three

The Coast Inn had started out in life as a private home on a huge tract of land. Now, over a hundred years later, the stately Victorian stood on a narrow slice of land on the ocean side of Pacific Coast Highway.

The constant whir of traffic roared in counterpoint to the ocean, which slammed into the rocky beach just below the inn's gracefully sloping back yard.

Sam drove into the inn's wide parking lot, pulled into a diagonal slot, and turned off the engine. Her hands fisted on the steering wheel until she determinedly relaxed them. She took a deep, calming breath. But she wasn't fooled.

She wasn't calm.

She wasn't peaceful. What she was, was furious.

A neatly buried deep-down, fury nibbled at the corners of her heart despite her efforts to quash it. "I shouldn't have to be doing this. Dealing with this. With *him*." She should have been able to leave the past precisely where she'd left it. But even as that thought stumbled clumsily through her mind, she had to admit, if only to herself, that the past was never very far away.

It walked beside her, shadowing her through holidays she couldn't share with her child. It stopped and sneered at her every August 8, when she was forced to mark the passage of another year—and wonder what her daughter was doing. What she looked like. What she was feeling. If she was happy.

All of those questions and more were a part of Sam's life. They'd become the underlying thoughts that lived just beneath her consciousness. They were with her always. She tortured herself, wondering if her little girl was now taking ballet lessons or playing soccer. If she preferred dirty jeans to party dresses.

If she ever wondered about her birth mother.

The hard, cold knot of pain and loss stayed lodged in her chest every moment of every day.

The past was a shadow that stayed just out of reach. Taunting Sam with memories that weren't real—just imaginary home movies she'd made of the little girl she'd held briefly and then let go.

Sighing, Sam stared out through the windshield at the sweep of ocean stretching out in front of her and squinted as the sunlight dazzled the surface of the water. Far enough out to avoid the slam of the waves against the shore, sailboats glided serenely under the cloud-dotted sky. Seagulls wheeled and danced in the wind. Closer to shore, surfers sat atop their boards, waiting for just the right wave. Sam knew exactly how they felt.

Here she sat.

Waiting for some unseen signal to tell her to get off her butt and go face Jeff.

She leaned her forehead on the sun-warmed steering wheel and closed her eyes, seeing him again. Not just this morning, but nine long years ago. It was all so clear. Her last glimpse of him as he marched out of their apartment, a duffel bag stuffed full of his clothes in his right hand. He hadn't stopped to look back at her.

Hadn't even lifted a hand in a good-bye wave. He'd just walked away.

And now he was back.

"But nothing's changed, right?" Sam blew out a breath and straightened up. Shifting a glance at the inn to her right, she imagined Jeff in one of the plush suites. Rich men liked having the biggest hotel rooms, didn't they? With hot and cold running room-service flunkies at their beck and call? She could practically *see* him, sitting at a table, poring over the *Wall Street Journal* and wishing he were anywhere but there.

Then again, maybe he didn't care.

Maybe seeing her again didn't affect him at all.

Sam wasn't sure which notion was more hurtful. If he hated seeing her again—or if it meant nothing.

And as she stared out at the water stretching on forever, Sam's mind drifted back, drawing up images that were all too clear.

At eighteen, Sam thought she'd found her world. Every time Jeff touched her, skyrockets went off inside her. He'd been her first lover and the magic she'd found with him had never been repeated.

That last night with him, heat surrounded them and dazzled every breath, every whispered word. They came together over and over again in the dark, bodies meshing, hands stroking, breath mingling.

His body claimed hers and she gloried in the feel of him, sliding deep within. Climaxes rippled through her and still it wasn't enough. She'd wanted more, always more. Of him. His kisses, his caresses, his voice, whispering in her ear how much he loved her. How much he would always love her.

She'd held him close, trapping his body within hers,

as if a part of her had realized, even then, that happiness that sharp, that sweet, couldn't last.

And it hadn't.

"Well, doesn't really matter what he's feeling now, does it?" she muttered and clambered out of the truck. Her knees were still a little weak, the force of that memory still quaking within her.

Dusting her damp palms against her jeans, she shoved her car keys into her pocket, grabbed up her purse and slung it over her shoulder, then stepped back and, because she needed to hit something, slammed the truck's door. Hard.

The only way to insure that Jeff Hendricks got the hell out of Dodge was to go see him, and sign his stupid divorce papers, *again.* She didn't owe him anything beyond her signature. But for her own sake, she would tell him about their daughter.

Would he give a damn? she wondered. Would he be tormented by the same "what-ifs" that danced through her mind day and night?

Would he even be interested to know that together they'd made a child and then lost it?

Jeff gripped the phone a little tighter, but kept his voice even. Just a matter of control. And control was the one thing he'd been weaned on. In the Hendricks family, control was damn near a religion, without all the messy supplication—after all, genuflecting will ruin the crease in your trousers.

The voice on the other end of the phone paused and he spoke into the breach. "It's being taken care of. Should be wrapped up by tomorrow."

With any luck.

Dammit, he had to get out of here.

He hadn't expected this mission to be as . . . *treacherous* as it was turning out to be. But then, he had a feeling that nothing was going to go as smoothly as he might have liked. Just seeing Sam again had been harder than he'd imagined. He hadn't counted on that punch of *awareness*. The slam of something hot and needy that had damn near staggered him, despite the threatening stances taken by her sisters.

Seemed that nine years wasn't long enough to put out *all* the fires within.

And just being here was already fanning those flames. He didn't want the fires burning again. The last time he'd surrendered to the heat, he'd been reduced to a pile of ash. A hard lesson, but one he'd etched into his brain to keep him from ever giving in to his emotions again. Besides, the past—which he rarely allowed himself to revisit—was done. Over.

The voice drifting through the phone receiver demanded his attention. "Right," he said, forcing himself to concentrate on the conversation at hand. At least long enough to say good-bye. "Tomorrow. I'll call you in the morning."

He hung up, letting his fingertips rest on the receiver as if trying to keep the connection to his present as a safeguard against the past. But the thread was frayed and he couldn't quite hang on. Jeff felt as though he were a particularly meaty bone being fought over by the dogs of his past and his future. And the jaws of each were sharp enough to tear him to pieces.

"A damn mess," he muttered. All because some miserable little county clerk had decided *not* to do his job. Jeff just wished he had the man's scrawny neck between his hands for five minutes. But the minute he considered it, Jeff reminded himself that he was a reasonable, civilized man. And Hendricks men never lost their tempers. Never gave in to the urge for violence, no matter the temptation. "So maybe I'd just turn the little bastard over to Mike Marconi, then stand back and watch."

Despite everything, he smiled to himself at the mental image. Hell, the Marconi women were nothing if not . . . exciting.

Exciting. Sam's face rose up in his mind, and once again he saw her pale blue eyes glare at him. Even in memory, she could shoot daggers at him like no one else ever had. Daggers, hell. She'd stabbed him through the heart. And he had the scars to prove it. Deliberately then, he turned his mind away from Sam and everything she represented and shifted a look toward the adjoining room. The low-pitched murmur of the television made him smile again, for different reasons. And he remembered just what was really important in his life.

Soon enough, this would be over and he'd be back in San Francisco. Back where he belonged. Where his life waited. Until then, the old inn where he was staying was comfortable, furnished in a style that made him think of a family summer home. The walls were covered in softly striped wallpaper and the gleaming wood floors were polished to a high shine. A wide balcony overlooked the cliff and the raging ocean some thirty feet below. The sliding glass doors separating the balcony from the main sitting room were open and the white sheers fluttered in the cold breeze as if dancing in tune to the ocean's beat.

Jeff surrendered to the restlessness inside him, stepping out onto the wooden deck and letting the wind slap at him in fierce welcome. He dropped both hands onto the whitewashed railing, his fingers curling over the cold, damp wood as he stared out at the swells rising out at sea. Froth churned on the water's surface and then danced skyward as the waves punched against the shore below the inn. A handful of surfers rode the breakers in toward the beach, then kicked free and paddled back out to wait for the next ride. Sameness.

There was a comfort in that. One he appreciated even more today, now that the regularity of his life had been interrupted. Squinting into the afternoon sunlight, he spotted the storm clouds hovering on the horizon. Though it was summer, he thought it appropriate for how his day was going that black thunderheads were gathering for an assault. Why not? He'd already made it through a different sort of storm at the Marconi place. Why shouldn't the heavens open up on him, as well? Hell, the way things were going, he should expect a hurricane. Class 12.

Seagulls shrieked overhead, and with the muted thunder of the ocean, he hardly heard the knock on the hotel room door. Probably would have missed it entirely, but for the excited, familiar squeal that immediately followed.

"I'll get it!"

Turning, Jeff headed inside in time to see his own personal little hurricane racing to the door.

"Hey," he called, "what did I tell you about opening doors—"

Too late.

Like every other female in his life, this one had a mind of her own. Laughing, the little girl yanked the door open before Jeff could stop her. And then Sam was there, standing in the doorway, shock glazing her eyes.

Sam's heart stopped.

She actually felt it jolt hard, stop, then start up again with a thudding roar that pounded in her ears and rattled her soul.

Staring down into a small, smiling face with pale blue eyes just like her own, Sam *knew*. Knew without the slightest doubt that *this* was her daughter. Her child. The one she'd given up nearly eight years before. The one she'd come to tell Jeff about.

Jeff.

Still reeling, she forced herself to tear her gaze from the child who was a mini-Marconi and look at the man stepping into the room from the balcony. The scent of fresh flowers and the sea filled the room and a sharp, cold wind entered with him. Sam thought he looked . . . annoyed.

Her world had just been rocked and *he* was pissed?

"Hi, who're you?"

A small voice, confident, happy. Sam looked back at the little girl and wondered how she ever could have *stopped* looking at her. She was perfect. Her dark reddish-brown hair was pulled into pigtails high at the sides of her head and the ends of her thick, wavy hair hung past her shoulders. She had bangs cut just a little

crookedly over big blue Marconi eyes and her mouth
was curved in a wide smile, displaying a missing front
tooth.

Oh God.

Who am I? she thought desperately. *I'm your
mother.*

Pain knifed through Sam, leaving her breathless in
its wake. Throat tight, lungs labored, Sam couldn't stop
watching the child—as if half-afraid the little girl
might vanish. She drank in the sight of her daughter
and thought she might drown in the joy of it. Dismiss-
ing Jeff as though he weren't even there, Sam commit-
ted this first sight of her child to memory, etching it
into her brain so that not even time would be able to
erase it.

Sam struggled for air. Fought for it as a dying man
battles to stay alive just one more minute. Her heartbeat raced, thundering in her chest. Her stomach spun
wildly as though she were on one of those weird carnival rides that turned you every which way but loose.
She slapped one hand to the doorjamb to keep herself
steady even while trying to find her voice.

"I'm Sam," she finally said, ignoring the child's father as he moved into an openly protective stance just
behind the girl. "Who're you?"

"I'm Emma Hendricks and—" She stopped and
looked back at Jeff for one more heart-stopping moment. "This is my daddy and Sam's a funny name for a
girl."

"I guess it is," she said, and silently congratulated
herself on managing to get another sentence past the
horrible, tight knot in her throat. *Emma.* Her daughter's name was *Emma.* A pretty name. One she might

have chosen herself if she'd had the chance. Sam's eyes filled for missed chances and empty years and she blinked frantically to keep them at bay. Not that she worried about crying in front of Jeff, but she didn't want her vision to be blurred. Not now. Not when she finally had the opportunity to actually *see* the child she'd once held briefly in the crook of her arm.

Oh God, the child she'd wondered about and prayed for, for eight long years, was standing in front of her, smiling at her—and seeing a stranger.

Emma wore pink shorts, a white short-sleeved T-shirt with pink ribbon around the neck, and bright blue Barbie sneakers with white ankle socks. She had a Band-Aid on her right knee, and freckles across her nose.

And Sam thought she'd never seen anything more beautiful.

"Are you here to see my daddy?"

Daddy.

Strange how much power one little word contained. The joy within receded under a tide of anger that slowly rose inside her. "Yes," Sam said, aiming one more brief look at Jeff. He was stonefaced—no expression of apology or shame to be seen. And dammit, he should be ashamed. He hadn't wanted Emma. Hadn't wanted *Sam*. He'd thrown away what they'd had and then, like a rat-bastard-lying-weasel-dog, he'd slipped under Sam's radar and stolen their child without bothering to tell her. *He'd* been able to love their daughter freely. *He* hadn't been haunted by decisions made by a scared eighteen-year-old. *He* hadn't spent every birthday, every Christmas, every Easter, wondering where she was and if she was safe. No, Jeff had been there, with their daughter, watching her grow and change.

God, she wanted to scream. She wanted to kick something. Break something.

But mostly, she wanted some answers.

Now.

"Yes, I'm here to see your *daddy*," Sam said tightly, wondering if he could hear the ice in her voice. If he could see the fury in her eyes. If he cared.

"Go to your room, honey," Jeff said.

Emma's little face screwed up in a tiny mask of disappointment/pouting/temper. "Daddy, you said we could get ice cream."

"We will," he said, stroking one hand over the back of her head. "Later. First, Sam and I have a few things to talk about."

A vise clamped around Sam's heart and squeezed as she watched father and daughter together. Their easiness with each other was touching and, oh, so hard to look at. If things had been different . . .

Oh yeah, they had to talk, she thought. That's for damn sure. They had plenty to talk about and it would be much better for everyone if Emma were nowhere around when they did.

"Good-bye, Sam," Emma said, and turned toward the door on the right. As she walked, she managed to drag her feet as if they were both chained to anchors. Clearly, she didn't want her father to miss the fact that she was disappointed. And just as clearly, Emma had inherited the Marconi flair for drama.

As soon as Emma was gone, Sam could breathe again. However, her whole body ached, as if she'd been tackled by a three-hundred-pound linebacker. She'd had her feet knocked out from under her and her breath slapped from her chest. Shaken, she kept a firm grip on the doorjamb, just in case her knees suddenly decided to give out.

"I wasn't expecting to see you," he said. His voice rumbled through the room, sounding like far-off thunder.

"I guess not," she said quietly, watching him walk across the elegantly appointed room. As she'd expected, he'd taken a suite. The wood gleamed, crystal vases were filled with fragrant flowers, and warm colors and overstuffed furniture made for a soft, cozy space.

And for as much as Sam gave a damn, it could have been a concrete cell painted beige.

He closed the door on Emma, shutting the girl out of whatever they might have to say. Then he turned and walked back toward Sam. His expression carefully neutral, he kept his gaze on hers and waited for her to speak first.

"She doesn't know me," Sam whispered, her gaze shifting now to the closed door standing between her and her child.

"Why should she?"

Sam snapped him a look and hissed at him. "I'm her mother."

He was unimpressed. "You *were*."

New pain, fresh and sharp as a well-honed blade, sliced through what was left of her heart. Her fingers dug into the doorjamb until she wouldn't have been surprised to see half-moon indents from her nails pressed into the wood. "I gave her up so that she could have a family."

"Spare me." He laughed shortly and stepped nearer, closing the space separating them until he could whisper harshly and be sure she heard. "You *gave* her to my mother."

"What?" Sam finally understood that old cliché about "seeing red." A crimson haze surrounded her vision, clouding everything in a shimmering wave of pulsing fury that pounded and rippled in time to the beating of her own heart. When she thought she could speak without blowing the top of her head off, she whispered, "Are you out of your mind?"

He sneered at her. No other word for it. The expression was one tyrants and despots reserved for the peon who made the mistake of crossing them. And he had it down cold. Must be in the genes, she thought wildly. Grow up rich and learn that sneer from the cradle up.

"Drop the act, Sam. No point in it now, is there?"

There went the top of her head.

She punched him. Hard. Her fist hit his chest and bounced off like a bullet ricocheting off a brick wall and it didn't help a bit. "You *are* crazy."

A muscle in his jaw twitched and a flash of memory blasted through Sam's brain. Jeff had always been one of the most . . . *controlled* human beings she'd ever met. That had been part of his fascination for her when they first met. Since she'd grown up in a houseful of people who shouted more often than they spoke, meeting a man whose aplomb was rarely shaken had been . . . intriguing. The one sign he'd shown of temper was that jaw twitch. And with enough of a push, she knew she could make him surrender to the anger and give it free rein.

That would suit her just fine. The way she was feeling at the moment, there was nothing she'd like better than a good old-fashioned screaming match.

But even admitting that to herself, she couldn't give in to the urge. Not with Emma . . . *Emma* . . . right there, in the next room. She had to find a way to fight in *his* style. Cold. Controlled. Reasonable.

It wouldn't be easy. What she was feeling went beyond pain. Beyond fury. Beyond anything she'd ever known before.

Reaching out, she grabbed a fistful of his crisply starched shirt and dragged him out into the hall. He came willingly enough, then pulled the door to quietly behind them. When they were alone, she released her grip on his shirt and gave a furtive look down the short hall to make sure no one else was within earshot. They were alone. Sunlight streamed through the leaded-glass window at the end of the hall and laid intricate patterns on the deep burgundy floor runner. More flowers, in a vase atop a table just below that window, sent the almost cloying scent of roses into the still air and Sam's stomach churned.

Ignoring the sensation, she focused on him. On the man she'd once loved more than anything else in the world. The man who'd walked away from her without a backward glance.

Old pain simmered deep inside, blending with the fury that still bubbled in her blood, and together they formed a mixture that nearly choked her. "Don't screw with me, Jeff. If I murdered you now, I'd find a way to get away with it."

"Nice," he said, nodding. "Good to know you're still making idle threats."

"Who says they're idle?"

"Jesus, Sam."

She shook her head and lifted one hand for silence. When she had it, she sputtered, "Just what did you mean in there? I never gave my baby to your mother. I *thought* I'd arranged for her to have a family."

His eyes narrowed. Dark slits of pure fury. The muscle in his jaw twitched again. "Don't screw with me, either, Sweet Cheeks. If you didn't give Emma to her, just how did I get her?"

She swallowed hard and tried to breathe at the same time. Not easy. "That's the million-dollar question, isn't it? I specified to the adoption attorney that I wanted her to go to a good home."

"She did."

"With two parents."

"She didn't need two," he said and shifted his long legs until they were braced apart, like a man standing on the deck of a wildly bucking ship at sea. "She had *me*."

God, how could the pain keep coming? Wasn't there a saturation point? One at which her body would simply say, *Sorry, no more pain here. We're full up. No more room*? Apparently not. Her nerves danced, her brain raced, and her stomach did a quick somersault that made her wish she carried barf bags in her purse.

"How did she *get* you is what I want to know."

"You know damn well how."

His eyes. Anger splintered in those dark centers and flashed like a warning beacon. But she couldn't pay attention. There was too much she had to know. Too much she had to say. And if he wanted to fight, then she'd be happy to oblige him. Sam couldn't remember any other time in her life when she'd been balanced quite so neatly on a razor's edge. She felt as though if she tipped too far one way or the other, she'd fall into some slimy black hole and just sink to the bottom.

How did this day manage to keep getting crappier?

Taking a deep breath, she told herself to fight for calm. She remembered her mother's voice always telling her daughters, "Think before you speak." Unfortunately, Mama had been disappointed on that one. The Marconi girls tended to jump feet first into the fire and only then worry about how to stomp out the flames. "I know that I gave her up for adoption *after* you sent me divorce papers."

He stared at her for a long minute, then shook his head and laughed shortly. "Nice try. *You* sent the papers, babe. I was in London. Remember?"

She swayed, as if his words had had a physical as well as an emotional impact. Oh, she remembered everything. In vivid, digitally enhanced color. She remembered meeting him, falling desperately in love in a few short weeks, and knowing, absolutely *knowing*, that she would never be happy unless they were together.

Their families had argued against it.

The Marconis, concerned that their eighteen-year-old daughter was far too young to get married, tried reasoning with Sam. It hadn't worked. Jeff's mother had tried a different tactic. She'd threatened to disinherit him. But he hadn't been bowed and his mother eventually caved in as he'd been so sure she would.

Memories rushed through Sam's mind, staggering her with the onslaught of lost passion and buried pain.

But she couldn't stop it. She felt it all again. Saw it all again. Saw herself as a young bride, living in a tiny apartment, and for the first couple of weeks everything was great. But then reality crashed and took them down with it.

Didn't matter, she thought. Nothing mattered now. Nothing but Emma.

"I sent you a letter, Jeff. Telling you about the baby. You sent it back to me. Unopened."

"Bullshit."

"And," she added, as if he hadn't spoken at all, "you sent along a set of divorce papers."

He shook his head, but something in his eyes shifted, changed, softened from anger to suspicion. "No I didn't."

"Somebody did," she snapped, leaning toward him. "And I've still got my returned letter to prove it."

He scraped one hand across the back of his neck. "Assuming that such a letter exists," he said tightly, "why the hell would you keep it?"

"As a reminder."

"Of what?"

She looked up into his eyes. "It reminds me of the mistake I made in trusting the wrong person."

He winced.

She didn't care.

"Show me," he said.

Chapter Four

"I don't believe this," Jeff said, clutching the un-opened, nine-year-old envelope. But he did. Dammit, he did. Standing in Sam's old bedroom in the Marconi family house, he half-expected one of her sisters to charge into the room swinging a chain saw. And right this minute, he couldn't even say he'd blame them.

They'd left Emma back at the inn. The owner's sixteen-year-old daughter had been happy to earn another twenty bucks babysitting. And this was definitely something he and Sam had to do alone. Just the two of them.

For years, he'd told himself that he and Emma had been lucky to escape Sam. She'd divorced him and given their child away. She hadn't wanted either of them in her life. And he'd made peace with that long ago. Now he was forced to face the idea that all of it had been a lie. That his own mother had orchestrated everything from behind the scenes. "Damn her."

"Huh? Damn who?" Sam's voice, insistent, cracking, as if she were about to snap in two. All that was holding her together were the tight bands of anger he could practically *see*.

His hand tightened on the still-sealed envelope and

his gaze fixed on the too-familiar scrawl across the front of it. "My mother."

God, how it cost him to admit this. To acknowledge that Eleanor Hendricks would go to such amazing lengths to get her son away from a woman she'd always considered unsuitable. Rage swept him like a brush fire consuming a hillside. It kept climbing, burning hotter and hotter, and there was no way of stopping it.

"Your—" She stared at him for a long count of ten and then stomped past him toward the window that overlooked the wide expanse of front lawn. An ancient oak stood in the center of the yard, sending gnarled, twisted branches out into a canopy of papery leaves that danced in the ever-present wind. From below came the muted music of a wind chime moving lazily in the breeze.

While she stared blankly out the window, Jeff stared at *her*. Nine years and she looked even better than he remembered. And God knew, he remembered way too well—on those rare occasions when a memory of her flitted through his mind. He tried to *not* remember. What was the point, after all? But with Emma growing into a miniature version of her mother, was it so surprising that thoughts of Sam kept cropping up?

Those few, amazing weeks of their marriage had been the one and only time in his life that he'd let go. That Jeff hadn't allowed himself to be ruled by the Hendricks dogma, "What will people say?" At nineteen, he'd discovered passion and the freedom of being himself—or at least being the man he'd become when he was with Samantha.

She had staggered him.

Literally.

The first time he saw her, she'd run him down in her successful attempt to catch a wildly thrown football. When she helped him up, he'd looked into her pale blue eyes and fallen all over again.

Unfortunately, they hadn't been able to see past their own passion far enough to know that the only thing waiting for them was pain.

And now the past had come back to bite him on the ass.

Feeling as though he were in enemy territory, he took a quick look around. He'd only been in this room . . . *her* room . . . once before. The night they'd come to tell her folks they were getting married.

The room hadn't changed much, either. The walls were still painted a deep green and bookshelves stuffed with paperbacks were painted a paler shade of the same color. Her bed was covered in a quilt that looked homemade and the same framed posters of Paris and Hawaii hung on the walls. He remembered teasing her about the disparate pictures, but she'd told him then that fantasy trips all had one thing in common. The fantasy.

But Sam had been *his* only fantasy.

And look where that had gotten them.

Gritting his teeth, he said, "You sent this letter to me, my mother returned it to you along with the divorce papers." Just like Sam'd insisted at the inn. Saying it aloud didn't make it any easier to handle. But there it was. "When you signed and returned them, Mother forwarded them on to me—with your signature on them." He shoved one hand through his hair, then let it drop to his side. Helpless. God, he'd always hated that feeling and right now it was choking him. "I thought *you* wanted the divorce."

She laughed shortly, harshly and the sound slapped at him. "Perfect."

He walked up behind her. Close enough to touch. But of course, he didn't. "She played us both."

"And Emma?" Two words—a world of feelings. She kept her gaze locked on the nearly hypnotic dance of the leaves beyond her window. It was as if she couldn't bear to look at him. Her hands fisted and unfisted at her sides as if she were subconsciously looking for something to grab onto—and couldn't find it.

Jeff moved to one side of her, keeping a safe distance from the energy and fury pumping off her in thick, emotion-packed waves. He leaned against the wall and watched her as he said, "Mother brought Emma to me right after she was born."

"God." She swayed slightly and he almost reached out to steady her. Would have if he'd thought for a minute his touch would be welcome. Yet Jeff knew she'd rather topple onto the floor than take any help from him at the moment.

"She said you gave her the baby. Said that you didn't want any part of me." And the pain he'd felt that day came racing back to remind him just how much caring for someone that deeply could hurt. Even beyond his too-stupid-to-live teenage pride, Sam had torn something from him he'd never gotten back. She'd taken his belief that he could be wanted for his own sake.

Sam's gaze snapped to his. "And you believed her?"

He stomped on the rise of temper inside. "Why wouldn't I? I tried to call our apartment but you were gone."

"I moved out when you left."

"So I guessed." But he didn't tell her how her leaving had terrified him. "I called here, but your sisters wouldn't give me a number to contact you."

"I told them not to."

"So." He nodded sharply. "We were running in circles, going nowhere . . ."

"And your mother swooped in on her broom and finished us off."

"I'd argue with that, but it's too close to true."

"Close?"

He blew out a breath of pure frustration. "What do you want me to say? I'm *sorry* that I got Emma? I'm *not*."

She shook her head hard enough that her hair swung out in an arc around her head. The last of the sunlight caught it and inflamed the strands, making that reddish-brown mass look like dark fire.

"You *left* me," she said.

"It was a break," he argued, feeling the futility of it even as he kept right on swinging.

"Right." She snorted a laugh. "Four months in London. *Without* your new wife. Heck of a break."

"I took a course at Cambridge, for chrissake." Jeff came away from the wall. He shoved both hands into his pockets. He hated feeling as though he were treading water in a tank where the water level kept rising. "We needed time apart. You know that." When she refused to acknowledge the truth of it, he snapped, "I needed space."

"Time away from me, you mean."

"Maybe," he admitted. "Maybe that's what it boiled down to. Hell, I didn't know what else to do."

She looked up at him, old pain and accusation glittering in her pale blue eyes. "We should have communicated. You should have talked to me."

The absurdity of *that* had him laughing out loud, though it didn't make him feel any better. "Jesus, listen to you. I was nineteen," he said, keeping a tight rein on the anger churning within. "I didn't *do* talking."

"You could have tried."

But back then, Jeff knew, he hadn't been interested in talking. Any time he was near Sam, all he'd been able to think about was stripping her out of her clothes and tossing her onto the nearest flat surface. Amazing how *some* feelings never really go away.

With that thought came blind panic and he surrendered to the adult version of sticking his tongue out. "Yeah? Well, so could you."

Astonished, she blinked at him. "Are you seriously going to try to say that to me?"

He knew what she was talking about and he had an answer for it. "Yelling doesn't count as communicating."

"It does in my family."

"*My* family's different."

"Ha. Well, I guess that's a fair statement." She grabbed the envelope from the dresser top where he'd tossed it and shoved it back into the top drawer of an antique chest. "My family shouts. Yours lies and steals children."

"She didn't steal Emma." Christ, had he really come around to trying to *defend* his mother? "You gave her up."

"God," Sam muttered, crossing her arms over her chest and holding on tightly enough to make her knuckles white. "I could cheerfully kill your mother right now."

"Too late," he said tightly. "She died a couple of years ago."

"I'm sorry."

"No you're not."

"No," she said, nodding. "I'm not. I'm frustrated. I'd like to look her in the eye and then spit in it. I'd like to run her down in the street, then back up and do it again. I'd like to—"

He understood. Hell, he'd like nothing better than to face down the old bat himself. But he couldn't. And since it was pointless and he knew Sam, Jeff interrupted the litany before she could get on a roll. "Why'd you give Emma up?"

She blew out a breath and tightened the death grip on her own arms even further. "I didn't have a choice."

"No choice?" he countered. Waving both hands to encompass the big old house and the family she'd told him so much about, he said, "What happened to the great Marconis? They wouldn't support you? They *made* you give Emma up?"

"No."

That wasn't nearly enough. He wanted more. Wanted to get into the head of the eighteen-year-old girl she'd been and find out just why she'd thrown everything away. Why she'd been so eager to lose not only him, but their child. He told himself it shouldn't matter to him. It was nine years ago. They were different now. *He* was different, now. But it did matter.

Too damn much.

"Then why?" he demanded, grabbing her upper arm and pulling her around to face him. "Why would you give her up? You used to talk about having a houseful of kids. I remember because it terrified me. I can't imagine anything making you walk away from your child. *Our* child."

"I don't owe you an explanation." She released her death grip on her own arms and used both hands to push at his chest until she was free of him. But Jeff could still feel her. His fingertips still hummed with that too-brief burst of electricity that arced between them.

It had always been like that with Sam. Instant awareness, the buzz of lust and the thirst for more. Once had never been enough when it came to Sam. They'd walked through most days like sleepwalkers because they'd been awake half the night devouring each other. Those memories were suddenly all too vivid in his mind, and with a hell of an effort, he deliberately shut them down.

Get a grip, he told himself. This wasn't about him and Sam. Not now. It hadn't been for a long time. There was no "them" anymore.

"Maybe you don't," he admitted, his voice cool, reserved, as he fought for his legendary control and then found it, wrapping it around him like a cashmere blanket. "But you sure as hell owe Emma one and I'd like to hear it."

She stiffened. From the tips of her toes to the top of her head. It was as if she'd suddenly been nailed to a wall. She was so still, the only way he was sure she was drawing breath was that she hadn't toppled over from lack of oxygen. Her features were frozen, but her eyes were alive with memory. With pain. Regret.

And for a minute, Jeff felt bad about asking. But

dammit, didn't he have a right to know? He'd spent the last nine years thinking that the woman he'd thought he knew had been a stranger. He'd believed that what they'd felt, shared, enjoyed, had been a lie.

Didn't he at least deserve to know the truth? Didn't they *both* deserve that?

She inhaled sharply. "What have you told Emma about me?"

He sighed. Apparently, her truth was going to wait for another day. Pushing one hand through his hair again, he answered, "I said her mother wanted to keep her, but she couldn't. I told her you loved her."

Sam's shoulders drooped as if the weight of the world had just slipped off, leaving her exhausted. "Thanks for that much."

"I didn't do it for you. I did it for Emma."

She nodded. "Thanks anyway."

"You're welcome."

She leaned forward, unlocked the window, and lifted the sash. Instantly, a cold sea breeze darted inside, as if it had been poised on the other side of the glass, awaiting its chance. The muted roar of the ocean sounded like a heartbeat and the wind chime jangled with abandon.

"I want to see her," Sam said, never taking her gaze off the gnarled trunk and branches of the tree in front of her.

"You have seen her." Stupid. He knew just what she meant and he should have been expecting it. But then, how could he have? He'd assumed all these years that Sam wasn't interested in their daughter. Now . . . things were different. Now, she'd want to know the child. Spend time with her.

And he wasn't sure how he felt about that.

What was this going to do to Emma? How would it affect his daughter's life? "I don't know if that's a good idea."

"A good idea?" She whipped her head around and pinned him with a steely look that stabbed right into his heart. "I don't even *know* her, Jeff. She's my daughter."

"She's my daughter too and, dammit, I'm not going to have her life disrupted."

"Disrupted?" She turned to face him. The breeze lifted her russet hair into a dance around her head. Her shoulders were squared and stiff and her chin was tilted at a defiant angle that he remembered. She looked like an ancient warrior about to fight to the death and Jeff knew that nothing between them was going to be settled today. Moreover, nothing would be decided without a battle.

But as Emma's father—the only parent she'd ever known, no matter *whose* fault it was—it was up to him to protect her.

"You think I want to hurt her?" Sam asked. "My God, you've had her for eight years. I just found her again."

"It's not that easy, Sam."

"I'll tell you how easy it is," she said quietly, but firmly. "You want me to sign new divorce papers, right?"

Alarm bells went off in the back of his head, but what the hell could he do about them? He had no choice but to hear her out and brace for the worst. "Yeah, of course."

"Well, I won't sign."

Damned if he couldn't practically *hear* the first salvo opening the war. "What?"

"I'm not going to sign. Not until I've spent time with Emma. Not until we figure out a way between us that I can be a part of her life."

Something hard and ugly settled in the pit of his stomach and Jeff wasn't proud of it. But Emma was *his* daughter. They were a team. A unit. And the thought of suddenly having to share the little girl with her mother hit him hard. It shamed him to admit even to himself that it was panic—and jealousy—rattling around inside him like a marble in an empty coffee can. He didn't want Sam getting to know Emma because *he* might lose a piece of his daughter's heart to her.

And he didn't know if he could take that.

Sam watched him and he wondered for a moment if she could tell what he was thinking. Then she spoke and he was sure of it.

"You're going to have to get used to sharing her, Jeff."

"Or?"

"Or," she said, giving him a smile that had nothing at all to do with humor, "we stay married."

The threat hung brazenly in the air and he could see that she was pleased with her well-aimed shot. So he could hardly be blamed for enjoying the look on her face when he leaned in close and said, "That can't happen. I'm engaged."

"You bet, Grace. Monday morning, without fail." Jo nodded as she talked, as though the older woman on the other end of the phone line could actually see her. It didn't pay to take chances. For all she knew, Grace Van Horn was clairvoyant. The woman did always seem to call the house at the worst possible time. What else was that but a psychic link to the universe? "Right. Sam will handle the details and the work crews will start arriving about eight."

Grace Van Horn, rich, irritating, and the customer who was destined to be the reason the next three months were already being called the summer of hell, kept talking, outlining her newest ideas for making their lives miserable. Great. Grace had already changed her mind three times and they hadn't even started work yet.

But they were used to this, Jo reminded herself. She and her sisters had been dealing with customers and potential clients for years.

Hank Marconi had started Marconi Construction when his daughters were little girls. They'd always gone to job sites with Papa and by the time they were teenagers, the Marconi girls could hold their own with any construction crew. Eventually, they'd all joined the business permanently, each of them with their own specialties, and Papa couldn't have been prouder.

Although dealing with clients was almost second nature now for the three sisters, Grace was a special case. A blinding headache burst into full-blown life behind Jo's eyes. Might as well get used to it, she thought. She'd be living on caffeine and aspirin for the next three months.

"Got it," she said, agreeing now to anything, since she knew full well that by the time Monday morning rolled around, Grace would have updates on her updates. "Circular staircase from the patio to the second story."

No helicopter pad? she wanted to ask, but didn't, silently congratulating herself on her restraint. Really,

Grace was great. Fun to talk to. A little weird, but weird was fun. Usually. Until she made a mess of Jo's files. All of her neatly compiled records and estimates and— She sighed and turned toward the coffeepot on the counter, suddenly needing sustenance. Empty. Perfect.

"Right. The wrought-iron balcony railings should be yellow to match the house." She made another note on her Van Horn file, for all the good it would do her.

Honest to God, if Jo had Cash Hunter in front of her right now, she'd drop-kick him into the next century. If he hadn't done his voodoo act on Tina, then the Marconis would have a real honest-to-God secretary to deal with Grace. But then, Jo thought wildly as Grace rattled on and on and on, maybe that's why Tina quit. Maybe it hadn't had anything to do with Cash's mysterious sexual hypnotism powers.

Something to consider.

Heavy footsteps pounded down the stairs and Jo shifted her gaze to the doorway between the kitchen and living room. It sounded as if trained elephants were marching on parade. But it was worse than elephants.

It was a giant rat.

Jeff Hendricks stormed down the last of the stairs, across the room, and out the front door like a man on a mission. Jo ran across the kitchen, still clutching the receiver of the ancient blue wall phone to her ear. The coiled blue cord brought her up short with a jolt strong enough to wrench her neck, just before the doorway. But she was close enough to see Sam, right behind Jeff, and she didn't look good, either. Temper vibrated all around her like a downed electrical wire jumping and skittering against the street.

Grace was still talking, but Jo had stopped listening. It wasn't only temper chasing her younger sister. There was something else. Something deeper. Something *big*.

Turning, she walked back across the kitchen, fighting free of the twisted blue cord as it tried to wrap itself around her.

"Right, Grace," she interrupted the older woman firmly. "I know. Don't worry. Monday. We'll be there."

She hung up, despite the fact that the older woman was still talking. She'd pay for that come Monday, but right now, it didn't seem important.

"I can't believe this," Sam was saying, standing on the threshold and facing her past. "After nine years, you're still reacting in the same way? You just walk away?"

"Why the hell do you care?" Jeff shot back.

Jo moved quietly into the living room, listening openly. The word "secret" didn't exist in the Marconi universe.

"You're *engaged*," Sam shouted, throwing both hands high and wide before letting them slap down against her sides. She couldn't even believe this. She'd been feeling like the scarlet letter–bearer for *dating*, for God's sake, and her *husband* was engaged?

Her brain spinning, she felt the world lurch crazily to one side, then right itself when Jeff started talking again. He stood at the bottom of the front steps and looked up at her. "We've been 'divorced' for nine years."

"Yeah," she argued, knowing that it made no sense,

"but now I find out we're still married and you're engaged to somebody else all in the same day. Excuse me for needing a minute or two to process."

He laughed, looked around the empty yard as if checking to make sure they were still alone before saying, "You're amazing. You don't want to be married to me and you're pissed that somebody else *does*."

Maybe.

Maybe that's what she was feeling. But it was hard to tell. There were too many emotions crashing around inside her like out-of-control bumper cars. God. She was married. Her daughter was no more than ten miles from her house. And her *husband* was engaged. No doubt to a Miss High Society Perfection 2004.

He had his career, a nice life, and their child.

What did Sam have?

New paintbrushes?

"Dammit."

"Good answer."

She scowled at him. "I wasn't talking to you."

"Naturally. Call me when you're ready to sign the papers."

He turned for the street and his black Expedition, parked at the curb. She stopped him cold with one sentence.

"I'm not signing, Jeff. Not until we work something out about Emma."

He stopped and looked back at her over his shoulder. His dark blue eyes shone with some emotion she didn't even want to identify. His jaw worked and the muscle there twitched violently a couple of times. This was costing him. But she couldn't seem to care.

"I'll call you tomorrow," he said tightly, then left, without another look at her.

Shaking.

She was shaking so hard her eyeballs were bouncing in her head.

"Sam?" Jo stepped out onto the porch behind her. "Did I hear that right? The weasel-dog's engaged?"

Sam laughed shortly. "Yep."

"This just keeps getting weirder."

"There's more."

"What's left?" Jo demanded.

Sighing, Sam realized that it wasn't over yet. Now she had to tell her family what had happened.

"What's wrong?"

She glanced at Jo, opened her mouth, then slammed it shut again. For this part of their conversation, she'd rather be inside where Mr. Bozeman couldn't "accidentally" overhear them while he was trimming his roses. She turned and went back into the house, with Jo as close as her shadow.

"Okay, you're starting to worry me now." Jo grabbed her sister's arm, pulled her into the room, and then pushed her down onto the sofa. "When a Marconi can't talk, she's either dead or—hell, I don't know anything else that could shut up a Marconi."

Sam dropped onto the cushion like a stone, bounced, then settled. Her hands in her lap, she inhaled deeply and blew it all out again, ruffling the dark red bangs that hung in her eyes. "Shock will do it."

"She speaks. A good sign. So tell me." Jo looked around the familiar, yet empty room. Sunlight slanted through windows, illuminating an inch worth of dust on the coffee table. Nope. No one else was here to help. She was on her own and Sam wasn't making this easy. Maybe she should go run after Mr. GQ and beat some answers out of him. Mike was better at the tough stuff, though, and she wished her youngest sister were around. "Dammit, Sam, don't make me beg. What is it?"

"I saw her."

"Her?" At least she was talking. That was good. She wasn't making sense, but speech was a step in the right direction. Jo dropped to one knee in front of her sister and looked her dead in the eye. "Her who?"

Sam looked up at her. "My daughter."

"Oh, my God."

All the air in the room disappeared. It was the only explanation for the sudden blast of light-headedness that had Jo swaying and then toppling over to land on her butt. The landing jarred her teeth and she shook her head as if that would somehow clear things up. It didn't. "Where?"

"With him. With Jeff."

"*He's* got her?" She shot a look at the wide-open front door. "I should have chased his ass down."

"He's always had her. He's raised her."

"But how?" This didn't make any sense. That baby had been given up for adoption. Turned over to a private attorney and— "How did he—"

"His mother."

"What?" She shook her head. " 'Bitch' doesn't seem like a big enough word."

"It'll do." Sam's gaze sharpened, then focused on Jo's. "All I know is Emma—that's her name, Emma—

looks just like us. Same eyes, same mouth. Oh God, Jo. She's mine and she didn't even *know* me."

Jo watched as Sam's anger faded into misery, swamping her with feelings she'd kept carefully blocked for years. All of them had suffered with her. Wondered with her. And couldn't come close to actually *knowing* the pain that Sam had lived with.

"Oh man. I don't even know what to say." Jo went up on her knees again and pulled Sam close. Wrapping her arms around her, she held her while Sam sobbed, her body shuddering with the force of a grief she'd never really recovered from.

It wasn't something anyone in the family talked about. But losing that baby had cost all of them. And none of them had ever forgotten the little girl who should have been a part of their lives. She was there, always. A shadow in the house. A ghost at the table. A phantom on Christmas mornings. She was birthday candles that had never been lit and fairy tales that had never been read.

All of the Marconis felt that absence keenly. Naturally, Sam most of all. Though she tried to hide it from her family, Jo knew that a part of Sam had been missing since that long-ago August 8, when she'd held her baby close and then given her up. Losing her daughter had carved out a slice of her soul that she'd never been able to recover.

"Oh God, look at me." Sam sniffled and pushed back out of Jo's arms. A smile that was more sheer determination than anything else crossed her face. Admiration for her younger sister bloomed inside Jo and pride was right behind it. "I just found her and I'm acting like it's the end."

"True." Jo forced a smile to match her sister's. She'd play this any way Sam wanted to. And anything big sister could do to make things easier, she'd do it. "So what's next?"

Swiping her fingers across her cheeks, Sam wiped away the last of the tears, then dusted her palms together as if ridding herself of the pain that had caused them. A hesitant smile wavered on her mouth and then strengthened as she sat up straight. "It's not the end of anything, Jo," she said and her voice took on a note of fierce resolve. "I'm getting another shot at this. She's back in my life, and I'm not going to lose her again."

"Not a chance."

Sam grinned. It was watery and still a little shaky but it was filled with a kind of joy Jo hadn't seen in her sister in way too long. "Wait'll you see her."

"She's one of us, huh?"

"Oh yeah."

"Not a surprise. Marconi genes are hard to defeat."

Sam nodded. "That's something Jeff's going to have to learn."

Chapter Five

It was too early in the morning to be dealing with this.

Sam took a deep breath and gripped the cardboard cup holding the last of her coffee a little tighter. What she wouldn't give for a refill.

Grace Van Horn, tiny tyrant, smiled benignly, like some benevolent good fairy. But Sam wasn't fooled. She'd been down this road before. Three summers ago, in fact, and the nightmares were *still* close enough to give her cold chills.

Short and trim, Grace was sixty and looked years younger. She was dressed in pale brown slacks and a lemon-colored silk shirt. Her snow-white hair was styled close to her head and her dark eyes sparkled with enough ideas to drive construction crews to strokes. The remodeling magazines Grace held clutched to her chest made Sam want to jump back into the truck and peel out of the driveway, leaving behind nothing but tread marks.

Under the best of circumstances, a summer of working for Grace was trying. Grace, a huge animal lover, gave her menagerie the run of the place and construction crews spent most of their time moving cats out of the way, chasing off dogs, shooing chickens, and trying desperately to keep the goats and sheep from eating the equipment.

But now, Sam didn't even have the luxury of a concentrated focus. Instead, her brain kept wandering far away from construction, to settle on Jeff and Emma.

She was *married*.

And having a hard time getting past that.

Plus, trying to think about work when all she wanted was another look at her daughter was nearly impossible.

"I'm so excited to be getting started," Grace said, sweeping her gaze across the gathered Marconi sisters and their crew, waiting in trucks parked in the driveway. She practically vibrated in her eagerness. "It's going to be a wonderfully creative summer."

Someone groaned.

Sam was really afraid it had been *her.*

When Grace started throwing the word "creative" around, it was time to hide. Since her husband's death ten years before, Grace had made it her mission in life to transform her home into a miniature version of the Winchester Mystery House.

Rumor had it that in 1881, a medium had convinced Sarah Winchester that she was being haunted by the spirits of those killed by the Winchester rifles her husband's company produced. The medium had assured Sarah that if she built a grand house for the spirits to visit, she could appease them—and that as long as construction of the house never ceased, Sarah would be safe. And for the next thirty-eight years, it worked, as she kept construction crews working around the clock, seven days a week—weekends and holidays included.

That amazing house, in San Jose, was a rambling

mansion filled with doors that opened to nowhere and staircases that led to ceilings. One of the wealthy woman's favorite pastimes was having her workmen tear rooms apart and redo them over and over again. The day she died, the work crews simply left . . . some of them abandoning half-driven nails in the walls.

Sam understood how they must have felt.

The Winchester house had begun as an eight-room farmhouse and by the time Mrs. Winchester died, there were 160 rooms, decorated with Tiffany stained-glass panes, solid silver doorknobs, and gold chandeliers. After her death, several storerooms filled with priceless treasures had been discovered—the contents never having been used. The house was now a historical monument, drawing thousands of tourists every year.

Grace's place was on a smaller scale, but not for lack of trying.

Built over a century ago, the big Victorian had stood proudly, as a testament to its owner's financial status as well as his taste for overblown gingerbread detailing. Then the bottom fell out of the cattle market and the house's owner sold it to a woman intent on making a different sort of name for herself.

As a cathouse, the Victorian was, arguably, the best bordello north of Los Angeles. Tucked away in the trees, the Victorian had worn its scandalous mantle with pride. Far enough outside of town that the church-going ladies could pretend it didn't exist, it was also close enough that the husbands of those ladies could find the house blindfolded.

Over the years, the house changed hands countless times, and every owner had been determined to leave their own stamp on the place. More land was purchased, forests cleared, and vineyards planted.

The house itself remained pretty much in its original condition, until Grace crowned herself Amateur Architect. Now, new rooms tumbled off to each side of the original structure, giving the impression of a stately old woman spreading the skirt of a dress that didn't suit her. And with its eye-searing, sunshine-yellow paint, dark green trim, and white accents, it looked as though the old woman in an ugly skirt had been forced to wear too-bright makeup on top of her other indignities.

"It's so exciting that the work's beginning," Grace was saying, "and the summer people will be arriving on Saturday—"

Sam's attention snapped back to where it had better stay, if she wanted to survive.

"—so we'll need to keep the construction away from the west wing and—" Grace was still talking.

Oh God. Sam gave herself a mental head slap. She'd forgotten about the summer people. How she could have managed that, she didn't know. Maybe it was wishful thinking. Maybe it was her brain being too full of Emma and Jeff. Maybe it was because she just didn't need one more thing on her list.

Grace's "summer people" arrived every year about the same time. A handful of women, friends for years, had grouped together to spend their retirement years driving around the country, following the good weather. Whenever they stopped, they did odd jobs or visited friends. Here at Grace's funny farm, the women would spend their time shearing the sheep and the cashmere and angora goats that had the run of the place, and carding their wool.

At least the summer people would help keep the goats and sheep out of the way. Though Emma would probably love it here with all the animals.

Emma.

Sam rubbed at the spot between her eyebrows and had the distinct impression she wasn't getting rid of her headache, but massaging it to help it grow.

"—I've got some ideas about the back bath, too," Grace said, then stopped and looked around. "Where's your father?"

Sam, being the duly elected—if not completely happy about it—representative, spoke up. "Papa will be back tomorrow, Grace. He went to—"

"Las Vegas," Grace interrupted, nodding, "of course."

Jo frowned. "How'd you know that?"

Grace's features went serenely blank. "Why, one of you girls must have told me."

"When could we have told you that?" Mike asked. "We just got here and—"

Sam cut Mike off before she could finish. How Grace had picked up Papa's vacation plans on the local gossip train wasn't really important. "If you want to show me your notes, Grace, we can have the guys get started."

"Of course. Just come right over here." Grace walked past them to an iron bench and table set under the sweeping shade of an elm that had to have been at least a hundred years old. She spread the magazines on the table and flipped open the first one to the page she had marked. "If you'll look at this, dear, you'll see that I want to go a different route in the back bedroom."

"Yes, but—" Sam winced and took a long gulp of her too-cool coffee. Oh, she'd be needing gallons of the stuff to deal with Grace. They'd talked about this job just three days ago and everything had been settled. The wood had already been ordered. Scratch that, she thought, already dreading her phone call to the lumber company. Of course, the upside to that was *they* were used to dealing with Grace, too. The people at Wright Wood were probably expecting her call.

Shooting a desperat "help me" look at Jo, Sam frowned when her older sister deliberately glanced away and did everything but whistle and rock on her heels. Fine, Sam thought. So much for solidarity among sisters. Clearly, she was on her own.

Grace talked and Sam made notes even while her brain went off on a tangent all its own. She hadn't been able to stop thinking about Emma. About Jeff. It was all so surreal. Nine long years and then suddenly they were both back in her life. She had to find a way to make this work. To reach the child she'd thought lost to her forever.

To survive Grace long enough to get to know her daughter.

"I think a parquet floor is the way to go in the new library."

Oh boy. "Parquet, uh-huh." Sam groaned and kept writing.

A cold wind blew up and rattled the leaves overhead. She tried not to think of it in "foreboding" terms. After all, once the disaster hit, it was just *boding . . .* nothing *fore* about it.

"I'll get the boys to unload," Jo said, still studiously avoiding Sam's gaze as she stalked across the lawn toward the drive.

Sam sighed and called back, "Tell 'em it's the east wing this summer."

"Right." Jo lifted one hand and kept going.

They'd have a talk later about this. But for now, Grace was still talking and it paid to listen up when she was on a roll.

"If you girls want to get started on the library, you could have some of the men start on the second kitchen. We'll need new cabinets and I'm thinking a purple granite countertop."

Purple granite? "Sure, Grace. We can do that."

Grace tapped one finger thoughtfully against her chin. "Or maybe marble. We'll have to see." Then she stopped and grinned conspiratorially. "It's going to be a wonderful summer, Samantha." Slowly, though, her grin faded as she took a closer look. "Honey, are you okay?"

"Fine." Sam could lie when she had to. She'd just never been very convincing. Now Mike . . . *there* was a woman with a flair for lying. She'd invented more stories than Mark Twain on his best day.

"If you'll excuse me for saying so, that's a load of horse hockey."

Sam blinked in surprise. This was the closest Grace had ever come to actually swearing. A memorable moment. Laughing, she said, "Grace, you never cease to amaze me."

"That's very nice, dear, but an evasion nicely said is still an evasion."

How did Mike pull off the lying so well that no one

ever called her on it? Sam was going to have to take lessons. "Honest. I'm fine. A little tired, maybe." Comes from lying wide awake in your bed all night, with visions of your ex-husband dancing in your head.

Sugarplums—whatever the hell they were—would have been much safer.

And to clear that picture from her mind she spoke up fast before Grace could work up a full head of steam. "You know what, Grace? Jo will be taking care of the paneling in the library, why don't you go show her what you have in mind?"

Distracted, Grace snatched at the suggestion like a kid grabbing for the last piece of candy in a bowl. "Good idea."

Sam watched her go and tried to feel guilty. She failed. She'd just tossed her older sister to the lions and all she felt was a small twist of satisfaction. That said something about her, didn't it? But what did that matter when she could watch Jo face the determined little woman like a condemned man waiting for the first bullet to strike flesh?

Life was good.

"Does my mommy want me now?"

Jeff scraped one hand across his face, then looked at his little girl. This had been so much harder than he'd ever thought it would be. But then, that wasn't really a fair statement, was it? Because he'd never imagined having to have this conversation.

The living room of their suite at the inn was filled with morning sunlight and the soft sigh of the ocean breeze, dancing across the balcony and into the room. The ocean's heartbeat sounded loud and steady and

Jeff tried to match his to it. At least that would keep him breathing. "I told you, M&M," he said, using the nickname he'd called her since the first time she was laid in his arms. "She *always* wanted you. She just couldn't keep you when you were a baby."

Now, that comforting statement he'd been giving his child since she was old enough to understand had new meaning for him. After hearing Sam's story and *sensing* the truth in it, he was forced to reevaluate the anger he'd kept for her all these years. And with that reevaluation came a whole new fury, directed solely at his mother.

The great Eleanor Hendricks. The woman who'd ruled her family and her world like a dictator with all the bashful charm of Idi Amin. Jeff's father had danced to her tune and hadn't found freedom until he'd dropped dead of a stress-related heart attack at fifty-eight. Though Jeff had missed him, he'd also missed the buffer zone his father had provided. Without her husband to concentrate on, Eleanor had focused her abundant energies on whipping her only child into shape.

And dammit, he'd *allowed* it. It had been easier than fighting back. Easier to go along and not make the waves that would have eventually drowned him.

Now, he was paying the price. All last night, he'd paced the confines of the suite, wishing for a chance to confront his mother. Since Emma had come into his life, he'd pulled away from Eleanor, refusing to let his daughter be ruled by the same velvet fist he'd always known. But that pulling away hadn't been enough. There should have been more. She should have been made to see just how much misery she'd caused.

Because that wasn't going to happen, Jeff had to deal with his own frustrations. But that could wait. There was something—someone—much more important at the moment.

"Your mom always loved you, Emma. Just like I told you." It cost him. Giving his daughter the mother she so desperately wanted and needed was costing him more than he'd ever thought it would. If that made him a selfish bastard, well, he'd just have to learn to live with it.

Emma nodded solemnly, as if she were considering his words carefully. Reaching up, she tugged at the end of one of her pigtails and twirled it around her fingertips. Her one front tooth worried her bottom lip and Jeff wished he didn't have to do this. Didn't have to face his baby and shake her world.

Dammit, he was the *dad*. The guy who was supposed to make sure Emma's life was safe. Happy. He'd done a pretty good job of it over the years too, even if he did say so himself, and it really gnawed at him that he was being forced into this.

For eight years, Emma had been everything to him. He'd made sure his work didn't swallow his life. He'd wanted her childhood to be different from his. Better. There were no rigid rules she was forced to adhere to. There were no piano lessons or French lessons. She was allowed to be a child—the best gift any adult could provide—and until today, the biggest challenge she'd ever had to face was deciding which teddy bear to sleep with at night.

And dammit, he resented the hell out of this situation.

Yes, he could see Sam's side in all this, and if he

could have, he'd have faced his mother down and made her pay for screwing with his life. But there was no chance for satisfaction there.

And if he expected to get back to his life—the one he'd built for himself and Emma—then he had to bend.

Or for damn sure, Sam would break him.

Sunlight washed over the room. The scent of the sea hung in the cool morning air and the ocean repeated its age-old dance against the shore. The inn wasn't home, but at least it didn't have a sterile, generic hotel-room feel to it. Of course, anywhere he and Emma were together *felt* like home to Jeff.

He waited. The silence worried him. Emma was never quiet for long. It simply wasn't in her nature. Watching her now, looking so much like her mother, he was forced to admit that Sam had passed along more than her eyes and her smile. She'd somehow, *in utero*, given Emma the gift of gab.

Smiling to himself, he thought no one he'd ever known had talked as much or as loudly as Samantha Marconi.

Until Emma had come into his life.

And now that his child was sitting so still, so silent, his insides churned.

At last, Emma turned her big blue eyes up to him. "If she wants me now, does that mean she can keep me now, too?"

Dammit.

Jeff reached out, scooped the little girl up off the floor, and settled her on his lap. Inching back farther against the cushions, Jeff held her close and rested his chin on top of her head. She smelled of shampoo and daydreams and he loved her more than his life. He'd walk in front of a truck for her. Crawl across broken glass.

Sacrifice a section of his heart, so hers could be whole.

"Yes, honey," he said, staring across the top of her head to the framed Monet print hanging on the wall opposite him. "She can keep you in her life now."

"So I have a mommy, too?" she asked, just to make sure, her little fingers plucking at the fabric of his shirt. "Like Isabel?"

Jeff smiled to himself. Isabel Feinstein, Emma's best friend and the model against which all things were measured.

"Yeah, honey. Just like Isabel."

"That's good." She shifted and tipped her head back to smile up at him and his heart rolled over in his chest. "Can I have pancakes for breakfast?"

The abrupt shift in subject eased the tightness in his chest. Crisis solved. She'd be okay. And that was the only thing that mattered to him.

"We'll both have pancakes."

"No way am I cooking tonight," Sam said, pulling a Diet Coke out of the fridge and popping the tab.

"Well, don't look at me." Mike stepped up to the refrigerator. "Hand me one of those."

Sam did. "What about Jo?"

Mike shrugged. "Said she had somewhere to go, then she was headed back to her place."

"So it's just us for dinner." Sam eyed her younger sister. "I'll flip you for it."

"Heads or tails?"

"Heads."

Mike dug a quarter out of her battered jeans, flipped it into the air, and caught it one-handed. Slapping it down onto the tabletop, she lifted her hand, then crowed. "Tails never fails. I want pepperoni—and no mushrooms."

"Dammit," Sam muttered, closing the fridge door with a bump from her hip. "How do you do that?"

"It's a gift." Mike dropped into the closest chair and propped her elbows on the table. Opening her soda, she took a long drink before glancing at Sam again through narrowed eyes. "You're going to Terrino's, right?"

"There's another place in Chandler for good pizza?"

"True." She took another swallow, then shoved herself to her feet again. "And that gives me time for a shower before you get back here with food." Strolling out of the kitchen, she tossed back, "Take your time."

Scowling, Sam picked up Mike's quarter and shoved it into her own pocket. She'd consider it a tip.

Still clutching her Coke can, she stalked through the living room and hit the screen door with the flat of her hand, hard enough to slap it against the side of the house. One day, she thought, she'd actually win a coin toss with Mike.

Then all thoughts died as a black Expedition pulled up out front. Instantly, her insides churned into a writhing mass of what felt like venomous snakes. Jeff's car. Her hands went damp and her heartbeat jumped into a gallop.

Sam was more than ready to go another couple of rounds with Jeff. She'd spent all day trotting back and forth between Grace and the work crews. She'd had to reorder paint three different times to keep up with Grace's changing opinions, and to top everything off, one of the goats had eaten her boot lace.

So she was more than prepared, Sam told herself. Anything he had to say, she'd stand up to. Any fast ones he tried to pull, she'd stop.

She was completely ready to deal with Jeff.

Not so ready to meet her daughter for the first time.

Oh sure. They'd actually *met* the day before. And that first brief glimpse of the child she'd loved and ached for would remain in her heart forever as a tiny miracle.

But yesterday, Emma hadn't known that Sam was her mother. Today was different. Should have been special. She should be at least *clean* for this meeting.

Though if she admitted the truth, she wouldn't have backed out of this meeting if she were covered in mud.

She was halfway down the front steps before she saw the little girl. Sam's heart slammed hard into her ribs and left her breathless. The world did a strange sort of dip and roll, but she had a feeling no one else noticed.

Emma was wearing blue jeans with a tiny yellow T-shirt. She looked small and sturdy and so damned pretty. Her Barbie tennis shoes practically bounced in place as she waited for her father to come around the front of the car to join her.

Oh God.

He'd really brought her.

She smoothed her nervous hands across her work shirt. What were you supposed to wear when being introduced to a child you hadn't seen since she weighed seven pounds six ounces? Surely not battered Levi's, a stained work shirt, and Frankenstein-worthy work boots.

This was supposed to be a moment she'd remember

forever. She didn't want to remember smelling bad or having a dirty face. And oh God, she didn't want her daughter to turn up her nose at first sight of her mother.

His fault, Sam thought. He should have told her they were coming. Should have let her get prepared. Should have— It wouldn't have mattered.

She might have been neater if she'd had warning, but she'd still be just as nervous as she was at the moment. In fact, she hadn't been this agitated since Nick Candellano had tried to sweet-talk her out of her panties when she was sixteen.

She'd survived that—Nick had, too, barely—she'd survive this.

Sam wiped the palms of her hands against her thighs and told herself to breathe. Good advice, since small black dots were beginning to dance in front of her eyes. Atta way, Sam. Faint at the child's feet. Good first impression.

Behind her, the screen door opened.

"Sam?" Mike spoke into the weird stillness. "Everything okay?"

"Yeah." She didn't turn around. Couldn't have, even if she'd wanted to. Sam couldn't stop looking at Emma. Even when Jeff came up beside the child and took her hand in his much larger one, all Sam could see were two pale blue eyes so much like her own.

So many nights, she'd dreamed of this. Thought she'd know what to say. How to act. What to do.

Turned out, though, she didn't have to do anything at all.

"Mommy?"

One sweet word and the wall that had been sealed shut around Sam's heart for nine long years tumbled.

She felt the impact of each cold brick as it tore away from her heart.

And the pain was almost as huge as the joy.

Almost.

"Emma." Sam took a step and stopped.

"Oh, my God." Mike's voice, awed.

Sam hardly heard.

She took another hesitant step and finally glanced at Jeff. He nodded and she took that action as a blessing of sorts. One more step. Sam took a deep breath, then smiled.

Emma pulled free of her father's hand and grinning, ran across the rest of the space separating them. Flinging herself into her mother's arms, Emma was a solid, warm weight that filled all of the gaping holes inside Sam.

She clung to her daughter, inhaling her scent, imprinting this moment on her memory. Evening sunlight was warm and golden. From down the street, she heard the McCall kids practicing on their skateboards. Behind her, Mike was coming closer. But all Sam could focus on was the overwhelming sensation of actually holding her child.

"Oh, Emma, I'm so glad you're here," she whispered, running her hands up and down the girl's back as if to assure herself that this wasn't a dream. She was terrified that she'd wake up and find herself in her own bed—as she had so often over the years—alone and crying.

But it was real and the strength in the small arms now wrapped around her neck convinced Sam that this time, she could believe. This time, she could hold and be held.

This time, her tears would come from a full heart, not an empty soul.

"Let me look at you," she said, and pulled back, reluctant to break that close contact, yet needing to see her daughter. "You're so big."

"I grow like a weed," Emma said proudly. "And I lost my tooth." She bared her teeth for a close inspection, then said, "The Tooth Fairy gave me a *whole* dollar for it. Daddy says that's 'cause I'm special so my teeth are special, too."

More than special, Sam thought.

Perfect.

She was perfect.

Chapter Six

The first stars were out.

Lamplight spilled out the back door screen and lay like a slice of daylight in the encroaching darkness. The leaves on the trees rustled like whispers in the ever-present ocean breeze. And next door, Mr. Bozeman was playing armchair contestant again, shouting out the answers to questions asked on *Jeopardy*.

Sam sat on the top step of the porch beside her daughter and wanted to pinch herself—just to make sure it wasn't a dream. Jeff had left Emma here with a promise to pick her up in two hours. And now that he was due to pick their daughter up any minute, Sam felt greedy for more. Would there ever be enough time to make up for all the years she'd lost?

Half-listening to her daughter's rambling, Sam studied the girl and realized she'd never learned so much about someone so quickly.

By the time dinner was over, Sam knew that Isabel Feinstein was Emma's best friend and the owner of a pair of red tap-dancing shoes that Emma coveted with her whole heart. She also knew that Jeff's condo in San Francisco was big and pretty and the housekeeper, named Julia, let Emma have cookies when she came home from school. She tried very hard not to think about a woman who was being *paid* to give her daughter cookies.

Emma wanted to be a race-car driver and a princess when she grew up and she thought her daddy was even more handsome than Ashton Kutcher—a statement with which Sam was forced to agree.

The little girl hadn't stopped talking since she'd walked in the front door. She'd eaten two slices of the pizza Mike had gone to pick up—after carefully plucking off the pepperoni and sausages. She loved dogs and had already attached herself to Papa's big golden retriever, Bear. This was a mutual attraction, since Bear hadn't lifted his huge head off Emma's lap in more than an hour.

"Daddy said that you love me."

"Oh, I do, Emma." Sam skimmed her fingertips through her daughter's thick pigtail. Her hair felt as soft as a breath. "I always have."

"Even when you didn't know me?" Small hands stroked the big dog's head.

"I always knew you," Sam said, hoping that somehow this little girl would understand. "In my heart. You were always there."

"Yeah?" Emma turned big blue eyes up to her and Sam saw the shine of tears glimmering in the pale light.

Oh God, don't cry. That's all Sam could think. She didn't want her daughter crying on their first—what was this? A *date*? Could you make play dates with your own kid? And could she get further away mentally from the subject at hand?

"Oh yeah." A twinge of something sharp and sweet twisted in Sam's chest. "Always."

Sam owed Jeff big for this. Despite everything that still lay unspoken between them, he'd made this situation so much easier than it might have been. And yet this was not a happy ending, she reminded herself. Not yet. There were still too many things to talk about. To agree to.

Just because Jeff had allowed Sam some time with their daughter didn't mean he'd be willing to share custody. And Sam wasn't willing to settle for anything less. She'd swallowed the heartache and walked away from her daughter eight years ago—she wouldn't do it again.

"Do you love Daddy, too?"

Whoops. Stop paying attention for a minute and crash, boom.

"Um . . ." *Brilliant.*

"You had me," Emma said, "and Isabel says only people in love can have babies."

Thank you, Isabel. How old was Isabel, anyway? She'd have to remember to ask Jeff. "Is that right?"

Emma nodded and stroked her small hand over Bear's head again. The dog, apparently tossing dignity to the wind, almost purred. "Isabel says that babies happen when mommies and daddies say 'I love you.'"

"Well . . ." She wondered frantically if Isabel had any insights on the whole nuclear fusion thing. Think, Sam. Think. She wasn't about to head into sex education class here, but if she didn't say something—

"So you had to love Daddy to have me."

Ah. A chink in the armor. Sam jumped at it. "I did love your daddy." Oh God, how she'd loved him.

Fiercely, passionately. He'd been her first thought in the morning and her last thought at night. When he touched her, she could have sworn she saw stars, and when he kissed her . . . Whoa. Stop the presses. Turn those old memories off. But even as she told herself that the past was long gone, her body was lighting up like a Fourth of July fireworks finale. She actually *felt* heat rush to fill her cheeks and then dribble down inside her to warm up a completely different area.

Which was, considering the current circumstances, *way* inappropriate. Sam took a long, deep breath of the cool evening air and wished it could put out the fires raging inside. But she had a feeling that nothing was cold enough to manage that entirely.

"Don't you still love him?"

What she was feeling had nothing to do with love, she thought. But then, she couldn't tell her daughter that, now could she? Sam looked into those eyes and tried to find a safe way through this emotional minefield. And just for a minute, she wished Mike were still hanging around. But her younger sister had gone upstairs after dinner, to give mom and daughter some time together.

Taking another, deeper breath, Sam blew it out slowly before saying, "I'll always love your daddy for giving me you, Emma. But it's different now."

"I know." The little girl sighed dramatically and laid her head down atop Bear's. That only lasted a minute, though. The big dog snuffled, turned its head, and whipped out its tongue to give her a swiping kiss across the face. She giggled, then sobered again and said, "Isabel says that mommies and daddies don't always live together."

"Isabel sounds—" *Dangerous,* Sam thought. Good

ol' Isabel had an opinion on everything. But she didn't say that, she only added, "Smart."

"Oh, she is. Isabel's eight already and on her birthday we went to the movies and had popcorn and candy, and how come you didn't want me when I was a baby?"

The subject changed so abruptly, Sam's head spun. These were the questions she'd somehow imagined her daughter asking her. But she'd thought that she'd have time . . . *years* . . . to come up with the answers.

Sam had never expected to connect with her daughter while she was still a child. In her dreams and imaginings, this meeting had always taken place after Emma was grown up. She'd heard the stories. Adopted children searching out their birth parents. And she'd always thought their reunion was years away, if ever.

Now that it was here early though, she didn't know how much to tell Emma. She was only a baby. She didn't need to hear her mother talk about an evil old witch-faced grandma who'd stolen so much from them. She needed truths. But the kind of truths that a child could understand. There would be time later for details. "I did want you, Emma." She spoke quickly now, hoping to ease away any doubts the child might be feeling. "I really did. But I wanted you to have a family and—"

"But you have a family. Aunt Mike and Aunt Jo and Grandpa and Bear and—" She paused and looked around as if searching for someone else. "Don't I have a grandma, too?"

Another ache in her heart. "No. My mom died just before you were born." And that was a big part of the reasons that had convinced an eighteen-year-old girl to make the biggest sacrifice of her life.

"Oh. My daddy's mommy died too, so maybe they're friends."

Sam doubted it, but managed to keep from saying so aloud. Her own mother—a sweeter, warmer woman never lived—was probably running a bingo game in heaven. While Jeff's mother was no doubt somewhere a lot warmer, desperately wishing she had sunblock strong enough to withstand the flames.

"So how come you didn't keep me?"

Sighing, Sam lifted Emma's hand and held it. Rubbing her thumbs across the back of her small, soft hand, she said, "I wanted to, baby. I really did. But—" She stopped and thought about it for a moment before saying, "There were some problems here and—"

"Was I a problem?"

"Oh no." Sam smiled widely and pulled Emma in close for a hug. This she could give her. This truth was pure and simple. "No, honey. You were never a problem. You were a gift I couldn't keep."

Jeff looked at the old house, lamplight shining in the windows, and just for a minute, he remembered his first visit here. Nine years before, he'd stood in just this spot, looking at the house and tugging nervously at his collar. But he'd had Sam beside him then. Leaning into him, hugging him tight, reassuring him with a laugh that her family would love him—because *she* did.

The sun was shining and in his memories it always seemed to be that way. Was it real? Or was it because when he was with Sam, the world looked brighter? Didn't matter now.

They'd walked up those porch steps together, and he'd heard the family inside. So different from his own. Here, there was laughter and shouting and a TV turned up way too loud. The scent of something mouthwatering drifted through the screen door and Sam said, "Lucky you. Mama's making her world-famous sauce."

Then he followed her inside and the noise stopped. Her sisters, her mother, and finally, her father, all turned to look at him and Jeff knew what it felt like to be on a glass slide under a microscope. Nerves rattled through him, but in an instant, it was over.

Sylvia Marconi, tall, slim, still lovely, hurried to him. "Let me see him, Sam," she said, smiling as she took his hands in hers. She studied him for a long moment with frank, warm brown eyes, then nodded. "I like you," she said firmly and kissed him on both cheeks.

It had felt as though someone had just hung a medal around his neck. Nerves slipped away, he took a deep breath and smiled. Impossible to do anything else when faced with such open welcome.

"Thank you, Mrs. Marconi."

She laughed and he instantly knew where Sam had gotten her full-throated, rolling yet musical laughter. "Call me Mama. We're family." Then she flicked a quick glance at her husband. "Papa, leave the football game and come meet Sam's young man."

Then it was a blur of voices, faces, smiles. Sam's sisters jumped right in, giving him warm hugs and making him feel at ease. Jeff had never experienced anything like it. The warmth of the house surrounded him and the Marconis swept him up in the flood of emotions.

Hank stood up, a barrel-chested man with a thick head of gray-flecked brown hair and a full steel-gray beard. Stretching out one hand to him, the older man winked. "Glad you're here," he said, with a wicked glance at his wife and daughters. "One more man in the house evens things up a little."

The family had welcomed him, but they still hadn't approved of his and Sam's marriage. They'd insisted the two of them were too young. And looking back, he thought maybe they'd been right. Didn't matter now though, one way or the other.

Jeff inhaled sharply, deeply, then blew the air out of his lungs in a rush. A twinge of regret pinged inside him like a steel ball in a pinball game, bouncing off rods and pins, racking up thousands of points. But there was no "win" here.

The afternoon that still lived in his memory was long gone and his welcome at this house, long revoked. That bothered him more than he would have thought. A soft ocean wind drifted past him, spearing curious fingers through his hair. Overhead, the leaves of the old oak rattled like an old woman's bones in winter. And Jeff shoved his hands into his pants pockets.

He hadn't expected to feel . . . so *much.* Sure, he'd anticipated his reaction to Sam. But he hadn't known that he would miss her family, as well. Nine years ago, Mike Marconi had been only sixteen and Jo nineteen. He hadn't known them well or long, but he'd felt their acceptance. They'd treated him like an older brother.

Now, Jeff thought grimly, Mike had already made it plain that she'd like nothing better than to pick up a nail gun and use him for target practice. Jo surely wouldn't be any happier. And he was sorry about that.

Hell, he was sorry about a lot of things.

Straightening up, he marched up the flower-lined walk and stomped up the steps. The point was, the past was gone and the future had yet to be mapped out. And dammit, he wouldn't let regret push him off course. What mattered now was Emma. Not the wispy, fragmented emotions of too many years ago—but a little girl who didn't deserve any of this shit.

The stereo was on and Bob Seger was growling about old-time rock and roll. Through the screen, Jeff saw past the dimly lit living room to the bright kitchen beyond. He lifted one hand to knock just as a woman danced to the kitchen counter, shook her bootie for emphasis, then shimmied in time with the music.

And he was caught, as he had been so many years before. She moved with a freedom and unselfconsciousness that he'd always envied.

His hand stilled.

His heart pretty much did, too.

Sam still had great moves.

And one terrific butt.

"God." While he watched, she did a fast dip and spin, then rocked her jeans-clad hips to the beat Seger provided. Jeff couldn't take his gaze off her. He'd nearly forgotten how she liked to dance in the kitchen. Her dark, fiery hair swirled around her shoulders and when she lifted her arms skyward, a kitchen towel clenched between her hands, the hem of her dark green T-shirt rose, giving him an all-too-brief glimpse of tanned skin.

Naturally, he shouldn't be noticing Sam—not the way he was, anyway. Dammit, he was engaged. To a woman who had the right to expect better. Jesus, was he really going to stand here and let his hormones drag him down a road he'd already crashed on?

Sure, he knew better. But he couldn't seem to help himself. Couldn't seem to tear his gaze from Sam's seductive dance. She wasn't even trying—yet he felt a raging need crawling inside him.

He unfisted his hand and laid it against the screen door. He couldn't interrupt. Didn't want to shatter this moment when she didn't know she was being watched. When she wasn't angry or defensive or ready to kick his balls into his throat. Just for this one moment, he wanted to enjoy seeing the woman he remembered. The woman who'd swept him into a sea of passion that had, eventually, drowned him.

That thought doused whatever embers were flickering to life within. He made a fist and knocked three times. Hard.

Instantly, she whirled around and her gaze fixed on him. Embarrassment and suspicion crossed her face in quick succession before her features composed themselves into a perfectly polite, perfectly poised, blank. She tossed the dishtowel onto the counter, glanced behind her, and then headed toward him.

Loose limbed and graceful, even when her spine was stiff enough to snap, Sam Marconi was the kind of woman who could bring a man to his knees. But she'd done that to him once, as he vividly remembered. Wouldn't happen again.

"A dancing carpenter?" he asked, and could have kicked his own ass for getting things off on the wrong foot. One thing to keep from getting sucked into a sexual haze—something else again to pick a fight with a woman who could make his life miserable.

Her eyes narrowed. Jesus. He remembered that look all too well. Ready for battle and hunting for scalps. Quickly, he lifted both hands in surrender. "Sorry. Look, I'm just here to pick up Emma."

Emma. He'd spent the last two hours wandering around "downtown" Chandler, thinking about what his daughter might be doing. What Sam was telling her. Stupid, but it had felt like the longest two hours of his life. For the first time, he'd been locked out of something involving his daughter. For the first time, he'd known that someone else had as deep a claim to her as he did himself.

And it wasn't sitting well.

Sam nodded, reached out and opened the screen door. "Come on in. I'll get her. She's out back with Jo and Mike."

Both of her sisters were there. Great. With the fortitude of a gladiator, Jeff managed to keep from groaning. But his features must have told her what he was thinking.

Her mouth twitched. "Don't worry. My sisters won't kill you in front of witnesses."

"Comforting. What about your parents?"

Sam inhaled sharply. "Papa's so happy to get a chance to be with Emma, he's willing to overlook you."

Briefly, Jeff mourned the loss of the older man's respect. He'd enjoyed Hank Marconi. Enjoyed having a father figure who wasn't steeped in years of guilt and family duty. "What about Sylvia? She ready to kill me, too?"

"Mama's dead," Sam said, all light in her eyes dissolving.

"God, Sam . . ."

She stepped back as he stepped in. Shoving her hands into the back pockets of her jeans, she shrugged and tipped her head to one side. "Just before Emma was born."

He hadn't known. Hadn't kept tabs on her or her family. He'd wanted to put it all behind him. And he'd succeeded. Now, a twinge of grief snaked through him, for Sylvia, for Sam, for him. For all of them and for what might have been.

"I really am sorry."

She nodded. "So'm I."

"I liked Sylvia a lot."

"She liked you, too," Sam said, gaze fixed on him. "Which just goes to prove that even Mama could make a mistake."

"Ouch." Her barb hit home and made the guilt flare just a little. Deliberately, he tamped it down. "And are you ready to kill me?"

"Haven't decided yet."

A long minute ticked past and the music kept rolling out around them. Guitars, drums, and raspy voices filled the room and made it seem . . . crowded. Sam walked around the end of the sofa and turned the volume down. When she looked back at him, she took a deep breath and said, "Emma's great."

"Yeah. She is."

"You did a terrific job with her." She wrapped her arms around her middle.

That admission had cost her. He could see it in her. And damned if a part of him didn't swell with pride.

Why should it please him to hear her say he'd raised their daughter well? Why should what she thought of him mean *anything*? It had been years since they were together.

But, he silently admitted, it hadn't been years since he'd thought of her. How could he avoid thinking of Sam? Every time he looked at his child, he saw her mother's face. "She's everything to me, Sam."

"She is to me, too." The words burst from her as if she'd been holding them in all night and finally lost the battle. As she spoke, she came back toward him, her steps as hurried as her words. "I know you don't believe that. Because I gave her up. But she's *always* been everything to me. She's never been out of my head, my heart. Not for a minute."

"I do believe it," he said, unable to deny what he could see so plainly in her eyes. He'd told himself for years that Sam hadn't wanted either of them. That he and Emma had been a mistake. One she'd eagerly corrected as soon as she could. He'd been wrong. He understood that now. "But it doesn't change what is, Sam. Emma's mine."

"And mine."

A ripple of anger swam uneasily in the pit of his stomach and he forced himself to contain it. "I have full custody," he reminded her with a calm he silently congratulated himself on.

"For now."

Shock slapped him back a step. He'd expected her to want visitation rights and had even convinced himself that they could agree on something reasonable. A week or two in the summer—the occasional weekend. But *joint custody*?

"You can't be serious."

Her pale blue eyes narrowed again and he could almost *hear* the starting gun going off, signaling the beginning of the battle.

"I've missed eight years of her *life,* Jeff," she said, her words an oath that was all the more powerful for the whisper it was delivered in. "I missed her first words, her first step, her first laugh. I wasn't there for her first day of school. I wasn't there to give her cookies when she came home—your housekeeper does that."

"Julia is—"

"Doesn't matter how wonderful Julia is. She's not me. She's not Emma's *mom.* I've missed too much already, Jeff. I won't miss any more."

His control slipped a little further and he scrambled to hang on to it. But she was threatening everything he held dear. Everything that mattered. "I'm not giving her up."

"I'm not, either."

He shoved both hands through his hair, and snorted a choked-off laugh. "You already *did.*"

"Nice shot," Sam muttered, and headed for the kitchen.

He was right behind her, his stride longer, and when he caught her, he grabbed hold of her arm and spun her around to face him. He yanked her close. So close, he could taste her breath on his face. So close, he could see her pulse pounding at the base of her neck. So close that the urge to be *closer* grabbed him by the throat and squeezed.

"Why?" His voice was a growl. A low roar of raw emotion. "Why are you the one woman in the world who can get to me like nobody else?"

She threw her hair back from her face, planted both hands on his chest, and curled her fingers into the fabric of his shirt. "I'm not trying to get *to* you, Jeff. I'm *trying* to get *through* to you."

Damn. Her perfume wrapped itself around him. Filled his head. Confused his senses. Stirred up flames until he felt the heat spreading through every inch of his body. He didn't let her go. *Couldn't* let her go.

Because he'd never really said good-bye?

Because she'd never left his mind?

Because he was an idiot letting his dick do the thinking for him again?

Or all of the above?

"That's what makes me nuts, Sam," he said, his voice hard, low, amazed. "You never *had* to try. You just do it. Always did."

Some of the starch left her spine. Her shoulders slumped and she almost leaned into him. Almost. Her hands relaxed against him, her palms lying flat on his chest. Jeff could have sworn he felt the imprint of her hands on his skin.

"What did that ever get us, Jeff?" she asked quietly.

"Emma, for one thing."

She smiled all too briefly. "But we lost *us*."

True. Though he'd be a liar if he didn't admit, at least silently, that he'd wondered often, over the years, what might have happened if they'd stuck it out. If one of them had only dug in their heels and demanded that the other *listen*. But they'd been too young. Too eager to blame. Too quick to quit.

And now it was too late.

Wasn't it?

God, she felt good.

"Jeff . . ." She shook her head even as he lowered his head to hers. Even as his mouth hovered just a breath away from hers. "We can't do this—"

She was right.

It was stupid.

And he absolutely *had* to. "Call it a nine-years-late good-bye kiss."

His mouth met hers and the flash of something hot, familiar, and overpowering hit him hard and fast. His body went tight. His blood pumped. His body tightened and his breath strangled in his lungs. Desire, *need,* was so overpowering, he felt his knees rock.

Then the guilt kicked in, slamming into him with a punch solid enough to steal what was left of his breath.

Instantly he let her go and took a step back. It wasn't far enough, but it was all he could manage.

"Sorry," he muttered, scraping one hand across his face as if he could wipe away the kiss and the memory of it. She looked as shaken as he, but true to her nature, she'd never admit it. Already, any semblance of softness had dropped away, like shadows disappearing when a light flicked off.

"That solved nothing."

"Didn't expect it to." He didn't know what to do with his hands. Now that he wasn't touching her, they felt empty.

"So what was the point?"

"Jesus, does there have to *be* a point?"

"Usually."

"Well, not this time."

She continued as if he hadn't spoken at all. "Because if you're trying to soften me up, confuse me with some lame-ass kiss designed to remind me of happier days—"

"You think I *planned* to do that?"

"Please." She snorted. "You always had a plan."

"Oh, that's good. Coming from you."

"What's that supposed to mean?"

He stared at her. "Aren't you the one who once told me we'd have five children and then listed their names and where they'd go to school?"

She flushed. "That was different."

"Oh, *your* plans are okay?"

"You are so far off the subject here."

"What exactly *is* the subject?"

"Emma."

Worry stirred inside him. "We'll work something out."

"Damn straight."

"Never give an inch."

"You got that right."

In a weird sort of way, he almost admired that. He must be a masochist.

"There's something else."

"What?" Wary, Jeff waited.

"I want Emma this weekend."

"I don't—"

"You've had her for eight years, Jeff. I want time with her. I *need* time with her."

He heard the desperation in her voice. Read it in her eyes. Felt it pulsing off her in thick, emotionally charged waves that wrapped around him and drew him close. He could fight her on it. He could hurt her and make Emma miserable. Or he could be a good guy.

Dammit, he hated being the good one.

"All right."

Sam was already beginning to argue when she realized that he'd agreed. It threw her off stride, but not for long. She smiled, flashing the grin that he remembered so clearly. The one he'd never been able to forget.

"Thanks."

He nodded, but even while she was still smiling, he wanted to make one thing clear. "This doesn't mean anything's settled."

"I know."

He wouldn't give up his daughter and Sam was just as determined. And in a vicious game of tug-of-war, didn't the rope sometimes snap?

Emma.

In the middle of a battleground and oblivious to the warring sides.

"Make no mistakes, here, Sam. I'm sorry if you're regretting giving our daughter up. And I'm sure as hell sorry that my mother was the architect of all this misery." He pulled her close again and loomed over her until her head fell back, but her gaze was still fixed on his. "And I'm willing to let you and Emma get to know each other. Spend time together. But I'm *not* going to relinquish full custody of my daughter without a fight."

She pulled free of him and rubbed her upper arms, where a clear, red imprint of his fingers was staining her skin. Nodding, she met his gaze. "Okay, then. Buckle your seat belt, Jeff. 'Cause this ride's about to get *real* bumpy."

The weekend was starting off great.

Thanks to Sam, Emma was soaking wet, smelled like a dirty dog, and had a brand-new scrape on her knee.

The harbor was filled with boats. Small skiffs with colorful sails bumped up against rich men's toys, and farther down the dock, as though they were living on the poor side of town, were the fishing boats. Like ugly stepsisters of the sleek yachts aboard which weekend sailors partied, the commercial ships were battered and worn. Rust spots stained their hulls and the smell of fish was never completely washed off, no matter how hard the deckhands scrubbed.

Yet Sam preferred the commercial fishing boats. At least they were hardworking and honest. The pleasure boats were pretty and stylish, but they'd never withstood heavy storm surf and daily wear and tear like the workingmen's boats. Just like people, she thought, as she watched Emma run along the boardwalk in front of her. *Give me a good peasant over an aristocrat anytime. At least you know where you stand with them.*

Unlike dealing with the movers and shakers. With Jeff. *Dammit.* He kept popping into her head. As she acknowledged that truth, she felt a slow hum and burn sizzling inside her. Ruthlessly, she stomped it out, mentally jumping up and down on the embers with both feet.

Jeff wasn't important now. Emma was. Only Emma.

Her *daughter* was happy. Healthy. And currently chasing an ugly little dog with one missing ear, a sloppy grin, and the smell of fish embedded in his fur. Homer was short on looks but long on personality, and he'd never met a kid he didn't like.

"Mommy!"

"Right behind you, honey!" She hurried, catching up just as Emma and Homer approached the battered ship that Homer's owner called home.

The boats alongside the dock creaked and swayed with the soft rippling of the water. Seals gathered on the rocks and swimming just below the dock barked and flapped their fins for the tourists tossing baitfish at them. The combined scents of the sea and fish and deep-fried churros being sold from the cart at the end of the dock filled the air.

Summer in Chandler, and as far as Sam was concerned, the best one in a long time.

"You two walk to China or something?" Hank Marconi leaned on the railing of the ship docked on her left and grinned at Sam and Emma. His thick gray hair bristled around his head, his beard looked tidy, and his pale blue eyes sparkled with delight as he watched his granddaughter scramble up the wide plank leading to the boat deck.

"Homer wanted to," Sam called back. "But we got tired."

"We got lunch ready." Hank grinned at his daughter, then turned and swung Emma up into his arms, cuddling her close to his barrel chest. God, Sam remembered what that felt like. To be held so close to Papa that you were sure nothing could ever hurt you. And she was so grateful that her own daughter was getting the chance to experience that wide, loving safety net, too.

"Lunch? Who cooked?" Sam asked as she walked up the ramp. "You or Antonio?"

"McDonald's," her father said with a wink. "It's special for my girls."

Thank God. Antonio Miletti, Papa's oldest friend since Anthony Candellano had passed away several years ago, was a nice man. But Emeril he wasn't.

"Look, Papa!" Emma crowed, pointing past him to the patio area of Charlie's, the upscale seafood restaurant overlooking the harbor. "It's my daddy! Daddy and Cynthia!"

Cynthia?

Sam turned, followed her daughter's pointing finger, and had no trouble at all finding her soon-to-be ex-husband and his current fiancée seated at one of the small glass tables covered by snow-white tablecloths.

Instantly, Sam's gaze locked on the woman.

She even *looked* like a Cynthia.

Cool. Beautiful. Her soft blond hair was expertly styled so that when the sea wind mussed it, every hair fell back into place like soldiers standing guard. Her emerald-green silk dress clung to every curve (which were pretty damned impressive even from a distance), and she was leaning in toward Jeff as if she couldn't bear the table separating them.

Sam took a minute to look down at herself. Frayed denim shorts, battered sneakers, and a tank top stained with whatever was clinging to Homer's fur.

Oh yeah.

No contest.

Winner and still champion, Cynthia.

Chapter Seven

Jo ran her measuring tape along the base of the wall in the soon-to-be-torn-apart library and tried to shut out the noise drifting to her from the back of the house. "One more half hour and I'd have been finished," she muttered as she made a note on the pad she kept in the front pocket of her jeans.

When she stuffed the notebook back into her pocket, she released the stop button on the tape measure and smiled as the metallic tape raced across the floor and back into its shell. With Sam down at the harbor with Emma, Mike off doing God knew what, she'd stopped in at Grace's house to have a little alone time with her work.

On Monday, the crews would start tearing down the walls and pulling up the old floorboards, and a part of Jo wished she could have talked Grace out of it. There was something to be said for the old. For wood that had stood the test of time. Sure it was scarred, but refinishing would have taken care of that. But Grace was determined. She didn't want refinishing. She wanted *new*.

Good steady income for Marconi Construction . . . but the artist buried deep within Jo wanted to change the older woman's mind.

Going down on one knee, she smoothed the flat of

her hand across the pale oak floorboards. Part of the original structure, this floor had been in place for more than a hundred years. And now, it would be discarded—replaced by either the parquet Grace was talking about or, for all Jo knew, *linoleum*. But at least Jo could save the wood. She'd store it at her place until she could find a way to use it in something beautiful.

People had lived and died and dreamed in this place. Her fingertips caressed the scarred, worn planks, as she thought now of the cattle baron, and the madam, both of whom had walked here. "What stories you could tell, huh?"

"Talking to wood is the first sign."

A deep voice spoke up from behind her and Jo grimaced tightly. Dammit.

Slowly, she stood up, refusing to be embarrassed for being caught indulging her romantic side. Turning around, she looked right at the man standing in the open doorway, watching her. "First sign of what?"

Cash Hunter gave her a lazy grin and leaned one shoulder against the doorjamb. His thumbs were hooked into the front pockets of his jeans and his black T-shirt strained across a chest that was, she knew, broad and well defined. He wore dusty cowboy boots that looked as though the only thing holding them together was the memory of once being shiny new. And his face . . . rugged angles, sharp planes, high cheekbones . . . well, his face was too handsome for his own good and *way* too handsome for *hers*.

He lifted one shoulder in a shrug. "No way to tell without further investigation."

Jo ignored the hot little ball of need that had burst into life at the pit of her stomach. She absolutely refused to become one of Cash's conquests. Ridiculous that women all over central California were lining up to fall at one man's feet.

"How do you do that?" she demanded.

One dark eyebrow lifted. Amusement glittered in his nearly black eyes. "Do what?"

That ball of need in her gut iced over in reaction to his obvious ego. "Make every statement a seduction."

"Did I?"

"There it is again," she countered, throwing both hands high. "Seriously, do you *work* on your material, or does it just come to you?"

He laughed shortly and straightened up with a loose, easy grace that gave the impression that he was a man who moved slow at *all* things. Jo took a deep breath and would *not* think about that.

"What's wrong, Josefina? I worry you?"

She flushed. Nobody, but *nobody,* called her Josefina. Not even Papa. Wishing she were holding a hammer instead of a tape measure, Jo glared at him. "Not only do you not worry me," she snapped, "I don't think about you at all."

"Liar."

Her head whipped around and she blinked at him. "You are a pitifully deluded man."

"Yeah?"

"*Yeah.*" Jo started past him, but stopped beside him long enough to shoot him a hard look. "Not every woman in the known universe is susceptible to the Hunter charm."

He stared down at her and damned if Jo couldn't feel the heat sizzling in his black eyes. The man was a walking hormone.

"So you think I'm charming."

Walked into that one. "I think you're dangerous."

"Even better."

She blew out an impatient breath. Her peaceful, quiet morning shot to hell, Jo glared at him again. "What're you doing here?"

"Working." He looked amused again.

Working? He wasn't part of the crew she'd hired for the summer. In fact, Jo had made *sure* that he wouldn't be around. She had a lot of female carpenters and hadn't wanted to risk losing any of them to Cash's weird hypnotic powers. "You're not on my crew."

He smiled. One brief, tantalizing smile that should have been accompanied by a loud set of warning bells. "Yeah, I know. Grace hired me."

"To do what?" Jo demanded, already trying to figure out ways to avoid him.

He smiled as if he knew just what she was thinking. "First, I'm building a butler's pantry in the first kitchen."

"First?"

His smile widened and a flash of amusement sparked in his dark eyes. "After that, a cedar closet in the master bedroom."

Which meant, Jo thought with an inner grumble, he'd be at the house all summer. "Perfect."

"So I'm charming *and* perfect. Josefina, I'm touched."

"Aaargh . . ." A growl wasn't much of a comeback but it was all she could manage. If she stayed, she might have to kill him and that would only stain the great oak floorboards she had plans for. Besides. She had somewhere else to be. Stomping past him, she stormed out of the room and toward the construction noise still bristling outside.

She didn't see him watch her go.

Sam sat with her back to the *tres chic* restaurant so she wouldn't have to watch Jeff and *Cynthia* canoodle over their chardonnays.

It didn't help much. Because she *felt* them there. Only thirty short feet away, they were dining in seaside elegance, while here on Antonio's boat, Big Macs were the order of the day. Sort of underlined the differences between her and her not-as-former-as-he-should-be husband, didn't it? He was always champagne to her beer, Jag to her truck, old money to her no-money.

Nine years ago, she'd told herself the differences didn't matter. All that mattered was what they *felt*. Well, she might not learn fast, but she *did* learn. And no stolen kiss was enough to convince her otherwise. Besides, she thought, that kiss hadn't meant anything. Just a blip on an otherwise flat surface. There was nothing left between them. Nothing but a little girl they both loved and wanted.

The ocean breeze skipped over the surface of the water, swept across the deck, and then left again, rushing on to play over the tops of the other boats at dock. Tourists wandered the boardwalk and hung over the railings to watch the seals. A kid on a skateboard whizzed past, darting between the clumps of pedestrians, his board roaring and thundering over the worn, wooden dock. Everything was just as it should be.

Except for Jeff and Perfect Woman.

"You like the harbor, eh?" Papa asked, his gaze fixed on his granddaughter.

"It's fun!" Emma took another bite of her Happy Meal hamburger and tossed a French fry to Homer, sitting right beside her, trying to look as pitiful as possible. Which, considering his less than American Kennel Club looks, wasn't tough. "Mommy says we can watch the men fishing on the pier, too."

"Pier." Antonio scoffed and shook his head until his straggly white hair writhed in the wind like albino snakes. "You want to see fishing, I should take you out on my boat. We'll catch a whale."

Emma's eyes went as big as saucers.

Antonio leaned in close to the child and grinned. "When your mama was a little girl, I took her fishing. She caught a shark."

Emma shifted her gaze to her mother and the jaw-dropping admiration shining in her eyes warmed Sam all the way through. The fact that the shark had been a baby and only a foot long, and they'd released it immediately, really wasn't the point, was it?

"Can I go?"

Sam grinned and shook her head. "Not today, thanks, Antonio. We've got plans."

"So what's next for you two?" Papa asked, reaching out to tug one of Emma's pigtails as if ringing a bell.

"Mommy's taking me to a castle," Emma said, handing off another fry to the little dog wiggling beside her.

"A castle?" Papa's gray brows lifted high on his lined, deeply tanned forehead. Years of working in the sunshine had left their mark on his features.

"Castle's," Sam said, laughing. It had been Mike's idea for the three Marconi girls—four now, counting Emma—to meet up at Castle's Day Spa. A couple of hours of buffing, polishing, and female bonding in great surroundings. In general . . . a girls' day out. Glancing down at her less than fabulous outfit, Sam thought it had been a pretty timely suggestion. "I called Tasha last night. She said she'd make room for us."

"You're gonna pay somebody to paint your toes, little girl?"

Even though she was sitting beside her own daughter, Sam knew Antonio would always consider her a kid.

"You oughta come fishing with your papa and me instead."

"Thanks," Sam said, shaking her head. "But I think I'll pass. I know you two," she said. "You'd have me scrubbing the deck and washing down the bait tank."

Papa and Antonio exchanged resigned shrugs that told her how right she was.

"I could go," Emma said, dropping one hand to Homer's ugly head, as if already reluctant to leave him.

"You come with us next time, mouse," Papa said, before turning his head to look at Sam. "You be home for dinner, all right? *All* of you. Calzones tonight."

"What's calzone, Papa?" Emma asked.

"Oh! You don't know calzones?" Hank slapped one beefy hand to his heart and staggered dramatically until the little girl's laughter erupted like soap bubbles on the air. After a minute or two, he stopped, grinned, and tapped the tip of Emma's nose with his forefinger. "I'll teach you all you need to know about cooking, little mouse. You bring your mama home on time, eh?"

"We'll be there, Papa." Sam slid her sunglasses from the top of her head down to cover her eyes. Sunlight glanced off the water in blinding flashes. "Let's roll, Em," she said, holding out a hand for her daughter.

"We've got to get back to the house and clean up before we hit Castle's."

Emma scooted off the chair, then looked from the homely little dog to her mother. "Can Homer come?"

"He's going fishing," Sam said, folding her fingers over Emma's.

"I need him for bait," Antonio said on a laugh.

"Not really," Sam corrected quickly as Emma's eyes filled up and her chin quivered. "Antonio's just joking."

Emma didn't look convinced. "Can I show Homer to Daddy before we go? He's only right there."

Sam shot a look at the couple still sitting over a leisurely lunch. The purely female half of her was shrieking, *No way, don't go near them looking as bad as you do.* The purely Marconi half was shouting just as loudly, *Go face 'em down. You can take her.*

Emma was dancing in place, holding on to Homer's collar with one hand and her mother with the other. *"Please?"*

What the hell? Who was she trying to kid? Why would she worry about how she looked in comparison to the Perfect Woman? So what if Jeff saw her looking and *smelling* like a rag used to wipe up the deck of Antonio's boat?

"Okay," Sam said, then shot a look at her father and his friend. "We'll bring Homer right back, then you guys can hit the high seas."

But Papa wasn't looking at her. Instead, he was frowning at Jeff and the woman with him. Sam groaned inwardly but wasn't too worried. Papa would never say anything in front of Emma. Though she could tell just from the set of his chin that her father would like nothing better than to bull up the walkway and take a swing at Jeff. Nobody hurt one of Hank Marconi's girls and lived to do it again.

Dropping Emma's hand, Sam threw her arms around her father's neck and gave him a big, smacking kiss on the cheek. He'd always been there. Through thick and thin, that was Papa. As steady as the sun, and just as warm. "Thanks, Papa."

He squeezed her tightly, briefly, and tore his gaze from Jeff to focus on her. "You and my little mouse have a good time, okay?"

"We will." She stepped back, kissed Antonio, then grabbed Emma and headed for Jeff.

Once clear of the boats, Emma sprinted ahead of Sam, running up the wide boardwalk toward the restaurant. Homer, like an emissary from Ugly Smelly Planet, raced alongside her, his excited yips startling a pelican into swooping off his perch to cruise the ocean looking for lunch.

The crowd parted in front of the girl and the dog, as if by magic and Sam was given a clear view of Emma's reception. Jeff's whole face lit up when he spotted his daughter and Sam's heart flipped over in her chest. Cynthia the Perfect was less enthusiastic. Emma reached to give her a hug and Cynthia grabbed the child's hands and held them safely to one side as she bent to kiss Emma's cheek.

Scowling, Sam thought, *Bitch.* Instantly though, she told herself that she was overreacting. What woman wouldn't protect a beautiful silk dress from a grubby kid and a dirtier dog?

Forcing a smile, she walked up behind Emma and nodded first to Jeff, then to Cynthia. While Jeff forced himself to admire the ugliest dog on the planet for his daughter's sake, the beautiful blonde stood up and offered her hand.

Sam shook her head. "Better not," she admitted wryly. "I'm afraid Emma and I smell like the docks."

Cynthia's smile was warm and filled with understanding. "That just means you're having fun together," she said, half-turning to link arms with Jeff as he stepped up beside her.

Beautiful, elegant, and *nice,* dammit.

How was she supposed to hate the woman who was going to be Jeff's wife if she made herself so damn likable? Not fair at all. And then there was the whole neat-and-tidy thing Cynthia had going for her. Suddenly, Sam felt even more dirty and disreputable than she had before. Inwardly sighing, she told herself she and Cynthia could star in a road production of *Beauty and the Beast.* No question about who would play the Beast.

Thankfully, the restaurant patio was nearly deserted. Most people had no doubt opted to eat inside, out of the reach of the sun. Which meant that the startling difference between Sam and Cynthia wasn't put on full display. Small favors.

"I'm so glad to get the chance to meet you," Cynthia was saying. "Jeff's told me all about you."

"Has he?" Sam shot him a quick look, but Jeff's features were carefully, studiously, blank. What had he said? she wondered. What had he told his fiancée about the woman he was still married to?

"I have to say," Cynthia continued, her light laugh rippling around them, "I was a little concerned. You know what they say about someone's first love . . ."

You never forget your first love? Was that it? Sam

kept her gaze locked with Jeff's. His eyes were unreadable, so she couldn't be sure what he was thinking. But she had to wonder if he'd given any thought at all to that kiss a few nights before. Had it bothered him? Had he felt the sizzle and snap that had leaped up between them?

Or was it all in her imagination?

And oh God, remembering that kiss right now had a guilty flush rushing through her. Tearing her gaze from Jeff's, Sam looked back at the blonde and smiled. "Don't worry about me," she said. "I'm just the 'ex.'"

"Oh, but you're so much more," Cynthia said, and reached for Sam's hand. Holding it in both of hers, Cynthia said, "You're Emma's *mother*. That will always link us. We're family. We always will be."

Ye Gods.

Sam hadn't thought of it like that. Of course, she'd thought plenty about having her daughter back in her life. And how she was going to make sure that Emma *stayed* in her life. She'd realized that she would have to forge a new relationship with Jeff. One that meant they'd be able to be civil to each other over the coming years.

But she'd never once considered having to deal with Emma's stepmother.

Family?

Could this get any more awkward?

Her silence stretched on and on until even *she* noticed the quiet hanging between them. She had to say something. Be nice. Be polite. Despite feeling like the ugly duckling standing next to a particularly beautiful swan. "That's very kind," she managed to croak.

"Oh, it's not kindness," Cynthia went on, with a smile for Emma. "It's gratitude."

"Huh?" Brilliant, Sam. Just brilliant.

"I want to thank you. For having had the courage to do what was right for your daughter."

"I don't—" Sam shot a look at Jeff, as if hoping for help, but he shrugged and looked at Cynthia in bemusement. Apparently he didn't have a clue what she was talking about either.

"You had the strength to give Emma up—"

Sam swallowed hard and tightened her grip on Emma's little hand as if someone were going to try to take her away again.

"—and that allowed Emma to be a part of *my* life." Releasing Sam, she turned her face up to Jeff's and positively *beamed* at him. "I can't tell you how much that means to me."

Jeff smiled at Perfect Cynthia and it was as if both Sam and Emma had disappeared. They were invisible. Even Homer was being ignored and Sam knew darn well it was almost physically impossible to ignore Homer.

She felt like the intruder she was. Like a voyeur, watching a honeymooning couple.

And that kiss seemed even more nebulous now. How could it have meant anything when he was engaged to Perfection? And why was he kissing Sam anyway, if cool blonde was waiting for him in San Francisco? And why was she asking herself so many damn questions that didn't have answers?

"Emma," she whispered, "we've gotta go."

" 'Kay." Emma squeezed herself in between Cynthia and Jeff and threw her little arms around Jeff's knees. Cynthia skipped back a step or two and swiped the palms of her hands over her skirt.

Jeff hugged his daughter tightly, then when she slipped over to Sam's side, he stuffed his hands into his pockets. When he began to rattle the keys in his pockets, Sam's eyebrows lifted and he stopped, shooting her a nod and a wry smile.

"Great to meet you," Sam said, backing away like a servant from the queen. "I'm sure we'll be seeing each other again while you're here . . ."

"Oh." Cynthia spoke up. "I'm afraid not. I'm heading back to San Francisco this evening—" She reached for Jeff's arm again and leaned into him.

A spike of something not so nice flickered inside Sam as she wondered if the woman was incapable of standing upright.

"Already? Short visit," Sam said, still inching her way closer to escape. Way past time to make herself scarce. After all, what did she and Cynthia have in common? They'd both slept with Jeff? She frowned to herself at that thought, not much caring for the images that had leaped into her brain.

"There are so many wedding details to be seen to, I really shouldn't have taken today, either," Cynthia admitted, like a sorority sister sharing a secret. "But I just had to steal away to see my Jeff. You know how it is."

She leaned a little farther. If Jeff backed up suddenly, Cynthia would take a header onto the stone patio. Sam told herself she really shouldn't enjoy that image so much.

"Sure," Sam agreed. "I know how that goes." She was almost out. Homer was already running down the walkway, headed back home, and Emma was tugging at Sam's arm, trying to follow the dog. "Well, you two have a nice visit and—"

"I'll see you and Emma tomorrow," Jeff said, and his deep voice rumbled across the distance separating them and seemed to thunder deep inside Sam's chest.

Weird sensation.

Even weirder situation.

"Right. Gotta go." And Sam quickly became the first Marconi in history to run from a battlefield.

Chapter Eight

Jeff felt like a cheating husband.

Grimacing tightly, he shifted his stance, unconsciously pulling a bit farther away from Cynthia's clinging grasp. Was it guilt that had him moving away? Or a yearning he didn't want to acknowledge?

Hell. A few days with Sam Marconi and his world was once again spinning off its axis. But why should that surprise him? Nine years ago, Sam had jumped into his world and turned it upside down. No big shock that she could still do it without even trying.

"Are you all right?"

Cynthia's voice snapped him out of the haze wrapped around him. Glancing at her, he plastered a smile on his face and reminded himself that Cynthia had been damned understanding about all this. And it couldn't be easy, planning a wedding only to find out that your fiancée was still married to someone else.

He stared down at her. Cool and beautiful, she had her brown eyes focused on him and her mouth was curved into a concerned smile. Sunlight shone all around her, making the soft blond hair she kept short and tidy look golden. Her perfume, an expensive blend of flowers and citrus, lifted into the air and all he could think was how different she was from Sam.

Cynthia was candlelight.

Sam was *fireworks*.

Bastard.

"Jeff? Honey? Are you all right?"

"Yeah, I'm fine." He shifted his gaze back to Sam and Emma. Couldn't help himself. The ugly little dog was running toward a rusty bucket of a boat and his daughter was right behind it. But it was Sam his gaze locked on. Even in a tank top, worn-out jeans shorts, and smelling like day-old fish, she *sparkled*.

Cynthia spoke up again, as if trying to wean his attention back to her. "Samantha seems to be connecting to Emma very well."

"Yes," he said, his mind wandering down dangerous paths. "She does."

"Does that bother you?"

Bother him? It worried him in ways he wouldn't have thought possible. Yes, Emma and Sam were bonding and that was good. He knew his daughter needed that connection with her mother. But he could admit, if only to himself, that he felt as though he were losing small pieces of his daughter's heart to a woman who'd turned her back on them both.

Jeff turned to face Cynthia again, and looked down into her deep brown eyes. She was close enough to him that he could feel her heart beating against his chest. She leaned into him, pressing her breasts to him and giving him an excellent view of her impressive cleavage.

Jeff waited—hoping to feel the buzz of awareness that always hit him when Sam was near. It didn't come. In fact, that special something, that *spark* of need, of lust, had never been there between him and Cynthia.

Which was, he reminded himself sternly, one of the primary reasons he'd proposed to her.

Sounded stupid, he supposed, but he'd already done the buzz of attraction. The dazzling burst of need and passion and desperation. And it hadn't ended well. He'd learned long ago that the "flash" wasn't all it was cracked up to be. Flash faded too quickly—turning lovers into strangers and flames into ash.

Sam and he had been combustible. Jesus, the passion and the memories were suddenly so thick, so strong, he actually felt the top of his head catch fire. And just as quickly, guilt wrapped cold fingers around the base of his throat and squeezed. He was standing beside his fiancée and thinking about his wife.

Wryly, he acknowledged that not many men could make that statement.

Shoving thoughts of Sam to one side, he concentrated on the beautiful, elegant blonde smiling up at him. No, there was no buzz here, but there was . . . *peace*. What he had with Cynthia was quiet. Comfortable. And it would, he knew, in time become love. The kind of love that two people of similar backgrounds could share over a lifetime.

That brought him up short.

Jesus.

Sounded way too much like his mother. Was he finally becoming the stiff little prig she'd always tried to make him into?

No, he reassured himself.

He'd simply grown up.

No more castles in the sky.

No more building hopes on passion.

This time, he was going to do it right. This time, he'd make decisions with his head.

"No." He finally answered her question with a smooth lie and wondered if it should worry him, just how easy lying was becoming. "It doesn't bother me. It's important for Emma to know her mother."

Cynthia nodded and slid her hand along his arm until she could take his hand in hers. Her scarlet fingernails drew gentle patterns on his skin, as if she were branding him in some way. Marking him as her territory. Why that made him a little uncomfortable he wasn't willing to explore.

"And has she agreed to sign the divorce papers?"

"Not yet." As soon as he said it, he saw the flicker of worry dart across her eyes. Well hell. There was no reason for both of them to be tied up in knots. "Don't worry," he said. "She will. Sam's just as eager as I am to put our marriage behind us. We just have to work out the details."

"She wants custody, doesn't she?" Cynthia turned her head to stare down at the dock, where Emma and Sam were now lost in the wandering crowd of tourists.

"Yes, but she's not going to get it." Jeff knew that Sam would be willing to fight for her daughter. But if he had to pull out the big guns, use his wealth and connections to win this battle, then he would. He didn't want to hurt Sam. But if it came down to it, he would do what he had to do to keep his daughter safe. To keep the family they'd built intact.

"Jeff," Cynthia said, her voice hesitant, careful. "I know this is hard, but we have to think about what's best for Emma."

Irritation snapped inside him. "Emma's my main concern in this, Cynthia."

She shook her soft blond hair back from her face. "Oh honey, I know that. I'm just saying that we have to be fair. We can't be selfish with Emma, no matter how much we love her. Samantha *is* her mother and—"

He cut her off. He wasn't ready yet to be reasonable. He wasn't willing to admit just yet that Sam might have as big a hold on their daughter as he did. If that made him a bastard, then he'd just have to learn to live with that. "Let me worry about Sam, okay?"

"Of course." Her smile tightened, but that was the only sign that she was upset. Cynthia Fairwood would never even *consider* shouting at him. It would never enter her mind to pick up the object closest to hand and heave it at his head. She'd never think about kicking him in the shins and pushing him out of the house wearing nothing but his boxers.

His mouth twitched as he remembered Sam doing just that. Hadn't been funny at the time, but damned if it wasn't in memory.

Cynthia, though, wasn't ruled by her passions. And that was a good thing.

"Oh sweetie," Cynthia said, capturing his attention again. "I can't find the key to your place. Could you give me your extra?"

"Sure," he said, already reaching for his key ring.

"Good." She smiled and held out her hand, folding her fingers over the silver key when he placed it in her palm. "I just want to bring over a few things from my apartment. No sense in waiting till the last minute, is there?"

"No," he said, nodding, "guess not." He and Cynthia had kept their separate places, since Jeff had wanted to wait until they were married before bringing her in to live with him and Emma. It had been important to him and Cynthia'd agreed. Which was just one more reason for him to stop and appreciate her for who she was—rather than wishing she were someone she wasn't.

She looked up at him with absolute trust, with confidence, which was enough to make him feel like an absolute prick. She trusted him, had promised herself to him. And only last night, he'd *kissed* Sam. Cynthia was getting ready to *marry* him and his brain was full of Sam.

Cynthia, though, was concerned not only for his feelings, but for Emma's welfare and for Sam. She was definitely a better woman than he deserved. "I'll take care of it," he assured her. "I promise."

A slow minute ticked past before she smiled. "I know you will. Just remember, the wedding's in five weeks."

As she cuddled up to him, snaking one arm around his waist, Jeff muttered, "Now how could I forget that?"

Tapping her foot, Sam shifted impatiently and twisted to one side, checking to see if the line was even moving. She'd known the market would be jammed. It always was on a Saturday. *Should have gone to Monterey,* she told herself with an impatient glance at the Timex on her left wrist.

But she was pushed for time. As always. She'd left Emma at the house with Jo and Mike so she could make the emergency run to the market, before their appointment at Castle's. Her brain was racing, her heart full, and while she stood in line, Chandler buzzed around her.

Most small towns had an excellent grapevine, but here, the gossip chain was forged by the top three links. Abigail Tupper, Virginia Baker, and last but certainly not least, Rachel Vickers.

Abigail had sharp green eyes and the rumor was, she was so old, she'd actually had a ticket on Noah's cruise. Virginia, at seventy-five, had once been a little girl (hard to believe) whom Abigail had babysat for. Now, she had gray hair, mud-brown eyes, and a strange fixation on the Mafia. Rachel, in her late sixties, was the baby of the group, which some of the more mean-spirited in town insisted was the reason she hung out with the other two. So she could be the youngest, *somewhere*.

But Sam had always known the truth. Inside, Rachel was every bit as withered up and mean as the other two. The Terrible Three banded together in everything and considered themselves the social arbiters of Chandler. The fact that Chandler really didn't *have* a "society" didn't come into it. At the moment, the women were busily working on getting Rachel's husband re-elected mayor.

It would be Sam's great pleasure to vote for Jackson Wyatt this time around. Jackson, since marrying Carla Candellano and moving to Chandler, had really worked himself into the fabric of town life. Even though he was a lawyer, he managed to remain a really good guy, and frankly, Sam would have voted for Carla's dog, Abbey, before she'd vote for Mayor Vickers.

Her brain rocketed with these thoughts and hun-

dreds of others as she stood in line at Pezzini's Market.
The small grocery store hadn't changed a bit over the
years. Narrow aisles were stuffed full of everything
anyone might ever need, and every item was just
slightly overpriced. The best sandwiches in town came
out of Pezzini's deli area and the butcher department
was long on Italian necessities.

Conversations rippled through the knots of shop-
pers, rising and falling like the ocean's tide. Sam only
caught snatches of everything, which served to make
her both uncomfortable and curious. She knew darn
well that she and Emma were at the top of the hit parade lately, but so far no one had had the balls to confront her with questions.

Apparently, today would be the day.

"He's staying in the big suite at the Coast Inn."

Sam's ears perked right up and she slid a sideways
glance at the speaker. Should have known. Virginia.
How did the woman get her information? She never
went anywhere except the grocery store and the beauty
shop where she had her fat gray sausage curls cleaned
and pressed twice a month.

"I think he's a hit man."

Sam smothered a sigh and rolled her eyes. Virginia's
fetish with the Mafia was well known. She never
missed a gangster movie on TV and had been known to
make citizen's arrests of "suspicious-looking" tourists.
The sheriff, Tony Candellano, quite rightly ran the
other way when he saw Virginia coming.

"With that little girl along?" Rachel said. "Oh, I
don't think so. Besides, that suite is expensive. Not
many Mafia men make good money anymore."

Hmm. Sam's lips quirked. Apparently organized crime wasn't what it used to be.

"Isn't he from San Francisco? The Mob isn't in San Francisco, is it?" Rachel continued, shaking her head until the fire-engine-red bun on top of her head threatened to topple. While she spoke, she dipped one hand into the Ziploc bag filled with Vote for Vickers buttons she clutched to her overstuffed bosom. She handed the pins out like candy at Halloween wherever she went—whether you wanted one or not.

"I saw the girl yesterday," Abigail said solemnly, her voice managing to thunder with absolutely no trouble. Must have come from all those years of threatening small children. She was a retired elementary-school teacher and her former pupils, all of them retirement age or better, *still* went pale and terrified when bumping into her. That kind of power, Sam could admire.

Though she didn't share that ingrained fear. Abigail had retired long before the Marconi girls went to school—and besides, *nobody* scared a Marconi.

Deliberately, Sam turned her gaze to Abigail's.

The old woman lifted one gnarled hand to smooth a thin thatch of snow-white hair and said, "The child looked . . . familiar, somehow."

Nasty old bitch. No doubt hoping to shame Samantha somehow. Of course, anyone who saw Emma would see the resemblance to the Marconi girls. It was stamped on her little face.

Sam smiled, despite the nearly overwhelming urge to throttle Abigail's scrawny, creepy chicken neck. She herself didn't mind being gossiped about. Heck, living in a small town, it was bound to be your turn from time to time. And over the years, maybe she'd given the gossips a thing or two to chew on—not nearly as many as Mike, but she'd had her share. Still, she wasn't going to stand by and let her daughter be discussed while waiting in line to buy pork chops.

"She should," Sam said loudly enough to make sure every cat in the building heard her. After all, she wasn't ashamed. Why would she be? "She's my daughter. Her name's Emma."

"Your daughter?" Virginia's long nose actually twitched.

"Really . . ." Rachel practically vibrated with excitement. "That would make the mystery man at the Coast Inn your—"

"My ex-husband," Sam provided, and only winced inwardly. After all, whose business was it that her ex wasn't quite as ex as he should have been? The important thing here was Emma. If she was up-front about her little girl, then there'd be nothing to gossip about. The housewives littering Pezzini's Market would spread the word fast enough and then it would be done. They'd move on, looking for juicier tidbits.

"Oh my," Rachel breathed. "Have a button."

Sam took it—already planning on throwing it out the minute she left the store.

Amazingly enough, Abigail, the head link of the Chandler chain, looked almost *proud* of Sam. Which was just too weird for words.

"She's a lovely girl."

"Yes," Sam said, waiting for Abigail to drop the other shoe. Say something cutting. Something really mean. Something in character.

It didn't happen.

"You must be very proud."

Puzzled and clearly thinking she wasn't hearing right, Virginia looked at her leader and opened and closed her mouth, in a futile attempt to unblock ears that weren't blocked. Rachel looked lost. As if she'd suddenly found herself standing next to a stranger and couldn't figure out how she'd gotten there.

Sam knew just how she felt. She stared at Abigail for a long minute and tried to figure out what was wrong with this picture. The older woman's shrewd green eyes narrowed thoughtfully.

Then, letting her gaze slide from Sam's, Abigail said only, "Give my best to Henry."

Henry. Otherwise known as Hank Marconi or, as Sam liked to call him, Papa. She stared at the back of Abigail's head hard enough to bore holes through her papery skin and rock-hard skull. Why was the Holy Terror herself being nice? There had to be a string attached somewhere, Sam just wasn't seeing it. Somehow, or some way, Abigail was up to something.

Say hello to Henry? Sam smiled inwardly. Her father would cross himself when he got *that* message. He still had a healthy dread of his former teacher—the only person in the known universe to *ever* have called him Henry. Well, except for Grace.

Sam's brain continued to run in circles. Too much going on. Finding her daughter, discovering she was still married. Abigail being *nice*?

Surely a sign of the coming Apocalypse.

"Helllloooo, Samantha."

And speaking of Apocalypse . . .

She shivered and came up out of her thoughts to face Frank Pezzini. Or as Carla Candellano always called him, Fabulous Frank. The son and heir to the Pezzini family fortune and grocery store, he was also under the sad delusion that he was quite the ladies' man.

At five nine, with a balding head, a fat middle, and sweaty forehead, Frank would probably never find a woman who shared that opinion, but that wasn't to say he'd stop trying.

"Hi, Frank." Sam forced a smile. "I need two pounds of sweet sausage and two pounds of stewing beef." Order fast, make nice, then run for your life. Words to live by when shopping in Chandler.

"Making sauce, eh?" He nodded sagely as if he'd deciphered her cleverly coded shopping list.

Hell, he was Italian, as were half the people in Chandler. Of course you're making sauce when buying sausage and beef. Papa was planning a celebration tonight and he wanted to make his special sauce and calzones for the granddaughter he was finally allowed to know and love.

Which was why Sam was standing here being leered at. Seriously, next time, Mike could do the grocery thing. Sam was pretty sure Frank was a little afraid of Mike.

"That's right. Papa's cooking." Still being nice. But really, next time, if Mike wouldn't do the shopping, Sam'd take the time to make the drive to Santa Cruz or Monterey. A forty-mile drive was well worth it when compared to having Frank's dubious charms foisted on you.

"I've got some nice . . ." Frank paused for a wink. "*Ripe* tomatoes, too."

Oh, dear God.

• • •

"What difference does it make if my nails are Poppy Red or Crimson Harlot?" Jo demanded, waving one hand until her manicurist ducked for cover. "Who's gonna see 'em but me?"

"That's just so sad," Mike retorted. "Jo's losing her touch with men."

"I didn't say that."

"Yeah, when was the last time you—"

"Hello?" Sam called out, just before her younger sister could start prying into Jo's sex life. Not that she wasn't interested, but Emma was sitting right there with them, and damned if the girl was going to get a sex education along with her first manicure. "Small people present, remember?"

"She's a woman," Mike argued, winking at her niece. "Just a short one."

Emma grinned and took a sip of her strawberry milkshake. "This is fun," she said.

"Ah," Mike told her, "so young. And therefore it is up to us to *mold* you. This isn't just fun, my wonderful niece, this is female power. The sights, the sounds, the smells." She waved one hand to encompass the entire manicure/pedicure section of Castle's Day Spa. Taking a deep breath, she paused, then blew it out on a contented sigh. "In here, as it should be everywhere else, women rule. *Women* are in charge and *women* share the secrets of the universe."

"Oh brother." Jo groaned and leaned over to take a sip of iced tea through the straw jutting up from a frosted glass.

Emma giggled. "You're funny, Aunt Mike."

Funny, Sam thought, and a firm believer that a tough-talking, ass-kicking Marconi could also have buffed nails and soft heels. Mike might have been the best plumber in California, but when the workday was done, she was a full-time *girl*. She swore by being pampered and used every opportunity to drag her sisters along with her. Getting a niece thrown into the mix was just a bonus.

Castle's had come a long way since its former life as a three-chair hair salon off the kitchen of a big Victorian. But when Tasha Flynn married Nick Candellano, Nick had hired the Marconis to turn the whole house into a palace of indulgence.

Sam looked around, admiring their handiwork, while her toes were being painted an impossible shade of purple—Emma's choice. The walls were a rich butter yellow and the white crown molding around the ceilings made the rooms look taller and more elegant somehow. The downstairs half of the house was reserved for hair and manicures/pedicures. Upstairs were a series of private rooms, each painted in cool, soothing colors, designed with relaxation in mind, where talented masseuses could make any amount of stress dribble away on a groan of delight.

Soft classical music drifted through speakers tucked discreetly behind copper planters filled with tumbling ferns. Muted conversations from contented women played counterpoint to the music. And the tables at the Leaf and Bean concession near the manicure station were crowded with snackers.

In short, Castle's was a little slice of heaven. Even

with her sisters bitching at each other just for the hell of it.

"You shouldn't encourage her, kiddo," Jo said to Emma with a nod at Mike. "She'll have you in here once a month whether you need it or not."

Mike visibly shuddered. "Please. Every two weeks is not too much to ask."

"I have better things to do."

"Right." Mike nodded, admired her French manicure for a minute, then said, "Like your mystery appointments twice a week. Care to confess yet what that's all about?"

Jo sniffed. "In case you didn't know, the word 'mystery' means you don't get to know what it is."

" 'Mystery' also implies that *someone* will try to solve it."

Jo shot her a look that would have scalded a lesser mortal. But Marconis were made of sterner stuff. Grumbling, Jo said, "Do the words 'butt out' mean anything to you?"

Smiling serenely, Mike said, "Hello? Have we met? The name's Marconi. And to answer your oh-so-foolish question . . . not a damn thing."

Sam snorted.

"Didn't think so."

"Come on, Jo, give," Mike said. "What's got you busy two nights a week if it isn't a guy?"

"Broaden your mind," Jo quipped.

"Why?" Mike asked. "It's happy the way it is."

"You know—" Jo twisted in her chair to face her younger sister, despite the pedicurist grabbing her ankle to hold her in place.

Sam spoke up before blood could flow as freely as the scarlet polish on Jo's toes. "So, Jo. Did you get the final measurements out at Grace's?"

"Yeah." She flicked a warning look at Mike, who seemed blissfully unaware of impending danger. Sighing, Jo looked at Sam. "And Cash Hunter was there."

"What?" Mike sat up straight. "And you're not off to join a convent? Do good works? Prostrate yourself for humanity's sake?"

"I restrained myself."

"Another first."

"Does your jaw ever get tired?" Jo wondered aloud.

Emma giggled. "I wish I had a sister."

Jo smiled at her niece. "Sisters. A good idea, in theory."

Sam jumped back into her traditional role of peacemaker. "What's Cash doing there?"

"Besides irritating me?" Jo asked. "Grace hired him, or so he says. He's building a pantry in the first kitchen and a cedar closet in Grace's bedroom."

"So he'll be working there this summer, too?"

Jo shook her head at Mike. "Quick, aren't you?"

"This could be trouble," Sam said.

"If we keep Sandy and Barb away from him," Jo pointed out, waving her hands to dry the polish, "we should make it without losing anyone else."

"Is he a bad man?" Emma asked, eyes wide and interested.

"Not from what *I* hear," Mike muttered.

"*No,*" Sam said, ignoring her younger sister and focusing on her daughter. "Cash isn't bad. He's just really *friendly.*"

"Didn't seem friendly to me," Jo said, and Sam

couldn't tell if she was complaining or not. "Just irritating."

"That's because you're just contrary," Mike accused Jo. "Every other woman in town would like to be . . ." She shot a look at Emma. "*Friends* with Cash. So naturally, you want him shot."

"Not shot," Jo argued. "Castrated, maybe . . ."

"Seems a little harsh," Mike argued.

"What's cas-tated?" Emma asked.

"Oh boy." Sam slumped in her chair and let her sisters dig their own way out of this one.

A few days later, Sam was busier than anyone had a right to be.

The summer people, Chandler's very own set of wandering Gypsies, were camped out on Grace's property and their very presence was distracting. Two RVs, with a total of four opinionated women, were damned hard to ignore. The women had been friends for years and once all of their husbands had either died or been divorced, they'd banded together to travel the country and "see the sights."

Brightly colored awnings were stretched out over grassy areas outside their RVs. Tables, chairs, hooked rugs, and kerosene lamps were set out to resemble outdoor living rooms. Campfires burned all day and most of the night. One or all of them had a pot hanging over the flames at all times and there was an ever-present scent of something delicious wafting in the air.

The real chore, Sam thought, was trying to keep her work crews from taking breaks under those awnings every fifteen minutes.

The women worked with the goats, shearing the

wool and then combing and carding it. Not a pleasant job, since none of the animals particularly *wanted* to stand still and have their long, tangled, dirty, and oh, God, *smelly* hair combed. But then the yarn would be spun and sold to the specialty knit shop in town.

Sam watched them and a part of her envied their freedom. Their responsibilities ended whenever they left one town behind and didn't start again until they decided to park for a while. It seemed an easy, simple life, and since her own was tangled into knots, the thought of climbing into an RV and hitting the road was looking better and better by the minute.

"On the other hand," she murmured, her gaze sliding from the laughing women to the small herd of Grace's goats wandering in and out of the work area. "There's definitely a downside."

The goats were a whole new set of problems. They were everywhere. Dogs and cats people were used to. Chickens were irritating but avoidable. The sheep, as a rule, turned up their noses at hanging with people, but the goats . . . they were a sociable bunch. With the run of the property, they quite naturally had decided that the house and work area were the best spots to be. Bad tempered and spoiled rotten, the goats helped themselves to whatever had been left lying around and even Sam was astounded at what the blasted things would eat.

"I'm telling you, I laid my new list of supplies right here on the workbench." Mike pushed aside hammers, levels, and empty coffee cups, looking for the eight-by-twelve sheet of paper she'd set aside only moments ago. "Somebody moved it," she snapped, planting both hands on her hips and scanning the crowd for the guilty party.

Hammers pounded, saws whined, and women laughed. Yet, over all that noise, Sam heard a distinctive sound that had her turning around in dread. "Not *somebody*," she said on a sigh. "Some*thing*."

"What?" Mike turned, too, and instantly leaped. "You little shit, give me that."

Any other time, Sam would have enjoyed watching her little sister fight a goat for what was left of her list, now hanging from one side of the damn thing's mouth. But it was late, she was tired, and she still had to go pick up Emma.

Emma.

The bright spot in Sam's universe.

She was still finding it hard to believe. She had her daughter back. And it was as though the missing eight years had never happened. Everything was good. Everything was just as she'd always dreamed it could be.

Well, except for the fact that Jeff was here too and showed no sign of giving in on the custody issue.

Mike dug her heels in, wrapped both hands around the goat's snout, and tried to pry its jaws apart. Sam shook her head.

Jeff.

A curl of heat unwound inside her and Sam told herself to squash it like a bug. Unfortunately, her body wasn't listening. She could lie to everyone else and was actually doing a fine job of it. But there was no point in lying to herself.

Jeff still had the ability to twist her insides into a whimpering, pleading mass of *want*.

"Give it up, you hairy rodent," Mike threatened.

The goat snorted through clenched jaws.

Sam lifted her head and stared up at the startlingly blue summer sky through the leafy canopy above her. A soft wind blew past, ruffling her ponytail and sending a few stray locks of hair into her eyes. She brushed them back and took a deep breath. Her stomach growled as she caught the scent of what smelled like stew coming from a bubbling cauldron hung over one of the campfires.

"Dammit, stop eating my *list*!" Mike shifted her grip on the goat, grabbing its head between her palms until she could stare it dead in the eye.

It chewed.

Mike steamed. "Listen to me, you little rat bastard," she growled. "As far as I'm concerned, we can get the wool off you from the *inside* out."

The goat stared at her for a long minute, then, apparently deciding that paper wasn't an attractive enough snack to risk disembowelment, spat what was left of the list at Mike's feet.

Mike let it go and the goat scampered off for greener pastures, so to speak. As she bent down to pick up the sodden, stringy mass of pulp, Mike threw another glare at the animal. "Can you believe this?" She grimaced at the dripping mess in her hand, then lifted her gaze to Sam. Thoughtfully, she asked, "Got a taste for goat burgers?"

Sam laughed and checked her wristwatch. "No, but you go ahead. One less goat around here could only be a good thing. I'm outta here."

"Hey," Mike said, reaching out to pull Sam to a stop. "How come you get to leave early?"

"Gotta pick up Emma."

Mike grinned. "You're really enjoying saying that, aren't you?"

"Oh yeah."

Grin fading, Mike asked, "What about the weasel-dog? He lightening up on the custody thing yet?"

"No." Sam shoved her hands into her pockets and told herself that it was just a matter of time. It had been a week already. Jeff's wedding date was looming— something she really didn't want to think about, for reasons she didn't care to explore. So he was bound to cave soon. He *had* to, if he wanted to marry Cynthia Perfection. "He will, though."

"I still say you should talk to Jackson."

Jackson Wyatt was Carla Candellano's husband and a very good attorney. Sam knew Mike was right. She should get herself a lawyer to handle her side of this. And maybe she would. Eventually. If Jeff refused to bend. But for now, Sam wanted to handle this herself. To find a way to reach a compromise with Jeff. For their sakes and for the sake of their daughter.

"If I have to get a lawyer, I will," Sam promised.

"There's a dodge."

"I'm not *dodging* anything," Sam argued. "Jeff and I should work this out. Together."

"Hey," Mike said, "maybe he'll do what he did before. Run away."

"If he does," Sam reminded her tightly, "he'll take Emma."

"Then we hunt him down like the weasel-dog he is."

"Not really helpful," Sam pointed out, not seeing the humor in any of this.

"Sorry. But he can't win this, Sam," Mike said,

reaching out to slap her sister on the back. "Emma's as much yours as she is his. And as long as you don't go all sappy and hormonal on us, the battle's ours—" She stopped and stared.

Sam looked away.

"You're not."

Sam sighed.

The hum of activity around them drifted into the background as Mike's gaze narrowed on her. Sam wanted to shift position guiltily, like a burglar in a lineup.

"Oh, for God's sake," Mike blurted, throwing her hands high before letting them slap down against her thighs. "You're still hot for him."

"It's nothing," Sam said quickly, with a glance around to make sure no one else was close enough to overhear. Bad enough she was having this talk with Mike. She'd just as soon not have everyone in Chandler knowing that Jeff was still able to light up her body like a fireworks show. "I'm handling it."

Mike snorted and folded both arms across her chest, completely hiding the Marconi Construction logo. "Yeah, you *handling* him is what I'm worried about."

"Cute." Sam turned away, snatched up her purse and slung it over her shoulder, rifling through it one-handed to find her keys. "Nothing's going to happen, okay? He's *engaged*."

"Uh-huh. He may be engaged to Ms. Fabulous, but he's still *married* to you. That makes *her* the other woman."

Well. Sam hadn't really thought about it like that. And it might have been better if she hadn't. Her hormones didn't need any encouragement, thanks. Besides, she told herself sternly, they'd had their shot nine years ago. It hadn't worked. Their time was over—and it wouldn't be fair to *anyone* to try and change the rules now.

"All I'm saying is . . ." Mike broke off and huffed out a blast of breath on a disgusted sigh. "Speak of the weasel-dog and up he walks . . ."

Sam whirled around and watched Jeff and Emma approach the worksite. She hadn't expected him. And seeing him like this, completely unprepared, she felt a wild rush of something hot and liquid and dangerous flash through her. *Good Lord.*

"Oh yeah," Mike murmured, leaning in close. "You're gonna be just fine around him. No problems here."

"Go kill a goat."

Mike snorted, spared one quick, murderous look for Jeff, then stalked off.

"Mommy!" Emma raced right for her and Sam automatically bent down to scoop her up. Joy raced through Sam and worry drained away. How could she possibly worry about tomorrow, when *today* she was holding her little girl close?

Then Jeff stepped up into the dappled shade, smiled down at her, and Sam thought . . . *Oh yeah. That's how.*

Chapter Nine

He shouldn't have come.

Jeff knew that, but he hadn't been able to stay away. Nine years apart. A lifetime. An eternity. He'd become accustomed to thinking of Sam only as a memory, and he'd learned to live with the occasional pang. Now, seeing her was mesmerizing. He couldn't seem to get enough.

And that was dangerous.

For both of them.

The more time Jeff spent in Chandler, the harder it was to remember his daily routine in San Francisco. This world, this life, was so far removed from his. Here, there were no high-rises. No impatient clients or business lunches.

A flicker of guilt zapped him as he thought about all the extra work he'd put his assistant, Sallye, through lately. She'd canceled his meetings, rescheduled appointments, and managed to convey her displeasure at his suddenly cavalier attitude toward work.

Couldn't blame her for being surprised, he thought. In the last five years, since he'd taken over the reins of the family bank, Jeff had been the model executive. He'd balanced work and home and slowly turned himself into exactly the kind of man his mother had envisioned.

That thought hit him harder than it had the last time it had drifted through his brain.

Had he really become the Hendricks family scion? Was he just another link in the long chain of dutiful bankers he'd sprung from? Was that it? Was he destined now to spend his life in a buttoned-down world?

Dreary thought.

Which was why this time in Chandler was so damn appealing. Here, there were beaches and the forest and the small town where every storekeeper greeted you like a long-lost friend—rather than a hefty receipt on legs.

Here, Emma was happy.

Here, there was Sam.

Dammit.

"I was just leaving to pick up Emma," Sam said, her voice dragging him out of his thoughts.

"Yeah, well," he said, shoving both hands into his jeans pockets. "Emma wanted to show me Grace's goats, and . . ." *I wanted to see you . . .* God, he hoped to hell he hadn't said that out loud.

Sam smiled and the power of it slammed into Jeff and rocked him on his heels. He was rushing blindly through a minefield. And though he knew the danger was right here, all around him, he couldn't seem to care.

"She had a good time here yesterday."

"Yeah," he said, enjoying the fact that for the moment, there was no enmity between them. "It's all she's talked about." And he could admit, if only to himself, he'd felt more than one twist of envy when listening to his little girl talk about her aunt Jo teaching her how to hammer a nail, or about Mike showing her how easily faucets come apart, or about how her mother had given her a paintbrush and let Emma help paint a wall.

The Marconis were adventure. They were fun, new, exciting. Emma's daddy, on the other hand, worked in a *bank*. Boring. Especially to an eight-year-old.

"C'mon, Daddy," Emma said, squirming to escape Sam's hold. As she jumped up and down, Emma's sneakers sent up tiny puffs of dust around her feet. "You have to see the goats and Aunt Jo and Papa and Uncle Mike and—"

Jeff inhaled sharply, deeply, and caught the gleam of humor in Sam's eyes. Not surprising. She probably saw the hesitation on his own features. Talk about a minefield. Walking unarmed into the midst of Marconis couldn't be a healthy thing. "Enjoying this?"

"I shouldn't, should I?" Her mouth twitched. "But yeah. I am."

"Good that one of us is," he muttered.

"Daddy, don't you wanna see the goats?"

Please his daughter or avoid having confrontations with the whole Marconi family on their own turf? Tough choice. But he wasn't ready to leave yet anyway. "Sure, honey—" He broke off as Hank Marconi bulled his way through the crowd of people to join them.

Jeff steeled himself, knowing there was no way to get out now, without looking like he was running for the hills.

The older man glared at him through pale blue eyes that glittered with emotion. Jeff had been dreading this meeting. Nine years ago, Hank had been the one person on Jeff's side. The one member of either family who'd seen the love between Jeff and Sam and recognized that it couldn't be fought. He'd offered friendship then, and now, Hank looked like he'd enjoy nothing more than stepping back in time to knock Jeff's block off.

"Hank." Jeff nodded, took the risk and held out one hand.

Sam's father stared at him for a long moment. Tension simmered in the air between the men. An unspoken vow had been broken, he knew. Hank had trusted Jeff to make his daughter happy—and Jeff had failed miserably. It didn't look as though Hank were ready to forgive and forget, either.

Finally, Sam took a step forward and laid one hand on her father's arm. "Papa?"

He glanced at his daughter, then shifted his gaze to his granddaughter, staring up at him with a question in her eyes. Hank scraped one hand across his graying beard and rubbed his jaw like he had a toothache.

Jeff saw the older man crack. And he couldn't blame him. No man alive would have been able to hold out against Emma *and* Sam.

Reluctantly, Hank took Jeff's outstretched hand and shook it. "It's good you've brought Emma home to her family."

I'm her family, Jeff wanted to say, but clenched his jaw to keep from uttering the words. Like a child fighting over a toy, he wanted to stake his claim on his child. Wanted to tell them all that Emma was his. He didn't want to share her, dammit. She was all he had. The only real family he'd ever known. And it cost him more than he could say to see the way Emma was being sucked into the Marconi vortex. But watching his daughter with the people who loved her, he couldn't deny any of them that connection.

"I'm glad Emma got a chance to meet her *other* family."

Hank eyed him with a steely glare and solemnly nodded. Then he released Jeff's hand and deliberately turned to focus on Emma. Patting her head with a surprisingly gentle, beefy hand, he said, "Come with me, little mouse. There's someone I want you to meet."

"But I wanna show Daddy the goats."

Jeff spoke up quickly. "It's okay, kiddo. I'll catch up."

He watched as she waved and then skipped along beside her grandfather. The goats were there, wandering through a crowd of workmen who paused occasionally to swat one of them out of the way. Hank and Emma had joined an older woman wearing casually elegant clothes and dozens of ropes of beads around her neck. As he watched, the woman took off several of her own necklaces and presented them to Emma. The little girl preened, then did a quick pirouette while her grandfather beamed.

Even if Hank wanted to stomp Jeff into the ground, it was clear the older man was nuts about Emma.

"Well, that was pleasant," Jeff said, still feeling the sting of Hank's disapproval.

"You're alive," Sam pointed out. "So, *upside*."

He choked out a laugh. "True."

Tearing his gaze from his daughter, he looked at Sam. Dirt streaked her forehead. Dried lemon-yellow paint streaks decorated her dark green T-shirt. Her worn, faded jeans clung to her legs like a lover's hands. Like *his* hands used to.

Great.

Images filled his mind and he couldn't shake them. Suddenly, the past was closer than the present and far more clear than a future that hung nebulously out of reach. He blew out a breath, and told himself to ignore the steamy visions clouding his brain. And he'd probably have as much luck with that as he would in telling himself not to breathe.

Pushing a stray lock of red-brown hair out of her eyes, Sam looked up at him. "So. You want to meet the goats?"

He stared into those pale blue eyes of hers and knew he should leave. Knew he should get far, far away from Sam and the memories she stirred within. "Yeah. I would."

Cynthia made a careful note in her day planner, then tucked a fall of blond hair behind her ear. "Yes, I understand," she said, nodding to the person on the other end of the phone. "That'll be fine. We'll be there Friday. About seven. Yes."

The caterer was still talking when she hung up the phone. Now that the details were set, she really didn't want to listen to the man tout his flair with salmon one more time. Besides, she didn't want to have to try to convince the man again that Jeff would show up for this meeting. He'd already missed two and Cynthia was beginning to feel like an idiot, trying to explain why her fiancé was on the missing persons list.

Idly, she rested her fingers atop the receiver as it lay in its cradle and then tapped her manicured nails in a staccato beat.

Her nerves clanged inside her like a mission bell in

a hurricane and she suddenly couldn't sit still a moment longer. Jumping to her feet, she crossed the living room of her apartment, pushed open the French doors to the balcony, and stepped out.

Instantly, a cold San Francisco wind slapped at her. The incessant growl of traffic from the street below rose up to greet her, and from a distance came the lowing bleat of a ship's horn. On the horizon, storm clouds banked and gathered, swirling together until they were strong enough to make an assault on the city.

She sighed and dropped both hands to the cold iron balustrade, curling her fingers over the lip and hanging on as if it meant her life. "This is not supposed to be happening," she murmured, squinting into the wind and blinking back the tears filling her eyes. "Jeff should be here. With me. Emma should be having her dress fitted. We should be *happy*, dammit."

But she wasn't.

Her fiancé was spending entirely too much time with his wife, for heaven's sake, leaving all of the wedding details to her. All he was supposed to do was get the papers signed. Why was it taking so long?

Worry curled inside her, but she wouldn't acknowledge it. Instead, she smiled, turned, and went back inside. Sitting behind her desk again, she picked up the phone and dialed.

"This place is amazing," Jeff said, running the flat of one hand across a newly paneled wall.

"It really is," Sam admitted, then shot him a quick look. "Though if you tell my sisters I said so, I'll deny it."

She'd been giving Jeff a tour through Grace's Winchester Wannabe house and it had been like seeing it all for the first time herself. Hard place to work on, considering Grace's propensity for changing her mind all the damn time, but seriously, if you just looked at the house itself, it was great.

"See this?" she asked, bending almost in half to show him the detail work on the chair rail ringing the room. "She had this done by a woodworker up north." Sam ran her fingertips over the intricate carvings. "He's done stars and the moon and the sun in here, and then in the library he's worked out symbols from fairy tales."

"Incredible," he said, running his fingertips alongside hers. "Makes my condo in the city look damn boring."

Sam laughed and straightened up. "Anybody's house looks boring in comparison to Grace's. You should see the kitchens."

"Kitchens? Plural?"

"Oh yeah. Three of 'em at last count, though Mike swears they're multiplying at night." Sam grinned as she remembered her sister's colorful cursing only that morning. "She's redoing the pipes and installing new sinks and countertops in the second kitchen.

"And Jo's doing the new floor in the study."

Sam led the way out of the room and down a set of switchback stairs, which, mimicking a set at the Winchester house, boasted forty-four steps, each of which were only two inches high.

"This is just weird," he said.

"No, this is just Grace," Sam countered and, grinning, looked over her shoulder at him. He was right behind her. The damn steps were so tiny that there was hardly any distance at all separating them. Her grin faded as his gaze locked onto hers. She *felt* heat radiating from his body and told herself to hurry the hell up and get down those stairs. They were too alone, here. Too isolated. Too damn *close*.

"Sam . . ."

His deep voice seemed to echo in the nearly claustrophobic stairwell. It rattled through her body, shaking her bones and boiling her blood, and Sam told herself firmly to knock it off. She only wished she were listening.

She cut him off. "If you think this is something," she said quickly, letting her words tumble over each other in the hopes of keeping him from speaking again, "wait until I show you the stained-glass windows in the ceiling."

"Sam . . ."

He looked at her, really looked, and Sam felt the heat pour through her system like sunlight trickling through black clouds. Oh, she really didn't want to be feeling any of this. Didn't want to admit, even to herself, that Jeff Hendricks could still have any sort of pull on her. But here he stood and she felt every cell in her body standing up to do a little hip-hop.

"I have to go to San Francisco," he said, blurting out the news as if the words tasted bad.

Not what she'd been expecting. She wasn't sure if she was disappointed or relieved. Because all she could think was, *He's leaving.* Sam's heart stopped and a curl of panic opened up in the pit of her stomach. "You're taking Emma away? Now?"

From outside, the whine of saws and the rhythmic thud of hammers sounded soft, as if it were the rush of blood and the heartbeat of the house itself. Here in the stairwell, they were isolated and Sam felt confident enough to have her say without witnesses.

"You can't take her away from me yet, Jeff. I'm just getting to know her. I've hardly had any time with her at all."

"I know and—"

"I haven't signed the papers," she reminded him quickly, pulling out her big gun early. After all, when you had a decent weapon, why wait to use it?

"I know," he said tightly, his features suddenly taking on the hard mask of marble. "I didn't say I was taking Emma."

Sam drew an easier breath. Panic receded just a bit. "What are you saying?"

"I have to go. Take care of some business that can't be postponed any longer." He shifted his gaze back to her and Sam read the frustration in those dark blue depths. He didn't want to leave. And just how should she take *that*?

No way at all, that's how, she told herself. It wasn't *Sam* he was reluctant to leave. It was *Emma*.

"I'll be back on Sunday," he was saying, and Sam concentrated. "I thought," he continued reluctantly, "Emma could stay with you while I'm gone. She'd like it, I know."

"*You* don't, though."

"Hell no, I don't," he said. "Why would I?"

Bristling a little, she reminded him, "I'm her *mother*." He snorted. "*Now.*"

"Cheap shot, but accurate." She squared her shoulders and managed to look down her nose at him even though she had to look *up* to do it.

"I know." He pushed one hand through his hair, stared at her for a long minute, then said, "Sorry. Don't know why I said it."

"Because this whole situation pisses you off?"

One corner of his mouth quirked. "I believe I may have mentioned that."

"A time or two."

He sighed and shook his head. Sam curled her fingers into fists to keep from reaching up and smoothing his hair back from his forehead.

"The truth is," he blurted, "I've got things I have to see to in the city."

"Like Cynthia?" Ouch. Now why'd she go and say the name? Sam really didn't want to think about Jeff *seeing to* Cynthia.

"She's part of it. But there's also the bank."

"Ah yes," she said, shoving both hands into her jeans pockets. Surprise flickered inside her, but Sam hid it well. Nine years ago, he'd talked about breaking away from his family's business. He'd talked about being an architect. Designing the buildings of the future. Making a mark that was all his own and *not* being just a part of the family legacy. Apparently a lot of things had changed. And since she was sad for it, she snapped, "The Hendricks family bank. Still making your own money in a back room?"

"Funny." His features tightened.

"I could have done better," she admitted. "But it's been a long day."

He blew right past her statement. "I've been doing what business I can on the phone and via the Internet. But I have to get back. Take care of a few things in person." He looked at her. "I can take Emma with me . . . or leave her here with you. Your choice."

"I'll keep her."

"Thought you might."

Sam watched him. He looked as though he hadn't been sleeping and she wondered if his dreams were as frenetic as hers. She wondered if *she* haunted him as he did her. And she guessed she'd never find out. Which was probably a good thing. "Thanks."

Something flickered in his eyes and was gone again in a heartbeat. "You don't have to thank me."

"I know."

His mouth twitched, one corner tilting slightly. "This may be a breakthrough."

"Huh?"

"Us. Having a conversation without fighting."

"Hey, I'm Catholic. I still believe in miracles."

"I used to." His voice had dropped so that she could barely hear it even in the isolation of the stairwell.

But she strained toward him as if whatever he was saying was far too important to be missed. Her body was answering a call her mind refused to acknowledge. But it had always been that way between them. Even in the midst of one of their blistering fights, she'd be just as tempted to wrap herself around him as throw a sucker punch to his abdomen.

God, she wanted him.

He lifted one hand toward her face and Sam held her breath. His gaze softened, his mouth curved, he bent toward her . . .

His cell phone chirped.

Irritated, he straightened up, reached into his pants

pocket, and pulled out the flip phone. He glanced at the caller ID, then frowned as he answered it. "Cynthia. Hi."

The breath she hadn't realized she'd been holding slid from Sam's lungs in a rush. If his phone hadn't rung . . . If Cynthia hadn't called just in time to remind them both of her existence . . . what would have happened?

Sam's insides jittered and she sucked in air in a futile attempt to calm herself. As if that were going to work. Disgusted with herself, Sam turned her back on Jeff and led the way down the stairs. She heard him following her, his footsteps loud on the oak steps. His voice, that low rumble of sound that had always been able to slip inside her body and shake things up, sounded different to her now as she half-listened to him talk to his fiancée.

"I'll be there," he said. "Don't worry. We'll do the caterer's practice dinner Friday night."

Caterers.

Sam smiled to herself and remembered her own wedding to Jeff. A quick trip to a chapel outside Reno and the buffet dinner at Harrah's. So technically, she mused, they'd had a catered dinner, too.

"I'll be back in the city by nine. I'll come to your place, pick you up," he was saying.

Oh, Sam didn't want to think about him going to see Cynthia, the Beautiful, the Perfect, the Wonder Bride. She didn't want to think about the blonde scooping her fingers through Jeff's hair, pulling his head down for a kiss and— She stopped her brain right there, because there was no way in hell she was going to think any further down *that* road.

One small thread of consolation . . . apparently he and Cynthia weren't living together. So she didn't have to have *those* images in her brain. Cozy nights in front of a fire, tucking Emma into bed together, sliding into a big comfy bed and—*Stop.*

At the bottom of the staircase, they stepped out into the "small" study. Sam had always thought of them as Papa Bear, Mama Bear, and Baby Bear studies. And this one, the smallest of the three, was her favorite. She and Emma had finished painting the room only yesterday. The butter-colored walls looked warm and soft in the summer sunlight streaming through the high, arched windows. The mahogany casements gleamed with fresh polishing and the floorboards were waiting their turn with the sander.

She walked across the room to the windows, giving Jeff a little privacy to finish his phone call. The fact was, if he was going to say "I love you" to Cynthia, Sam didn't want to hear it. She'd just painted this room and throwing up in it would ruin the ambiance.

A minute or two later, she heard him come up behind her. She didn't turn. Didn't trust herself to look at him. Something had passed between them in that stairwell. Something tenuous yet powerful. And she could still feel the echo of it rippling inside her.

"I've gotta go."

Sam nodded, fixing her gaze on her daughter, playing in a splash of sunlight. "I know."

"I'll be back on Sunday."

"I'll be here."

"Sam—"

She closed her eyes. "Have a good trip."

"Right."

She heard him walk away and still she didn't turn. Then he was there, in the yard, swinging Emma up for a goodbye hug. As he left, Sam watched him and had to quash the urge to run after him.

Chapter Ten

The caterer's carefully prepared meal might as well have been cold oatmeal.

Jeff had dutifully eaten his share, made all the right noises, and smiled when Cynthia proclaimed the menu a winner. But if someone had held a gun to his head, he couldn't have told them what he'd just eaten.

Now, sitting in a sleek jazz club on the waterfront, he was having a hard time concentrating on the woman across the table from him. Cynthia had brought him here so he could see the job she'd done on the place.

A talented, creative interior designer, Cynthia was already making a name for herself in the city.

"What do you think of the place?" she asked, a bright smile curving her lips.

"You did a great job," Jeff said, meaning it. It was a small club, and she'd chosen red leather and stark chrome as the basics and built from there. It looked intimate and edgy. No doubt just what the owners had been looking for.

"Thank you." She lifted her martini glass and took a sip before speaking again.

Four musicians were crowded together on a too-small stage and teased hot, sultry music from their instruments. The steady thump of the bass fiddle beat in the room like an extra heartbeat and the audience, clustered around tiny, candlelit tables, swayed in time with the rhythm. Wall sconces held yet more candles and the flames flickered wildly in the swirl of chill air sighing through the air conditioner. Shadows danced on the walls as waitresses wearing short skirts and suitably bored expressions weaved in and out of the crowd, carrying trays burdened with martinis.

Cynthia, apparently oblivious to his wandering mind, was holding a one-sided conversation, bringing him up to date on the plans for the wedding.

His wedding, which was now, God help him, just four weeks away.

"The flowers are beautiful, Jeff," she said and he forced himself to pay attention. "Lilies of the valley, peonies, and sterling roses."

"Sounds nice," he murmured, figuring that it was an appropriate response. Hell, he didn't know a daisy from a weed, so what did he care? Dammit, not the right attitude, he told himself. Cynthia deserved better from him.

But what the hell was he doing? Sitting across the table from his fiancée, thinking about the woman who was still his wife. He scraped one hand across his face, trying to wipe away memories of Sam, but it just wasn't any good. She was with him all the damn time. So how could he marry Cynthia if he still *wanted* Sam? And if he walked away from Cynthia, was he any different from the man he was when he'd left Sam nine years ago?

Jesus, a man could go nuts thinking about this shit.

"It's all going to be beautiful, Jeff." Cynthia

snapped him out of his thoughts by tapping his hand with one manicured fingernail.

"Sure it is, Cyn." He looked directly at her, focusing only on Cynthia, determined to give her his full attention.

She tipped her head to one side, her blond hair swaying gently with the movement, as she studied him for a long minute. "Do you want to go back to my place?"

Christ, no. His instinctive reaction bulleted through him and all he could hope was that his feelings weren't etched into his features. But Jesus, he couldn't even consider going back to her place. Sleeping with Cynthia now that Sam was firmly rooted in his mind was just something he couldn't do.

He'd feel like a cheating husband.

And technically, he thought wryly, that's just what he'd be.

But it was more than that. Cynthia was beautiful, no doubt about it. But he didn't feel the flash of desire for her that just thinking about Sam could create.

What the hell was he supposed to do?

"No," he said finally and forced a smile he hoped she bought. "Let's stay. Listen to the music."

"All right," she said slowly, dragging the tip of her fingernail across the back of his hand. He was pretty sure she meant it to be seductive. What it was, was irritating, doing to his skin what the sound of nails on a blackboard did to his ears.

He pulled his hand free and picked up his glass of scotch.

"You're right," Cynthia said, her voice now a husky

whisper filled with promises. "We've hardly seen each other in two weeks and I'm talking your ear off about flower arrangements." She reached across the small, round table and this time covered his free hand with hers, to cut off his escape.

Her hand was cool on his and he realized how he missed the jolt of heat he felt whenever Sam touched him. Dammit, he'd convinced himself a long time ago that the heat was for fools. That the only thing a man got out of the fires of passion was a serious burn. And the good sense to avoid it the next time.

He looked at Cynthia and reminded himself just how perfect she was for him. She was good with Emma. An excellent hostess. Beautiful. She was smart, too, and always up for a debate—whether it was about literature or politics. She loved to travel—last summer they'd hiked all over northern Italy. They'd had a lot of good times together, he thought now.

So why was he looking at her soft blond hair and imagining Sam's reddish-brown mop? Guilt pinged inside him and had him giving Cynthia's fingers a quick, perfunctory squeeze. Then he let her go and took a quick gulp of straight scotch, sending a river of fire pouring through him.

"You're thinking about Samantha, aren't you?" Cynthia asked, giving him a kind smile and an understanding glance.

Good thing he'd already swallowed or he'd have been choking to death now. Damn. He thought about lying to her, then realized the futility of it. "Guess I was," he admitted, then tried to soften the blow by adding, "There's a lot to be thought out."

"I know," she said and leaned back into the plush red

leather seat. Toying with the stem of her crystal martini glass, she lowered her gaze to the tabletop before saying, "I've been doing some thinking, too."

Jeff winced. Of course she'd been thinking. He'd hardly considered how hard all of this was on her. And she'd been a damned good sport about the whole thing, considering the circumstances. "Cyn—"

She lifted her gaze to his and again he saw compassion glimmering in her eyes. It would have been a hell of a lot easier on him if she'd just been pissed. A loud Marconi argument would feel good about now, he thought, and just how twisted was that?

But his adrenaline was racing around with no place to go. Sam would have given him a fight. And she'd have pressed him until he'd lost his cool and joined in the shouting. It would have cleared the air, energized the two of them, and they'd have hopped off to bed to finish up with a grand finale.

At least, that was how it had worked once upon a time.

Cynthia was too controlled for that. If a problem was presented to her, she'd think about it for several days, likely discuss it with her shrink, and then come up with several neat solutions that wouldn't hurt anyone's feelings. He'd admired her even temper before. And wasn't he a bastard for now suddenly wishing it were different? For wishing she were different from what she was? For wishing she were Sam?

"It's okay, honey," she said. "I understand. You must be so torn about all that's happened."

"I am," he admitted and leaned forward, bracing both forearms on the tabletop. Christ knew he needed to talk all this out. But how could he do that without having to explain to the woman he was supposed to marry that he was still feeling . . . *something* for his wife? Nope. Cynthia was definitely not the confessor he needed. "I didn't expect to have to deal with anything like this."

She reached out and gave his hand a quick pat. "I know, but . . ." Her voice trailed off, hesitant.

"What?"

Cynthia inhaled slowly, then let the air out in a soft sigh. "I realize this is hard on you, Jeff, and it's just horrible, I know. Still, I hate to say this, but I just feel so sorry for Samantha."

Jeff blinked. The music went on, surrounding them with a warm flow of softly played jazz that swirled through the room like a summer wind. Around them, couples laughed and talked, and seconds ticked past as he waited for her to continue.

She bit her bottom lip, paused a moment as if to convince herself to go on, and then started speaking. "It's only that I can see how difficult this must be for Samantha." She smiled at his obvious confusion. "Oh honey, it's hard for us too, of course. But we have each other, don't we? And we have Emma. If you look at it from Samantha's point of view . . . well, anyone would feel bad for her."

Frowning now, he was more confused than ever. If anything, Sam had come out the winner in this. Despite his mother's machinations nine years ago, Sam had her daughter back in her life. She was holding the ace in this little hand of poker and she knew that he'd have to share custody of their daughter if he wanted that divorce. So why was Cynthia wasting any sympathy at all on Sam?

"What do you mean?"

She scooted around on her chair, then leaned toward him. "Think about it," she said, her voice a low hush of sound. "Samantha's in a very hard spot right now. To find she's still married to a man she didn't want? And added to that, she's being forced to spend time with a child she gave away."

Jeff scowled as Cynthia's words slapped at him. *Forced?* Hell, if anything *he* was being forced to share his daughter with a woman he'd thought betrayed him. "She's not being forced."

"Of course not, a bad choice of words," Cynthia said quickly. Her eyes gleamed quietly in the candlelight and Jeff tried to remind himself that she was on his side.

"I'm sure she's enjoying seeing Emma again, but Jeff, honey, remember, she gave Emma up." Cynthia paused again and seemed reluctant to continue. But she managed. "Samantha didn't *want* to raise Emma. She signed away all of her rights to her own *child.* So having the girl pop back into her life now must be an incredible intrusion."

He shifted in his chair and suddenly wished they were far away from this crowded room where the music was now just a distraction. Too many people sitting around enjoying themselves. Too many thoughts careening through his brain. An intrusion? Emma?

No. As kind as Cynthia was trying to be, he was sure she was wrong. And still, a worm of doubt slithered through his mind, his heart. "No," he said firmly, not really sure if he was trying to convince Cynthia or himself. "Sam *wants* Emma. Hell, she's holding off signing the divorce papers until we can come to terms on custody."

Cynthia smiled and shook her head sadly. "Jeff, you just don't understand women at all." She sighed, picked up her drink and took a small sip. "Don't you see? If Samantha admits the truth—that she doesn't want Emma—she'd look horrible—*heartless*—to her own family. She can't do that, no matter how she really feels."

He remained unconvinced and his expression undoubtedly said so.

"Honey." Cynthia sighed, then lowered her voice even further, as though she really disliked saying anything at all about this. "She *has* to at least pretend to be glad about having Emma back in her life. But I can't imagine that she is. Not for a moment."

Shaking his head, even as Cynthia's notions chipped away at him, Jeff told himself she was wrong. He'd seen Sam's face when she'd gotten her first glimpse of Emma. He'd been on the receiving end of the Marconi temper he remembered so well. No way was Sam *pretending* anything.

"No," he said, mind made up. "Sam was always honest. She wouldn't—"

"Honest?" Kindly, Cynthia stretched out her hand again and took his. "Jeff honey, I know you want to think the best of people . . . but was she honest with you, nine years ago?"

"She tried to be," he said, despite the old pain that reared up and took a bite from the corner of his heart. "I told you about how my mother lied about everything."

"You did," Cynthia said, rubbing her thumb over his knuckles. "But if we're going to be honest, let's

face it all. Sam wrote you a letter that was hijacked by
your mom. But if she'd *really* wanted you to know
about the baby, would she have given up after one attempt?"

"No," he admitted through gritted teeth, because
Cynthia was sitting there patiently, waiting for him to
respond.

"No." She smiled again and gave his hand a reassuring squeeze. "So what makes you think she's being entirely honest this time?"

Unwanted, a ribbon of uncertainty wound through
him, snaking its way through his body like a cold wind
sluicing off a mountainside. The music suddenly
sounded shrill and the candlelight dancing in the darkness made his vision swim uneasily. Chilled through,
he wondered if Cynthia was right. And then wondered
again how he could even consider it.

Remembering Sam with Emma, the joy on their
faces, he couldn't convince himself that Cynthia was
right about this.

But he'd been wrong before.

Hadn't he?

By the time Jeff dropped her off at her apartment—
without even bothering to come in for a nightcap—
Cynthia was so frustrated, she wasn't sure what to do.
Jeff was pulling away. From *her.*

She felt it.

Every day, things changed just a little more. His attention was scattered and his past was too tangled up in
his present while she was trying to build a future.

There had to be something she could do about it.

Samantha Marconi was causing too much trouble for them.

And Cynthia Fairwood wasn't going to sit still for it much longer.

She stepped out of her heels, and felt the cool press of the hardwood floors beneath her bare feet. A chill rippled through her as she walked across the living room toward the French doors leading to the balcony. Calm, controlled, she reminded herself to be *patient*.

She opened the doors and let the icy wind off the bay slap at her. There was a solution to this mess, she knew. All she needed to do was find the right button to push.

Sam had her daughter all to herself for a while.

She slid a CD into the stereo, turned up the volume, and smiled as Bonnie Raitt growled through the speakers. She moved with a sliding, dancing step and hugged joy close.

It felt good. Good to be back in her own place and to have Emma with her for three whole days. Outside, the last lingering light of day clung to the edges of twilight with a tight fist. The first stars were just beginning to peek out even as the dying sun sent streaks of crimson and gold slashing across the sky.

Inside though, lamplight held the coming night at bay. Her gaze swept the cavernous living room, admiring the pale wash of golden light reflecting on the newly sanded and varnished floor. A few scatter rugs were sprinkled around the room and the twin sofas she had facing each other looked a little lonely, with only a battered coffee table and two lamps to keep them company—but it was home.

Only a mile from the house where she'd grown up, it might as well have been on a separate planet. Which was a good thing. As much as Sam loved her sisters and father, she needed her own place. She'd bought the sprawling old bungalow a few months ago, determined to bring it back from the sad state of neglect it had slumped into. And she was well on her way.

Now that she had dead termites and a shining, re-done floor, she could get into the other things she was itching to do. Like expand and update the kitchen, paint every room, get a new roof, gut the bathroom, build a garage—just minor cosmetic changes, she thought, smiling to herself.

Tonight though, the house looked damn near per-fect. She felt a small whiplash of pleasure to see Emma's things scattered over the living room floor.

Most mothers—she hugged the word to her tightly—would be complaining, she guessed. Wanting the child to come in and pick up the piles of clothes and toys and a plate filled with cookie crumbs sitting alongside an empty milk glass. But Sam was loving it.

And she knew she had Jeff to thank for it.

Not just for this time alone with their daughter—but for raising Emma well enough that she was able and willing to accept her long-missing *mom* popping up out of nowhere.

Wasn't *that* a pain in the ass?

Her smile slipped a little as she wrapped her arms around her middle and held on. She didn't want to be indebted to Jeff. Didn't want to be faced with her past every time she looked into his dark blue eyes. Didn't want to remember what they'd had and what they'd lost.

But there was no way around any of it, was there? Not if she wanted Emma in her life. And there was nothing she wanted more. Even dealing with Jeff and the pain was worth it.

"Mommy?"

Sam's heart skittered and she smiled as she left the living room and walked barefoot into the kitchen, following her daughter's voice.

The little girl was kneeling on a chair pulled up to the old oak table. Bright light from the overhead fixture spilled down on her, illuminating the worn linoleum, ancient appliances, and the smiling child. There was flour in her hair, across her nose, and enough of it dusted down the front of her pale pink T-shirt to bake a loaf of bread.

Sam thought she'd never seen anything more beautiful. "How's it going?"

Emma grinned, and pressed a cookie cutter firmly onto the rolled-out dough. "I'm almost done. Can we cook 'em now?"

"You bet." Memories of baking cookies with her own mom galloped through her brain and Sam smiled, wishing her mother could know that Emma was home now. Where she belonged.

"And then we get to frost 'em, too?"

"Of course," Sam told her, walking up close enough to smooth one hand down the back of her daughter's head. So soft. "What good are cookies if they don't have lots of frosting?"

"This is fun." Emma threw her head back and shot another full-wattage grin at her mother, and Sam's heart did a somersault in her chest.

"Yeah, it is." God, how could she ever have thought

she could live without her child in her life? How had she managed to get through the last eight years without being able to look at her—touch her?

"Is Aunt Mike gonna come over and have some cookies?"

"We can call her if you want to."

"'Kay." Emma peeled the cookie shaped like a star up off the flour-covered bread board. Laying it carefully on the cookie sheet beside the others, she said, "An' Aunt Jo, too."

"Sure." Sam picked up the cookie sheet and walked to the oven she'd already preheated. Pulling open the door, she faced the wave of heat that spilled out and slid the cookie sheet onto the top rack. Closing it up again, she set the timer, then turned around to help get the next batch ready.

"Can Papa come, too?"

Sam laughed. The kid was a Marconi right down to the bone. Why have one person over when you can have a dozen? It's the Italian way.

"I think Papa's busy tonight," Sam said, remembering her father had said something to her about a late meeting with . . . She frowned thoughtfully. He hadn't actually *said* who the meeting was with. Funny, she'd been so preoccupied with Emma that it hadn't occurred to her at the time, but now that she thought about it, she wondered what the secrecy was about.

"Okay, can Daddy come?"

Sam winced. "Your daddy's in San Francisco, remember?"

"Yeah," Emma said, nodding so sharply, she sent a cloud of flour flying into the air. "But he could maybe come back and have cookies with us and see my new room and my Barbie blanket—"

Sam laughed as her daughter kept right on rolling.

"And maybe he could stay here too with you and me."

Whoops. That's what she got for not paying attention. "Uh, honey, I don't think your daddy would want to stay here."

"How come?" Small face, trusting eyes, solemn smile.

"Well." *Think, Sam. Think.* "He's staying at the hotel, remember?"

"Yes, but this is nicer."

"Thanks, but—"

"And maybe Cynthia could stay here, too, because she's marrying my daddy and he says she's going to be my new mommy, but if I already have you how come I have to have another one?"

Ouch.

Thinking about the perfect, elegant blonde being Emma's new *anything* was hard to take. Okay, fine, she was small enough to admit that Cynthia Fairwood was just a little intimidating. Admitting that, even to herself, made Sam stiffen her spine and scowl.

Be a grown-up, she thought firmly. *Do the right thing.* "Well, I guess you'll be lucky then, won't you? You'll have two mommies."

"Isabel says one mommy is a real mommy and the other mommy is a step."

Isabel again. One of these days, she was going to want to meet Isabel Feinstein. And buy her a lovely one-way ticket on a cruise ship to China.

"Yeah, technically, Cynthia will be your stepmother."

"I don't think she wants to be."

"What?" Instantly, Sam went on alert.

Emma sighed and patted a small twist of dough into a ball. "Cynthia says we're gonna be friends, not steps."

"Oh . . ." What was she supposed to say to that? Maybe Cynthia was trying to be a friend, not a mother. Which sounded good to Sam. But what if Cynthia wasn't looking to be a friend, she just wasn't interested in Emma? What then?

Emma stopped her thoughts cold, though, in the next instant. Turning, she wrapped one arm around Sam's waist and leaned in for a hug that squeezed her mother's heart and filled her soul. "You're a weasel-dog."

"What?" A short, sharp laugh shot from her throat as Sam looked down at her daughter.

Emma gave her a wide, gap-toothed grin and said it again. "You're a weasel-dog, Mommy."

"Okay," Sam said, still chuckling. Judging by the happy gleam in her daughter's eyes, she was willing to bet she wasn't being insulted. But damned if she wasn't intrigued. "Where'd you hear that?"

Emma blew out a breath that ruffled her bangs and sent puffs of flour into the air. "Aunt Mike says that's what a Marconi says when they think somebody's really great."

"Is that right?" Sam fought the smile tickling the back of her throat and told herself it was time to have a chat with Mike. "And why'd she tell you that?"

"'Cause I heard her call my daddy a weasel-dog and she said it means she really likes him."

"Oh . . ." *The light dawns,* Sam thought. Mike had

gotten caught and had faked her way out of it. Nice job, nitwit. "Well, it can mean that," Sam said softly, already planning on staking her sister out on the first anthill she could find. "But sometimes other people don't understand what we mean, so we only call people in the family a weasel-dog, okay?"

Emma shrugged and went back to rolling her ball of dough. "Okay."

Hey, she'd made it through her first mother-daughter crisis. And earned a gold star, she thought. She hoped. Mike, though, was a different story.

Slapping her dough onto the table, Emma flattened it with her small hand as Sam gathered up the rest of the dough and picked up her rolling pin.

"Are you gonna go away again?"

Sam's heart stopped. The question came so softly, so tentatively, she'd almost missed it. But she heard the worry in her daughter's voice and felt the ache in her own heart in response.

Dropping to one knee beside Emma, she cupped the child's face between her hands. "No, baby," she promised, willing her daughter to read her eyes and believe her. Even though she had no right to expect it. "I swear. I'm never going away again."

"Really?" Her one front tooth worried her bottom lip, tugging at it nervously.

Sam stared into those wide pale blue eyes so much like her own and felt a geyser of love pump through her body, swamping her with so many emotions it was hard to draw a breath. But she managed. This was too important not to.

"Really, honey. I'll always be your mom. I'll always be here. Always."

Emma studied her for a long minute while Sam's heart thudded painfully in her chest. All she could do was hope that her daughter would give her a chance. The chance to prove that things would be different for all of them now. Seconds ticked past, marked by the hum of the oven timer and the swish of wind-driven branches against the windows.

Then at last the little girl leaned out of her chair, falling into her mother's arms and tucking her head into the crook of Sam's neck. "I'm glad, Mommy."

"Oh, me too, baby." Sam's hands swept up and down her daughter's back in long, soothing strokes and she wasn't sure which of them needed those strokes more. "Me, too."

Chapter Eleven

"Hey," Mike argued the next day, "I call 'em like I see 'em."

Sam shot a glance over her shoulder, just to make sure Emma was far enough away that she wouldn't hear her aunt Mike's death rattle. Satisfied, she turned back and glared at her little sister. "For chrissake, Mike. Can't you control yourself around Emma at least?"

Mike squirmed a little, but held her ground. Her blond hair, pulled through the back of her baseball cap, hung in a thick braid down the middle of her back. Her Marconi Construction T-shirt was stained with grease, water, and God knew what else. A streak of grime strayed across the bridge of her nose, and as Sam watched, her sister's pale blue eyes narrowed.

"The son of a bitch, he's lucky that's *all* I call him."

"That's great," Sam argued, throwing her hands up high and letting them slap down against her thighs. "Much better. Emma's his daughter, too, you know. And if he gets pissy, he could make my seeing her a hell of a lot harder."

"He wouldn't." Not yet anyway, Mike told herself.

"He *might* if Emma starts talking about Aunt Mike calling him a weasel-dog."

Mike winced. "Fine. I'm sorry. I'll only call him that when Emma's not around."

"I appreciate the restraint."

"You should." Mike stood amid the rubble of the kitchen and wanted nothing more than to kick something. But what? If she kicked one of the rotted-out pipes, it would just spew a river of disgusting crap all over the place and she'd have to clean it up.

How the hell was she supposed to have a decent tantrum if she couldn't punch something? New pipes lay stacked against the far wall and the gaping hole where the porcelain sink used to be showed an excellent view of ancient pipes below and a mousetrap, long since snapped closed. She'd been working all morning and still hadn't had the chance to install the new stainless-steel sink or even to measure for the *purple* granite countertop. Purple, for God's sake. Then Sam shows up to ride her ass about calling a jerk a jerk and ruins what was left of a perfectly crappy day.

Sighing, Mike glanced through the kitchen window at her niece, sitting under a tree learning how to knit at Grace's knee. The older woman and Emma had really bonded, Mike thought. The two of them always had their heads bent together. Snow white to auburn, they were like twins separated at birth by fifty years.

But then, Emma had gotten to all of them. Papa hummed while he worked, Jo set aside her beloved ledgers for the chance to play on the beach, Mike herself had already taken Emma fishing, and Sam . . . Sam's heart was in her eyes every time she looked at the daughter she'd never thought to see again.

They were happy.

All of them.

But it felt . . . fragile. And Mike couldn't help wondering if she was the only one to realize it.

Shifting her gaze back to her sister, Mike reminded her, "You shouldn't be surprised that I want to drop-kick his lying ass. All of us wanted to punch his lights out nine years ago. And Marconis never forget."

"Don't I know it." Sam snatched a dirty rag from the back pocket of her jeans and wiped her paint-smeared hands on it. "The point is, Jeff's Emma's father. And we can't afford to piss him off until we get this custody deal settled."

Mike grimaced tightly. "Don't know why you're so worried about that. He needs you more than you need him."

"He has Emma."

"Yeah and he's *engaged*." Mike grabbed the rag from her sister, wiped the grease off her own hands, then stuffed the rag into her own back pocket. "He can't exactly marry his little bimbo until his first wife lets him go, so you're in the driver's seat."

"She's not a bimbo."

"How do you know?"

"She's too rich. Rich women aren't bimbos." Grumbling now, Sam continued, "She's gorgeous. Has class. Good taste in clothes. And to top it all off, bigger boobs than me."

Mike snorted. "*Emma's* got bigger boobs than you."

"Depressing, but true."

Sam's heart was in her eyes and Mike wanted to scream. She'd been doing a lot of thinking the last few days, and though she'd tried to keep her mouth shut, for a Marconi that was damn near impossible. Now, as she looked at her sister, Mike knew she couldn't hold it in any longer. "He's working you, Sam."

"What?"

Mike shook her head in disgust. Sam was just too damn nice. She usually expected people to do the right thing. She looked for the best in people most of the time, and most of the time she got jabbed in the eye with a sharp stick for her trouble.

Well, Mike didn't expect the best of anybody. She'd figured out a long time ago that people did what they had to do to get what they wanted. And Jeff was right at the top of the heap of all the selfish, self-serving, lying, cheating weasel-dogs she'd ever known.

She hadn't said anything, mainly because she didn't want to be the one to pop Sam's balloon. But nobody else seemed to be thinking what she was. No one else was looking at Jeff and wondering just what he was really up to. Even Papa had been blindsided by a tidal wave of love for his first grandchild.

Mike was glad to have Emma in their lives, too. The kid was great and God knew she wanted to see her sister happy. But she still didn't trust Jeff to not hurt Sam again. He'd done it before. What was to say he wasn't waiting for his chance to do it again?

"Earth to Mike." Sam shoved her, just to get her attention.

It worked.

"Fine." Mike whipped her hat off, yanking her braid free and sweeping her bangs off her forehead with one dirty hand. "I'll be the black cloud to your set of rainbows. The fly in your ointment. The bottle of salt to your open wound—"

"For crying out loud," Sam snapped, "can we do this without all the drama? Quit with the metaphors and get to the point, okay?"

"Okay." She slapped her hat against her thigh. "I think Jeff's setting you up."

Sam's head snapped back as if Mike had hit her. And dammit, that's just what it felt like she'd done. But *somebody* had to say it.

"What're you talking about?"

"For God's sake, Sam. Think about it." Mike fisted her hand around the brim of her cap, the stiff cardboard edge digging into her palm. Sam's gaze speared her and Mike felt as though she were propped up against a bullet-pocked wall, wearing a blindfold and waiting for the rifles to fire. But there was no going back now. "He shows up in your life again because he *needs* you. He needs that divorce so he can marry the rich bitch."

"She's not a bitch," Sam corrected, then added, "At least she doesn't seem to be, though I hate her anyway just on general principles."

"That's the spirit," Mike cheered. "Now if you could just do the same for *him*."

"I hated him for years. All it got me was an upset stomach and a headache."

"Yeah, and now you've stopped hating and started wanting again." Mike stared hard at her and knew she was right. Sam damn near vibrated every time the weasel-dog showed up. "Hating's safer."

"I know. And don't worry." She pulled in a deep breath, blew it out again, and said firmly, "I can get past the whole 'want' thing. It's just hormones."

"And isn't that what got you into this mess nine years ago?"

"No," Sam said firmly, meeting Mike's gaze and holding it. "It wasn't just hormones then. I *loved* him. Really loved him. It was more than wanting. More than anything I'd ever felt before."

"Oh, now I feel better."

"That was then, this is now."

"Wish you believed that."

Sam shifted a look at the little girl sitting in the shade of an old maple tree. A goat wandered close enough to sniff at the skein of yarn at Emma's feet, and laughing, the child snatched it up fast. Looking back at her sister, Sam said firmly, "I do believe it. He's not mine anymore. Maybe he never was. But what's important now is Emma. He's going to have to give me at least partial custody, Mike, or I won't sign. I don't know how you think he can screw me when I'm holding all the cards."

"Because you don't even know what the real *game* is." Mike stomped off a few steps before turning around and coming right back. "You're playing gin rummy and he's dealing five-card stud."

"Back to metaphors." Sam hit the heel of her hand against the side of her head. "You're not making any sense."

Mike blew out a disgusted breath. "He's being mister nice guy right now. He's letting the steam rise up between you because he can use it against you. He's letting you see Emma and not giving you any shit about it. Because he needs you."

"He's not that manipulative."

"Yeah? Well, what happens *after* you sign the papers?"

"Huh?"

"Once you've signed on the dotted line or whatever and he's married to Polly Perfection . . . what's to keep him from siccing his rabid, killer lawyers on you and snatching Emma right back?"

She didn't take any satisfaction at all from the way Sam's face paled. But at least Mike felt as though she'd made her point. "Bottom line is," she added, lowering her voice even though no one else was in the room, "he's rich enough to get away with anything, and what could we do to stop him?"

"Jeff wouldn't do that."

"You don't sound real sure of that," Mike pointed out.

"Why would he?"

"Why *wouldn't* he?"

Sam stared at her daughter across the yard from them, and Mike was pretty sure she could actually *hear* Sam's heart twisting painfully in her chest.

Dammit.

"I just want you to be careful," Mike said softly.

Sam nodded, folded her arms across her chest, and inhaled sharply, deeply. "I will be." Turning her head, she met Mike's gaze steadily and after a long moment said, "You're right."

She smiled. "Hey, there's a phrase I never get tired of hearing."

"Don't get used to it." Sam unfolded her arms, reached out and grabbed Mike, giving her a brief, hard hug. "You're almost never right, but when you are, it's right on the money. Can't believe I never considered it myself, but Jeff's been trying to get me to sign the divorce papers—and they're the old ones. There's nothing in there about custody of Emma. If I sign the ones he gave me, I'll be signing away my rights to her, *again*."

"What're you gonna do?"

"Whatever I have to."

"Sounds good. Ambiguous, but good."

"Hey, even I need a minute or two to put a plan together."

"Just tell me what you need."

Sam smiled and nodded. "Don't worry about it. I will." She turned and headed across the room, stepping gingerly over the discarded pipes. "But for right now," she said, pausing to look back at Mike, "I'm going to put the faux-suede finish on the library walls."

"And then?"

"Then, I'm going to figure out how to play five-card stud."

Pride rippled through Mike as she watched her sister. Sam'd been through a lot. Hell, for that matter, *all* of the Marconi girls had been through a lot—just in different ways. But they'd all come out the other side and were stronger because of it.

Jeff had no idea who he was dealing with.

"Cynthia likes cashmere," Emma said, hanging on the top of the wooden slats as though it were a trapeze and she was center ring at the circus.

"I bet she does," Sam murmured, trying not to think about the woman Mike had called Polly Perfection.

"But I don't think she'd like the goats," Emma continued as she jumped down off the wood fence.

"Not many people do." Sam thought of Mike's constant battles with the goats and hid a smile. Grace, though, liked to think of the animals as part of the décor. She always said that goats and sheep belonged in the bucolic countryside.

Sam walked beside her daughter and told herself she should be working. All around her, the sound of hammers and saws and the shouts of people trying to be heard over the whine of machinery told her that everyone but *she* was hard at it. But how often did she have the chance to just hang with Emma?

Thinking about that made her realize just how much more time Jeff and Cynthia would have with the little girl, and another twist of envy grabbed at her.

Cynthia was everything Sam wasn't. She was champagne, Sam was beer. She had a place in Jeff's life and Sam was no more than a blip in his memories. The woman was used to wearing cashmere, and the closest Sam got to that fine, soft wool was tripping over Grace's goats.

Her brain raced as she remembered what Mike had said earlier. Was Jeff only stringing her along? Being nice because he had to? Waiting for the chance to change the rules? A part of her wanted to deny it all, but how could she risk that? She had to stay on top of things. Had to keep one step ahead of Jeff just in case he *was* planning to turn on her once the papers were signed.

"The goats are funny, but they smell bad."

"Boy howdy," Sam murmured, agreeing wholeheartedly with Emma. "But even Grace can't convince the darn things to take regular baths."

Emma giggled at the thought of goats in bathtubs.

Then a moment later she said, "Aunt Jo said I could

help her hammer some stuff if you said it's okay, so is it okay and I'll be careful, too."

"Yeah," Sam said, running one hand across the top of her daughter's head. The tiny Marconi Construction T-shirt that Mike had had made just for Emma was already filthy. What was a little more dirt in the grand scheme of things? Besides, she had the distinct feeling that her little girl didn't get very dirty at home in San Francisco. There, she probably had piano lessons and ballet lessons and . . . who knew what else? Well, she couldn't compete with Jeff in that arena, but she could sure as hell see to it that Emma had actual *fun* here.

And, she thought, while Jo and Mike rode herd on Emma, Sam could head into town and take care of something she should have done days ago.

"Go ahead," Sam said, then was forced to shout as Emma scampered from the shed at top speed. "But be careful and no going on the roof!"

Two hours later, after a hurried consultation with Jackson Wyatt, attorney at law—and recent mayoral candidate—Sam figured she deserved a break. Standing in the middle of the sidewalk on Main Street, her head spun with all the information Jackson had given her. She was going to have to sit down and try to make sense of it all. Try to figure out just what she was willing to do—how far she was willing to go—to keep Emma in her life.

"Won't take much figuring," she muttered and ignored a tourist who walked a wide berth around the woman standing on the sidewalk talking to herself.

Scowling, Sam thought that if Jackson was right,

then she and Jeff were about to get into a good old-fashioned war. And she couldn't help thinking that it was generally the innocent bystanders—in this case, Emma—who ended up getting hurt.

But she'd do all she could to keep from dragging her daughter into the middle of this. She didn't want Emma put in the position of having to choose sides. No kid should have to do that. That didn't mean, though, that Sam was willing to roll over and play dead.

She'd fight if she had to. And if she fought, dammit, she'd *win*. After all, she only wanted to share in bringing up her daughter.

Wouldn't any mother want that?

Head pounding, mind spinning, she told herself she should head back to the job site. But her stomach was in knots and her nerves were skittering like live electrical wires downed after a storm. No point in facing Emma again until she was calmer. Though how she was supposed to stay calm when thinking about going into a custody battle with a man who had more money than God was something she hadn't really figured out yet.

Besides, with Jo, Mike, and Papa, not to mention Grace, all there, the little girl was in good hands.

Which meant Sam could take advantage of being in town.

Chandler was a small town by anyone's standards.

Small enough so that you couldn't walk down Main Street without having to stop and chat every few steps. But it was also big enough that you weren't forced to drive into Monterey to shop for groceries. Small enough to escape the notice of a chain coffeehouse like Starbucks—but big enough, thank God, to support the Leaf and Bean.

Glancing quickly to her right and left, Sam jumped off the curb and sprinted across Main Street, darting between the cars stopped at the light. She waved to Joe Hannigan, sitting in his truck, then grinned at Julie Davis as she stepped out of the bakery, carrying a box that undoubtedly held a birthday cake for her son Justin.

Everything was so . . . normal.

The sidewalks were bustling and shopkeepers' doors stood wide open in invitation to the tourists and their wallets. Sam smiled as she did a little bobbing and weaving between the people slowly meandering along the sidewalk.

Every year, the tourists flocked to town to take in the harbor and the art galleries and the eclectic little shops selling everything from pot holders stamped "California" to tarot cards and incense. The crowds were thick and noisy and Sam loved it. Made her feel as if she were in the middle of things. And today, the rush of people took her mind off—however briefly—her own problems.

Sam pushed open the door to the Leaf and Bean and paused on the threshold to linger over the fragrant aromas that reached out for her. Coffee. Good, rich coffee. And on top of that *amazing* scent came waves of tantalizing aromas . . . apples, blueberries, and oh, dear God, *cinnamon rolls*.

Polished wood gleamed in the sunlight streaming through the wide front windows. From the overhead beams, on silver chains, hung shining copper planters and baskets bursting with ferns and ivy—enough to start a halfway decent rain forest. The shop felt cozy, welcoming, and for Sam, just what she needed.

"Just going to stand there drooling?"

Sam grinned. She stepped all the way inside, closing the door behind her. Ignoring the scattering of people at the dozen or more small round tables, she kept her gaze on the blond woman smiling at her. Walking across the highly polished wood floorboards, she followed her nose toward the glass cases filled with muffins, rolls, bagels, and oh my, freshly made biscotti. Slapping one hand on the countertop, Sam said, "Stevie. Be a hero. One latte and a cinnamon roll before I fold up and perish."

"Easily done." Stevie Ryan Candellano finished wiping the already gleaming wood countertop, then set the cloth under the counter before turning toward the espresso machine. "Hey, I hear your daughter's in town."

Not surprising, Sam thought. No secret stayed that way in Chandler for long. Besides, her friends knew the whole story. Knew about how Sam had given up her daughter and knew the pain she'd been living with ever since.

"Yeah," Sam said. "She's great. Really."

"So when do we get to meet her?"

"Soon. I promise. I'll bring her in next weekend for some of your special hot chocolate."

"Good." The steamer hissed and spat as Stevie heated the milk until the surface of it frothed like a cloud.

"So how's Beth doing?"

"Hanging in," Stevie said with a half-shrug. "Mama's been over at Beth and Tony's nearly every day since the baby was born. I think Beth's ready for a little alone time."

Mama Candellano loved nothing more than her family, and with a brand-new grandson, she could hardly be expected to keep her distance.

"Well, Tasha's due next month," Sam pointed out. In fact, the whole Candellano family seemed to be having a population explosion. "Maybe that'll take the heat off."

"Off Beth and onto Tasha. Only fair." Stevie pulled the stainless-steel milk jug free, then wiped down the twin steamer rods with a clean cloth. As she poured the hot milk into a tall cardboard cup, then spooned a layer of foam on top, Stevie said, "Hey, tell Mike I need her to take a look at the sink here in the shop for me."

"She's dealing with Grace. Trust me, your sink'll be a vacation."

"I saw the summer people are back."

"Oh yeah, hip deep in goats over there." Sam reached for her coffee, then slid a sleeve over the bottom of it. "Grace is making Jo nuts, Mike's ready to mutiny over a purple granite counter, and Papa's useless, he just keeps grinning at Emma."

"Situation normal, then." Stevie laughed.

"Pretty much, and as far as I'm concerned, the world will be right again with a latte and one of your cinnamon rolls."

"Girl," Stevie said, "you're way too easy to please."

"Not how I remember it."

A deep voice, directly behind her.

The smile on Sam's face froze.

The world went still and her blood did a wild race through her veins in celebration. Dammit.

There went a perfectly good coffee break.

Turning, she looked right into a pair of dark blue

eyes and wondered why she hadn't sensed his presence. "Jeff."

"Sam." Everything in him tightened up and Jeff didn't know how the hell to stop it. She'd always had that effect on him and it was damned annoying to admit that she still had the ability to turn his hormones inside out. Although that was all it was, he reassured himself. Hormones. A purely chemical reaction.

Damned irritating.

"What're you doing here?" she asked.

"Same as you. Coffee."

"I *meant* what're you doing *here*? In Chandler. Aren't you supposed to be in San Francisco?"

"I came back early." Didn't really cover it, he thought. He'd raced out of the city as soon as he could manage it. He'd left behind a fiancée who was very quietly, very properly, pissed as hell and a backlog of work that had his secretary considering hiring a hit man.

And it didn't seem to matter.

He'd told himself he was rushing back to be with Emma. But she was only part of the reason. No matter what kind of bastard it made him, Jeff knew that for him, the real draw in Chandler was still Sam Marconi.

Chapter Twelve

"You never should have let her on the roof."

"Will you shut up already?" Mike shot Jo a quick, uneasy glance. "She's fine. No harm done."

"Yeah." Jo snorted. "*She's* fine. *You* won't be, as soon as Emma tells her mother. That happens and we're—I mean *you're*—dead meat."

Sunlight glanced off Jo's sunglasses and seemed to bounce right into Mike's eyes. Like she didn't already have a headache, thanks very much. Her stomach was still doing a roll and spin and her palms were still sweaty. Not that she was nervous or anything. Hell, no. Just that the summer heat had really been beating down on them, practically melting the roof they were sitting on.

The cast-iron weather vane—in the shape of Merlin, no less—stood stock-still atop the conical roof of the tower room, just twenty feet from them. No wind. No air. And the wide sweep of blue sky overhead didn't harbor the hope of a single cloud. The first of July had arrived and was already making them wish for fall and cooler weather.

But it wasn't the heat making her flinch. Mike's shoulders twitched as if she could already feel Sam's glare boring into her bones like a slow-moving bullet, determined to eke out as much pain as possible. It wouldn't be pretty. But hell, she could outfight Sam. And if it came down to it, she was pretty sure she could *outrun* her, as well. But just to get into the right frame of mind, she started using her best arguments. The ones she'd use on Sam as soon as she had to.

"What's the big deal? We went on roofs when *we* were her age."

Jo flipped her hammer into the air and caught the handle as it came down again. Keeping one eye on it and the other on Mike, she did it again. The solid smack of wood against flesh sounded like a heartbeat.

"Yeah, but *we* had Papa watching over us. Not *you*."

Mike thought about snatching the hammer on its next trip through the air and giving her sister a thump with it. But then Jo would just retaliate and Mike really didn't want to meet her date that night with a black eye. "You were up here, too, you know."

"Not a chance," Jo said, laughing, shaking her head. "You're not pinning this one on me."

"You're the oldest."

"That only worked when Mama pulled it. Not gonna help you this time."

"That's very nice. Thank you for your support."

"Hey, you've got my support," Jo assured her. "I'll even beg Sam not to kill you." Grabbing the hammer again, she took a good grip on it, positioned one of the roofing nails over a forest-green shingle and hammered it home. "After all, she kills you, and I end up having to deal with that granite counter."

"Love you, too," Mike sneered.

Jo laughed shortly, shook her head, and shifted around until she was sitting, knees drawn up, on the sharp incline of the roof. Arms wrapped around her legs, she dangled the hammer as she watched Mike. "You screw up, you pay. It's the Marconi way."

True enough. Mama and Papa had never minded their girls making mistakes. But they had expected them to take the consequences without an inordinate amount of bitching. But this was one session Mike would just as soon pass up. Hell, Sam hadn't been gone a half hour when her long-lost daughter had taken a nosedive off the roof.

Oh yeah. That was gonna go over *real* big.

"Emma had a great time," Mike argued, but that sounded weak, even to her own ears. Sam wouldn't care if her little girl was having fun or not. She'd only care that she'd taken a header off the roof.

"Yeah," Jo said, as if reading her mind, "until she fell."

Mike winced. "She had a life rope on, didn't she?" Thank God, she added silently, blessing the sturdy belt shaped like an infant's seat on a swing set that Emma had worn. She didn't even want to consider what might have happened without the safety precautions. Nope. Don't think about it.

"No harm, no foul." That heavy-duty seat had provided Emma with an E ticket ride and she didn't even have a bruise to show for it.

Although Mike was pretty sure she herself would be seeing Emma take that tumble off the edge for a long, long time. Her dreams would be full of it. And she'd relive over and over again her own wild dash to the edge of the roof only to look down into Emma's laughing eyes as the little girl swung like an auburn-haired pendulum at the end of the rope.

The kid had treated it like a big game.

"Christ," she admitted, slapping one hand to her chest, where she could feel her heart still doing a fast dance. "She scared the shit out of me."

Jo nodded, pulled off her sunglasses, and stuck one arm of them into the bib of the denim apron she wore over her work shirt. "Ditto."

Mike figured she'd lost at least ten years off her life in ten seconds flat. She only hoped they'd turn out to be old, ugly years. She didn't want to miss any fun, after all.

"Kid's amazing," Jo muttered, shaking her head and smiling now as she remembered how Emma'd wanted to go up on the roof and do it all again. "She may look just like Sam but she's got a lot of you in her."

"Yeah?" Mike grinned.

"Not so sure that's a compliment." Although it was. Mike might have been the baby of the family, but she'd always had more balls than the other two put together. If she wanted something, she went after it. Didn't always turn out great, but she'd never had to sit and wonder, what if? Of course, if she ever said that to Mike, there'd be no living with her.

"Sure it is," Mike said, her grin only getting broader. "You're nuts about me."

"Or just nuts."

"Goes without saying." Mike shrugged. "You're a Marconi."

"True." Jo shifted her gaze from Mike to the crowded yard below them. The summer people were still busy in the goat house, some of the crew were lazing about under the trees taking a break, and Papa and

Grace were huddled together—no doubt talking about the job.

She frowned.

Couldn't be a pleasant conversation. Not judging by the way Grace's chin jutted out or how fast words were tumbling out of her mouth. Crap.

"What's wrong?"

Jo pointed. "Look down there. Papa and Grace are getting into it, which can only mean—"

"Crap." Mike squinted into the afternoon sunlight as she stared at the couple standing to one side of the bustling crowd. "Think she's changing her mind about the job again?"

"I don't know," Jo said thoughtfully, studying her father and Grace as if she were watching a foreign movie with subtitles she couldn't quite read. "But it can't be a good . . ." Her voice trailed off as she caught a glimpse of something else. "Oh, for God's sake."

"What now?" Mike scanned the crowd below. She lifted one hand to block the sun.

"Look at that." Jo pointed with her hammer and felt a swell of disgust and fury pour through her body, thick enough to make the hammer shake in her hand. "Would you just look at him?"

"Him who? Jesus, who're we talking about?"

"Are you blind?" Jo reached over, grabbed Mike's chin in her hand, and positioned her head until she was looking where Jo wanted her to look. "Right there. Mr. God's Gift to Women is hitting on one of the gypsies."

"Huh? Oh. Cash."

"Yeah, *Cash.*" Jo shook her head as she watched him, unable to tear her gaze away even though it was none of her business what the bastard did—or rather, *who* the bastard did. As long as he stayed away from her crew, what the hell did she care?

But watching him drape one muscular arm around a woman who had to be twenty years older than him made her want to bean him with the hammer. Her fingers tightened on the worn wooden stock as she considered the odds of making that throw from this distance.

"That's Kate, isn't it?" Mike asked, squinting now.

"Looks like her," Jo muttered, remembering that Kate was the youngest one of the summer women, although she was in her early fifties at least.

"She's pretty," Mike said.

"Of course she's pretty," Jo snapped and could just barely make him out through the red haze crowding the edges of her vision. "Would he waste his time with a dog? I don't think so."

"What's it to you?" Mike asked.

"Nothing," she snapped. It meant absolutely nothing to her. Cash Hunter was an irritation. A thorn in her paw. A worm in her apple. "But for God's sake, can't he keep it zipped?"

Mike laughed shortly. "Doesn't look like the woman's complaining any."

No, it didn't. Which only made Jo more furious. Were all women that stupid? she wondered. Did no one but *her* see that the man had more moves than a chorus line? Did no one have enough self-respect to not want to be one of a *legion* of Cash Hunter victims?

The woman wrapped her arm around Cash's waist and leaned into him, her long black hair shining like a satin cape in the sunlight. She smiled up at him and

Cash, making his first move, dropped a kiss on the woman's forehead.

Jo quietly sizzled.

The man should have a warning sign hanging around his neck.

He should be shot. Okay, she amended, maybe not shot. But caged. And kept where women could pay a buck and stare at him through the safety of steel bars. He could be studied. Like any other dangerous animal.

"You're just jealous because you're not getting any."

Jo slanted her a look. "And you are?"

"This isn't about me," Mike pointed out.

"Fine. How do you know I'm not?" Of course, she wasn't, but that didn't mean she wanted that sad fact to be obvious to everyone.

"Please. Even *your* mood improves when you get laid."

Hard to argue with that one. But she tried. "There's nothing wrong with my mood."

"Nothing a night with Cash couldn't clear up."

"Right." Jo snorted. "One night with him and I go off to save the world? No, thanks."

Mike's blond eyebrows lifted. "Scared?"

"Not interested."

"Uh-huh."

"Shut up, Mike."

"Ooh. Good comeback."

"Don't you have something else to do? Someone else to toss off a roof?"

"How 'bout I start with you?" Mike grumbled.

"How 'bout you help me finish these shingles?"

"Who died and made you the boss, anyway?" Mike turned to grab up her hammer and a fistful of shingles.

"Mama did," Jo muttered, as her heart fisted in her chest.

"What?" Mike asked.

"Nothing," she muttered darkly. Grabbing her sunglasses, she shoved them back on and deliberately turned her back on Cash and his latest conquest. "Absolutely nothing."

"Yeah," Mike said, with another look at Cash and the woman, strolling through the dappled shade. "I believe you."

They took their coffee to the cliff park.

Not much of a park, really. It sat at the edge of town, a narrow strip of tidy grass bordered by a splash of summer flowers on one side and an iron fence on the other. Traffic on Pacific Coast Highway sounded out in a steady roar, but was drowned out by the wild crash and thunder of waves slamming into the rocks at the foot of the cliff.

Seals barked, tourists wandered, and in-line skaters whizzed along the sidewalk, buzzing by the unwary and making them jump for cover. Wind rushed in off the sea and tugged at Sam's hair, making her wish for the cap she'd left in the truck. Heck, if she was going to wish, then she'd just wish herself away from here. To somewhere safe. Where the heat that pulsed inside her whenever Jeff was around wouldn't be able to take hold.

Like the North Pole.

Taking seats opposite each other at a steel table-and-bench set with peeling red paint, each of them waited for the other to start. She'd be damned if she'd talk first. *He who speaks first loses power.* She wasn't sure where she'd heard it, but it made sense and she was going to fight her Marconi instinct to jump in and fill a silence.

Sam's insides skittered, but she kept her hands steady as she set her coffee cup down and began tugging at the cinnamon roll. Just because she wasn't going to talk, didn't mean she wasn't going to eat. Besides, when her nerves started jangling, it was like ringing a dinner bell. Her body craved food. Usually in great quantities. And preferably *chocolate*.

"You always did have a sweet tooth."

Her hands stilled and her gaze lifted, meeting Jeff's squarely. "Don't."

"Don't what?"

"Don't talk like you know me." She shook her head firmly, swallowed the knot in her throat, then deliberately popped a piece of the gooey roll into her mouth and chewed. "You don't have the right."

A short bark of laughter erupted from him as he slapped both hands down onto the tabletop. "Fine. I don't know you. I *did*, though."

She squirmed uncomfortably. Happened every time she remembered their past. Every time she let herself wander down a road that was filled with disappointment and regret. "That was a long time ago."

"You haven't changed that much."

Sam took another bite, wiped her hands on the napkin Stevie had jammed into the pastry bag, then reached for her latte. She had a quick sip and, fortified, told him, "I'm not that girl you walked out on, Jeff."

"I didn't walk out."

"Funny," she snapped. "Looked like you."

His lips flattened into a grim slash and his eyes narrowed into slits. "We've been through this. I went to London. To study."

"And nine years later, you're back. Tough course." She winced, hearing the strident tone of her voice and not much caring for it. It was Mike's fault, she thought. Making her wonder about Jeff's motives. Making her second-guess every word that came out of his mouth and weigh every word that came out of her own. "There's no point in going over it all again."

"Agreed."

"Yay us," she said, with a twist of a smile. "So how about instead we talk about what's important now?"

"We should be able to work something out."

"Gee? Think you can be a little *more* vague? Or is that the best you can do?"

"I don't know what you want me to say," Jeff blurted and pushed to his feet as if he couldn't sit still and have this conversation.

Sam knew just how he felt. She watched him stalk around the edge of the table, like a man who needed to move, but had nowhere to go. The wind caught his black hair and tangled it around his head. His short-sleeved blue shirt was the same deep sea blue of his eyes and his jeans looked new enough that she was convinced he rarely wore them.

He wasn't a part of her world anymore. He was just a visitor and the casual clothing he wore was nothing more than a costume, helping him to fit in with the locals. His reality was suit-and-tie, corporate America. A world where Sam would be as lost as he looked.

Blowing out a breath, she said bluntly, "I *want* you to tell me that you're willing to share custody of Emma."

He glared at her and the muscle in his jaw twitched spasmodically. His dark blue eyes flashed and he scraped one hand across his face in an obvious attempt to calm the temper sparking in his eyes.

"Just like that," he said flatly. "It's been just me and Emma for eight years and now you want to take her away from me?"

"You've had her in your life, Jeff. I missed all of it."

"Your choice," he reminded her, teeth clenched, jaw muscle working as if he were trying to chew rocks. "Not mine."

"I didn't *have* a choice." Frustration bubbled inside and Sam had to react. She wanted to throw something, kick something, and if he came one step closer, she'd be happy to use him for target practice.

Thankfully though, he seemed to have a pretty good memory of their time together, too, because he stayed just out of kicking range. Sam didn't know if she was relieved or disappointed.

Standing up, she walked across the postage-stamp portion of grass to the iron railing at the edge of the cliff. She closed her hands over the cold, damp bars, and held on as if the earth were being tipped harshly to one side and those bars were her one grip on reality.

Unfortunately, "reality" was six feet three, with broad shoulders, long legs, and thick black hair that made a woman want to run her fingers through it. She glanced over her shoulder at him. Even if it was just to hold his head still while you banged it against a door.

"I know that look," he said warily.

"Then go away."

"Can't."

"Won't."

"Whatever. We've got to talk and it may as well be now."

She snorted and ignored the flash of pain inside, concentrating instead on the ripple of annoyance riding atop it. "There's that king-to-peasant tone I admire so much."

"You're a snob, Sam."

"What?" Sheer dumbfoundedness had her gaping at him. She felt her mouth drop open and her eyes bug, but she couldn't seem to stop herself.

"You heard me." Jeff stepped up alongside her and grabbed hold of the iron railing, his left hand way too close to her right. "You're the one who was always making a big deal about my family being rich."

She fisted one hand, and in self-defense he quickly dropped his own over it.

"Easy enough to say money means nothing when you've never had to go without it."

"I guess it is."

She yanked at her hand and practically snarled, "Let go."

He laughed shortly and tightened his grip. "Not a chance. You've got a mean right hook, as I remember it. And since I can't hit you back . . ."

Scowling, she told herself not to notice the well of heat building up beneath his touch. She tried desperately to ignore the scattershot of lightning-like sparks that shot up her arm and into her chest. But her breathing hiccuped and her heartbeat started a trip-hammer pounding that made her head swim.

So not fair.

That Jeff Hendricks would be the *one* man who could do this to her.

Nine years since he last touched her and it was as if it were yesterday. Memories rushed through her brain and nearly staggered her. She had to get some distance. Had to keep Mike's warnings in mind and take charge of the hormones screaming at her to let go and enjoy.

"Fine," she grumbled, relaxing her hand under his. "No hitting. Just . . . let go."

He almost did. Then thought better of it and instead rubbed the pad of his thumb across her knuckles, sending waves of sensation rocketing around inside her. Dammit, he was doing it on purpose. Had to be. Was he really using her own body's reactions against her in an effort to get his own way?

"Jeff . . ."

"I missed you."

"What?"

He sighed and kept his gaze focused straight down, to the froth and foam of the waves as they crashed onto the cliff rocks and the small crescent of beach below. There was a handful of surfers, astride their boards, waiting for a good ride in, and just as many seals, diving slick bodies beneath those waves, looking for a meal.

The past swirled around him, cloaking memories in a velvety fog that made everything look a little softer, cleaner, kinder than it actually had been. But in the midst of those memories, Jeff was forced to stop and consider a harsher, more recent memory, as well.

Cynthia.

Trying to convince him that Sam had never wanted Emma. That she still didn't. That all of this scrambling to spend time with her daughter was merely to save face in front of her family.

200   MAUREEN CHILD

But he couldn't believe that.

Not of the Sam he used to know.

But hell. Had he ever really known her? Hadn't she given away their child?

"You missed me?" she asked, breaking the chain of thoughts threatening to strangle him.

"Hell, yes." He smiled tightly. "In London, there was no one to shout at me. No one to throw a lamp at my head." He looked at her. "No one to lock me out of the house in my underwear."

Her lips twitched.

"So yeah. I missed you."

She blew out a breath and Jeff knew he'd surprised her. A brief flicker of pleasure spurted inside him, then was smothered again just as quickly. It had never been easy to surprise Sam. She'd always been too quick. Just one step ahead of him.

A little out of reach.

Just like now.

"You never said so."

He shrugged and tried to remember himself, nine years ago. Crazy about Sam. Worried about the future and so damn scared he was going to fuck up his life and hers along with it . . .

"Young and stupid," he said, as if that explained it all.

"If you hadn't gone . . ."

"At the time," he admitted for the first time in, well, *ever,* "I thought if I didn't leave, then you would."

"What? Why would I?"

He turned his gaze on her and lost himself in the pale blue wash of her eyes. The sun kissed her hair, teasing out red streaks and spotlighting the few freckles crossing her nose. If possible, she was even more beautiful than she'd been then. And back then, she'd stolen his breath away every time he looked at her.

But just because he'd been crazy in love, that hadn't meant sunshine and roses. "Jesus, Sam, we fought all the time."

That had been new to him. In his family, discussions were held in moderate tones. Voices were never raised and passions were kept just as tightly under wraps. His parents had maintained a cool, restrained relationship with no highs or lows to complicate matters.

Sam was a revelation.

Her temper was a living, breathing, fire-spitting dragon that held nothing back. She shouted and cursed and flung whatever happened to be handy. Yet when the dragon went to sleep, the fire remained.

"Sure we fought. People fight," she said, as if she couldn't quite believe that he still didn't understand that. "But we always made up."

"There is that." When the dragon of her temper went dormant, the fire remained and her passion was all-encompassing. Jesus, he remembered those wild make-up sessions in the cramped bedroom of that tiny apartment they'd shared in Berkeley. There'd hardly been room enough for both of them in that bed, so they'd slept locked together, neither of them sure where one of them began and the other one ended.

It was the one time in his life he'd felt as though he'd found his place in the universe.

With Sam.

And then he'd lost it all.

"You should have stayed."

"Maybe." That was something he'd tortured himself with plenty of times over the years. If he'd stayed, would it have been different? Would it have gotten better? They'd never know. But he hadn't been the only one to make mistakes. "And maybe," he said, "you should have told me about the baby."

"I tried," she said stiffly, clearly indicating that this little cruise down memory lane was over. "Your mother hijacked the letter."

Not something he was going to forget. Ever. The trickle of anger inside him quickly became a flood with nowhere to go. It dammed up in his chest, backed up into his throat, and made it hard to draw breath. Eleanor Hendricks had escaped the consequences of her interference—as she had most of her life. Even from the grave, his mother was still reaching out to screw with him.

"Okay, forget my mother," he said tightly, though he knew that he'd never truly be able to forget what Eleanor had cost him—and Sam. "Hell, forget me."

"Be a lot easier if you weren't standing there every time I turn around," she muttered.

He ignored the comments, too intent now to stop, to be distracted.

"Why, Sam?" he asked, knowing that this one question had to be asked. Had to be answered before they could go any further. "Why are you so interested in having Emma back in your life now? If you want her so badly, why'd you ever give her up?"

"You wouldn't understand."

"*Make* me understand," he said, turning her in his grasp, his hands tight on her upper arms, pulling her close enough that she had to tip her head back to look up at him.

She shoved at his chest, but he wouldn't let go. Not

now. Not until they had this much at least out in the open. Where it always should have been.

"Explain it to me. You owe me that much."

"Owe you?" she echoed as she wrenched free of his grasp in a wild, frantic move. "I don't owe you anything."

"Maybe not," he conceded, his gaze locked on hers so that he could see the emotions churning in her eyes. He heard the hitch in her breath and spoke up quickly to cut her off before she could burst into a tirade. "Maybe you don't owe me *now*. But you owe the me from nine years ago. Tell *him*."

Chapter Thirteen

Oh, Sam really didn't want to go back there again. But hadn't she been steeped in the past for the last couple of weeks, anyway? Hadn't she been reliving every decision and revisiting every ache and pain?

She stepped back and away from him, needing the distance, and was desperately grateful when he didn't follow. Turning her back on the ocean, she walked the few steps to the beat-up red table and snatched up her coffee cup. She took a long swallow, using the caffeine as someone else would have taken a shot of whiskey for liquid courage.

Maybe he was right. Maybe she *did* at least owe him an explanation of everything that had happened so long ago. At the very least, didn't she owe it to *herself* to finally be able to say everything she'd wanted to tell him back then?

With the heat still roaring through her, Sam took her first tentative step into the cold fog of memory. "After you—I mean your *mother*—sent me the divorce papers, I didn't know what to do." Her fingers tightened on the cardboard cup and she concentrated on the warmth soaking into her palm. She clung to it as she would a life preserver tossed to her in a black, stormy sea. "I came home to tell the family."

"And they didn't want the baby?"

He sounded stunned and she couldn't blame him. If nothing else, the Marconi family was a close one. They would never have turned their backs on her and her child.

Sam sighed. "They would have. But I didn't tell them. Not until after."

"Why?"

Why. She looked at him and just for a minute saw the boy he'd been behind the eyes of the man. And her heart wept for everything that was lost.

"Because when I got home, I found everything falling apart." She gulped at her coffee again, but the heat didn't reach her this time. Just slid down her throat to churn in the pit of her stomach. "They hadn't wanted to worry me before. But Mama was sick. Cancer."

"Sam—" He took a step closer and she held up one hand to keep him at a distance.

She just couldn't handle the sympathy. Not now. Not if he really wanted her to finish. "With Mama sick," she said, and hurried her words as if rushing through the story would make the pain somehow briefer, too. "Papa had his hands full, trying to take care of her and keep the business running."

Rubbing at the spot between her eyes, she tried to tame the headache brewing there. But it was already raging and nothing could stop it.

"Jo left college, to come home and help out. Mike . . ." She shook her head and gave him a half-smile. "Mike decided to avoid dealing with Mama's illness by running away. When the police brought her back, she'd run again. The whole place was in turmoil. Mama was dying and it felt like she was taking the whole family with her. She was the center. The heart of us. And every day, we lost another piece of her."

He shifted position, dipped his hands into his pockets, and an instant later, she heard the coins and keys rattle together. She didn't even stop him. Somehow, that little irritation was almost a comfort as she kept talking.

"It was tearing Papa apart," she said softly and walked to the nearest steel trash drum and dropped her half-full cup into it. For the first time in her life, coffee was turning her stomach.

Then, facing the ocean, she stared out at the horizon and the clouds just beginning to gather as she continued. "He cried at night. When he thought we couldn't hear him." She shivered and blinked back a sudden sheen of tears that made the ocean blur and her head pound. She could still hear her father's quiet tears and the pitiful grief in the sound was still enough to shake her to the ground. "He's the strongest man I've ever known, yet he cried like a lost child at the thought of being without her."

"Sam—"

She shook her head and swiped one hand across her cheeks, impatiently wiping away her own tears. "Mama told me, *asked* me, to take care of them. To help Mike and to make sure Jo went back to college."

The wind sighed past her, trailing cold fingers along her arms, sending chills racing through her. Jeff stepped up close but still didn't touch her and she didn't know now if she was grateful or sad for it.

"Well," she said on a choked laugh, "I got one of those right. Convinced Mike to stop running, but couldn't sell Jo on going back to school. She was the oldest. She decided to stay home, help run the company. Nothing I said would change her mind."

"It wasn't your fault."

"Maybe not, but I still felt as if I were letting Mama down." She sighed softly, remembering. "I told them about the divorce."

He winced.

"Mama didn't say anything, but I could tell she was disappointed. Marconis marry for life, you know." Sam laughed a little, though there was nothing funny about any of this. "I couldn't tell her about the baby, too. Couldn't tell Papa. I thought about it." She sighed and remembered. "God, I thought about it all the time. I wondered if maybe if they knew about the baby, it would give them all something to hold on to. If it might give Mama some happiness in the midst of all the misery. But then," she said, shoving one hand through her hair, "I realized it would just make it harder on Mama. Knowing that there would be a grandchild she'd never see. Never hold. Never love."

Jeff opened his mouth to speak, but she rushed on. "Mostly, though, I thought about Emma. It wasn't fair to give her a single mother who was falling apart." Shaking her head, she shot Jeff a quick glance, then looked away again before she could read the emotions in his eyes. "I just couldn't become the proverbial straw to the Marconi family camel."

He laid one hand on her arm and, oh God, Sam wanted to lean into him. Just for a minute. And since the yearning went bone deep, she forced herself to ignore it.

"Sam, you should have called me—"

A short bark of laughter erupted from her throat. "Right. Pick up the phone and call the husband that didn't want me or my baby and say, 'Hey, would you mind coming home from London? Mama's dying and Mike's missing, I sure could use the help.' Sure. Good plan."

His features tightened and he shut up, which she was also grateful for. It allowed her the few minutes she'd need to get through the rest of it.

"I was the *good* one, you know? The middle sister who never caused any problems. Mama used to call me that all the time. 'Jo's the artistic one, Mike's the firecracker, and Sam's my Good One.'" She laughed again, but this time, even she heard the misery in it. "The one time I went against the family was to marry you and look how well that turned out."

"I see your point."

"Good." She inhaled sharply, drawing the cold ocean air deep inside her and holding it for as long as she could. "Anyway, ovarian cancer is fast, if nothing else. Mama died and Mike stayed home. She stayed miserable, but she stayed home. Jo worked with Papa and I transferred to Long Beach State. Stayed with my aunt Mary. Papa's sister. I managed to finish my courses, and graduate. Then I had the baby and—"

"Gave her up."

Memories reached up from her heart with icy fingers and took hold of her throat and squeezed. She could still feel the incredible feathery weight of her newborn baby girl as they laid Emma in her arms. So tiny. So furious at being pushed into the world. Her eyes were screwed shut and Sam remembered wondering what color her eyes would be—and knowing that she would likely never find out. She'd counted every finger and every toe. She'd run a fingertip along her baby's face as if imprinting her touch on the tiny child so that at least *something* of her would remain—if not in the baby's life, then in her heart. And then the nurse had swept in, scooped Emma out of Sam's arms, and walked away through a set of double glass doors and into a future Sam wouldn't be a part of.

Misery pumped through her bloodstream and made her want to fall to the ground under the weight of the pain. But she clung to the one truth she'd had to comfort her through the last eight years.

"It was the best thing for *her,*" Sam said, not really caring now if he believed her or not. *She'd* believed it at the time and she *needed* to believe it now and that had to be enough. Her dreams were already haunted with her own doubts and guilts. She didn't need to add Jeff's regrets to her own list. There were too many now, as it was.

"When I came home, I told them about Emma." She still remembered the shock, the pain, on her father's face as he realized he had a grandchild he would never see. "Papa said I should have told them sooner. That he would have raised my daughter. But it wouldn't have been right, Jeff."

She was still sure of that. No matter what. It wouldn't have been right or fair to ask her father to raise a child after his own were grown. When he was still grieving. When the foundations of the family were so shaken. "I was eighteen. I did what I thought was right. What I thought was best. For Emma."

"It *was* right for Emma," Jeff said.

She laughed shortly and risked a glance at him. "Sure, you can say that. You're the one who raised her."

"Are you really sorry that she came to *me*?"

Sam thought about it for a long minute, then shook her head again. As hard as it was to know that he'd had all the years with their daughter that she had missed, Sam knew that the truth was a simple one.

"No. If she'd gone to someone else, I never would have met her like this. Never would have gotten to know her. Or had the chance to love her face-to-face." She turned to face him and read understanding in his deep blue eyes. Her heart eased a little with that and she was surprised to find that it actually mattered to her, what Jeff thought of her decision.

"I wish I'd known. Wish I could have helped you back then." He lifted one hand and smoothed her hair back from her face.

Sam shivered at the touch of his skin on hers. Warmth trickled through her, easing back the chill that clung to the edges of her soul. His fingertips trailed down the side of her face, sculpting the curve of her cheek and the line of her jaw. She inhaled sharply and held it, telling herself that he was simply trying to comfort her. To ease an old pain.

But even she didn't really believe that. There was more here. How much more she didn't know. Didn't think she should explore. But her body wasn't listening to her head and she found herself leaning toward him.

She inhaled the scent of his cologne, a dark, rich fragrance that seemed to lift in the wind and reach for her.

His fingers dipped beneath her chin and tipped her face up to his. His gaze moved over her features with an intensity that turned the simmering fires within into raging infernos.

"I wish," he murmured, his voice a deep rumble of sound that barely carried over the crashing thunder of the ocean, "we could go back."

"But we can't," she whispered. No matter how many times she'd wished that herself over the last couple of weeks, she knew there was no changing the past. All they could do was live with it, try to make peace with it and the choices they'd made. "There's no going back, Jeff."

He nodded slowly, still staring into her eyes as though trapped there. "No. You're right. No past, then. No future. Only now."

And then he kissed her.

The man had a head like solid concrete.

Why did she find that so attractive?

Grace smoothed her hair, smiled to herself and walked a bit farther from the crowd of people. She didn't look back. She knew very well that Hank Marconi would be right behind her.

He didn't disappoint.

"Grace, I'm too old for this nonsense," he muttered, once they were out of earshot.

She stopped beneath the shade of a maple tree that had been standing on the property for more than a hundred years. Above her head, the leaves rustled gently in a puff of wind and sunlight peeked through the thick greenery to lie in lacy patterns of shade across the grass. Summer was just getting started and she was already having so much fun.

"Oh Henry, you'll never be old."

He flushed, his darkly tanned skin going a bit red in the cheeks and she wasn't sure if the heat was to blame or if it was her compliment. His gray hair and beard were neatly trimmed and his pale blue eyes sparkled even as he shook his head and his index finger to boot. "You're skipping around the point, Grace."

"Not at all. Everything is going along nicely, isn't it?"

"Yes, but—"

"And we're enjoying each other's company?"

"Of course, but—"

"Then there's no reason for anything to change, is there?"

He blew out a frustrated breath and looked around behind him, checking to make sure they were still as alone as they could be in a compound filled with people. When he turned back to her, he said, "You're a hardheaded woman, Grace."

She smiled, glad he was willing to let their argument end. She'd come to care for him quite a bit, but she wasn't ready yet to test the strength of their relationship by letting his children—and the rest of the town—in on it. Besides, there was something very . . . sexy about a secret love affair.

Still smiling, she stepped past him, out of the shade, back toward the lively crowd. And as she passed, she said, "That's why you love me, Henry."

Jeff had been hungry for the taste of her for days. She was in every dream, every waking thought. The essence of what she was, *who* she was, was with him at all times. Taunting him with thoughts of what might have been. Reminding him at every turn just how much he'd given up. How much he'd turned his back on.

As his mouth came down on hers, he poured everything he was into the kiss. Her mouth gave to him as she fell into the moment, the emotion. Then she sighed into his mouth and it was like a benediction.

She was everything.

And he was a damn fool.

Sam knew she should stop him.

Wasn't her brain shrieking at her to do just that?

Unfortunately, her body just didn't give a flying damn.

Wind raced, waves crashed, heart raced, and hormones stood straight up and danced.

She leaned into him, surrendering to the instantaneous burst of heat lighting up her insides like a neon sign in a Vegas night. Wrapping her arms around his neck, she held on, pressing herself into him, wanting suddenly to feel every inch of him melting against her.

Over the thundering beat of her own heart, she heard someone moan and was pretty sure it had been her. Oh God. She was lost. This wasn't a memory. This wasn't even the same kind of kiss she remembered. This was more.

Because *they* were more.

Older, but no wiser.

Her lips parted for him and the first hungry swipe of his tongue took her breath away. She sighed into him and he gave her his breath in exchange. His arms folded around her middle like iron bands, holding her tightly to him, as if he were afraid she'd suddenly bolt and make a dash for it.

But she couldn't have, even if she'd wanted to.

And she *didn't* want to.

Oh God, this was what she wanted.

What she'd wanted from the first moment she'd opened her front door and found him standing on the porch. Even when she'd wanted to brain him with a hammer. Even when she'd shouted at him and cursed him. Even then, everything in her had been racing toward this moment, whether she could admit it aloud or not.

He groaned and pressed her more firmly against him, taking her mouth, plundering her as if his life depended on his being able to taste as much of her as possible. And still it wasn't enough.

His hands slid up and down her spine, exploring, defining every curve, and she wriggled against him, wanting the exploration to go farther, deeper.

Sensations, feelings, coursed through her body and Sam let them run riot. It was better than thinking. Better than stopping to consider what the hell she was doing. Because if she did that, then she'd have to break away from him.

And she knew she didn't have the strength for that.

His mouth tore from hers and slipped down her throat, kissing, tasting, nibbling. Her nerves jangled crazily and every inch of her skin felt alive with possibilities.

Sunlight streamed down on them, adding even more heat to the tangled fury of the fire already engulfing them.

"Sam." He muttered her name thickly, in a voice choked with desire, with a hunger she recognized and shared.

Two skateboarders barreled past them on the sidewalk, the steel wheels on their boards growling almost as loudly as their appreciative catcalls.

"Oh baby!"

"Go for it, dude!"

"Oh God." Sam pulled free of Jeff's arms, and took a few shaky steps backward.

Jeff, breath heaving, shot a murderous look at the two kids who were already far in the distance, their laughter drifting in the air like a helium balloon cast adrift.

"I can't believe . . ." Yes she could. Of course she could believe it. Hadn't she just been thinking that this was perfect? What she'd wanted from the get-go? Oh God, Mike had been right. She was going to get all sappy and hormonal over him again. And then what would happen to the grand plan of keeping Emma in her life?

Lifting both hands, Jeff scrubbed his face with his palms, as if trying to wake himself out of a coma.

Some coma, Sam thought.

"I'm not sorry," he snapped.

"Who asked you?" she countered.

"I figure I know you well enough to know that already you're doing the 'We shouldn't have done that' dance."

Sam bristled, since that's exactly what she'd been doing, but she had no intention of letting *him* know that. "I told you. You don't know me. I'm not the same person I was nine years ago. Any more than you are."

"You taste the same."

"Oh jeeezzz . . ." Shivers. Shouldn't get shivers. Not a good sign. Dammit, Sam. Everybody makes mistakes. But you could at least have the sense to make *different* mistakes.

"I want you."

She flicked him a glance when she was fairly certain she wouldn't self-combust by meeting his gaze. "Yeah, I got the picture."

"You want me, too."

Hard to deny *that* one.

"Okay, yeah. I do." He took a step closer and she held up one hand. "But I also want chocolate to be labeled a diet food. So I guess I'm just doomed to disappointment."

"You don't have to be," he said tightly, and she could hear what this was costing him in the thickness of his voice. She felt the tension simmering off him in vicious waves that reached for her, tempting her back into the circle of his arms.

Oh boy.

Nope. Stop. Think.

"Did you forget a little something?" she demanded, walking a wide path around him as she headed for town. For Main Street. For *crowds*.

Man, did she need the safety-in-numbers thing right about now.

"Huh?"

"Your fiancée?" Sam reminded him, turning around to face him while continuing to walk backward. "You remember. Cynthia? Blond? Big boobs?"

His mouth, his fabulous mouth, flattened into a grim line. And his dark blue eyes shuttered. "Right."

"How quickly they forget," she muttered, disgusted, but still unwilling to look away from him.

"I didn't forget, I just—"

"What?" she demanded, throwing both hands high and wide. "Decided to go for the gusto? After all, it's not every man who can bed his fiancée one night, then zoom to another city and boink his wife the next night!"

"Who said anything about *boinking*?"

"Nobody," Sam said. "It was implied."

"It was a kiss."

That stung, even though she recognized it for the lie it was. She could see the truth in his eyes, feel it practically vibrating in the air around him.

Typical that he should deny it.

Even to himself.

"It was way more than a kiss, *babe*," she said, lifting one hand and pointing her index finger at him. "And you know it."

"So you admit it."

Her mouth snapped shut. Then she opened it again and snapped it closed one more time. Somehow or other, while she'd been doing all the talking, he'd laid a trap and she'd stumbled right into it.

He took two quick, long strides and caught up to her at the edge of the cliff park. Behind her, Chandler was going about its everyday life. Tourists wandered the sidewalk, stores did bumper business, and car horns honked in frustration. But here, on this small slice of grass, she was staring up into the eyes of a man who knew her past, shaped her present, and was still holding her future in doubt.

"I'm not admitting anything."

"Too late." He grabbed her hand. A small, tight twist of a smile curved his lips, then flattened again before she could get used to it.

"Let go."

"Not a chance."

"I mean it, Jeff." She kept her voice down, because hey, when a Marconi started shouting, there'd be no stopping and who needed the whole town as a witness?

"I'm feeling something for you."

"Duh."

He ignored that. "Something I don't want to feel."

"Well, isn't that the nicest thing anyone's ever said to me."

"Shut up, Sam."

She sighed. "Jeff, let's just call this whole thing a mistake. A stumble on memory lane."

"That'd be the easy way."

A short, sharp laugh shot from her throat, but there was no humor in it. Hell, there was nothing funny about any of this. "Then we sure as heck won't do it. We never did anything the easy way, did we?"

He nodded grimly. "Not so's you'd notice."

Carefully, gingerly, she wormed her way out of his grasp and took a step back, just for good measure. She considered it a small victory when he didn't grab her again.

This was all getting way more tangled up than she wanted it to be. She hadn't expected that kiss. Had wanted it, sure. But hadn't expected it. And now that it had happened, she didn't know quite what to do about it.

Sure, they were married.

Technically.

But *technically* he was engaged.

So the only way to back up, emotionally and physically, was to slap a barrier down between them, and she knew just the way to do it.

"I went to see a lawyer today."

Jeff's gaze flickered, then shuttered, and she imagined this was just the steely-eyed look he used to keep the peasants in line at his family bank. Wow. Hadn't taken long at all to change from lust bunny to danger man.

"Why?"

"Why not?" she countered. "Why should you be the only one with a lawyer?"

"I thought we were going to work this out between us."

"Yeah, well," she said, "I figured I needed someone on my side."

"This isn't a war, Sam."

"Yeah it is," she said. "Just a bloodless one. So far."

"Doesn't have to be this way."

The distance between them was lengthening. And she told herself it was for the best. Although a part of her already missed being held and kissed and *wanted* . . . there was no future there for her.

"What way?" she asked. "The way where I get a say in what happens? Yes, it does."

"You could have trusted me."

Regret shone in his eyes and for just a minute or two, Sam wished it were different. That *they* were different. That there was no Polly Perfection waiting for him in San Francisco.

She wanted, desperately, to be able to wipe out the

last nine years. But that was impossible. Too much had happened. To both of them.

"I guess that's the bottom line, Jeff," she said, and her voice held the sorrow she felt weeping within. "I don't trust you."

Chapter Fourteen

Her words hit him like a bunched fist.

Breath still wheezing, body still on full alert, Jeff felt something inside him crack and he wanted to damn her for it.

But how could he?

Why the hell should she trust him?

When she'd needed him most, he hadn't been there.

Okay, sure, his mother's fine hand had seen to that. But he could have gone to Sam anyway. Could have forced a confrontation and gotten the truth out of her. Instead, he'd let his pride get in the way and so lost nine long years.

And had anything really changed?

Hell, he was *engaged* to another woman and he'd just groped Sam in public like a randy teenager hoping to score at a drive-in. Jeff shoved one hand through his hair, scraping his fingernails along his scalp. The added pain didn't help any, but he figured he deserved it.

Sam's taste still lingered on his tongue.

Just as her words still echoed in his mind.

The pictures she'd drawn were so vivid, he could actually *see* her as she'd been, scared and alone. He felt as though he'd now been witness to Mama Marconi slowly dying. And he wished to hell he could step back in time and beat the crap out of his younger self.

But that was as impossible as what was happening between them now.

On the drive to Chandler from the city, he'd gone over and over everything Cynthia had suggested. That Sam wasn't really interested in Emma, but only pretending, in order to keep up a good front for her family. He'd told himself she was wrong.

Small consolation to know he'd been right. Yes, Sam really wanted Emma. And she'd hired a lawyer to help her in the fight.

Which left them exactly . . . *where*?

"Why is this so damn hard?" he wondered aloud.

"It was always hard with us."

He stared down into those pale blue eyes and knew she was right. They'd never been easy together. But hadn't that been part of the fun?

Fun.

Had he ever once had spontaneous, unplanned, just-for-the-hell-of-it *fun* with Cynthia?

Frowning to himself, Jeff considered it for a long minute and realized that the answer was no. Strange now that he thought about it, but usually the times he and his fiancée spent together were carefully choreographed ahead of time. Cynthia had said more than once that she enjoyed the planning of an event as much or more than she did the actual event itself. Theater dates, dinners at fine restaurants, mapped-out-down-to-the-minute day trips or vacations, like the one they'd taken to Italy. Cynthia didn't *do* spontaneous.

And he'd never noticed enough to miss it.

What did that say about him?

About *them*?

Hell of a time to think about this, he told himself as Sam continued to stare at him as if wondering where his mind had drifted off to. But dammit, could he help where he was when an epiphany struck?

Jesus. Think, he ordered himself. Just think about this. Cynthia. Him. Relaxed, *fun*.

Nope. No such animal existed.

Maybe he might have realized it sooner if they'd been living together. But with Emma in the house, Jeff had decided to wait until they were married before Cynthia moved in. With the result being, they didn't see nearly enough of each other.

They hadn't even had sex in weeks.

Christ. When had he stopped noticing that he was living like a damn monk?

And why hadn't he paid closer attention to the fact that he didn't mind not having sex more often? Cynthia was a beautiful, intelligent woman—but she wasn't the one woman in the world he wanted with every breath.

So what in God's name was he doing *marrying* her?

"Calling Jeff. Yoo-hoo!"

Sam slapped his arm when shouting at him had no effect, and Jeff jerked awake as if he'd been yanked out of a warm bed and tossed into an ice-cold swimming pool.

"What?"

"What what?"

He shook his head. "What'd you say?"

"Which time?"

"Huh?"

"Great." Sam nodded and gave him a mocking smile. "Terrific. We're talking about custody of our daughter and you're off in la-la land." Shaking her head, she turned away. "Let me know when you get back."

"I'm back now."

She glanced at him over her shoulder. "Doesn't look like it."

Probably not.

Crap.

He had so many damn ideas racing through his mind, he probably looked as if his head were exploding.

Which it was, so good for him.

There were a lot of decisions to make. Some of them sooner than others.

But right now, there was Sam.

Jeff reached for her, slapping one hand down onto her shoulder and stopping her in her tracks. She slipped out from beneath his hold, but didn't try to keep moving.

Small victory.

"I don't know what to do about making you trust me."

"You can't *make* someone trust you, Jeff."

"I know." He did know that. Didn't make it any easier to deal with, but he knew it.

"And I won't sign the divorce papers until we work out the custody thing."

"I know that, too." His fingers tightened on her shoulder and he swore he could feel her blood rushing through her body. "I'm willing to talk about sharing custody."

"*What?*"

She actually swayed on her feet.

Couldn't blame her. He felt a little stunned himself. All he'd been worried about was losing Emma. Losing that one connection to his child. But by sharing Emma with her mother, he'd be *keeping* his daughter, not losing her. The only sure way to lose his child at this stage of things would be to deny her access to her mother. Then Emma might come to hate him. And he wouldn't be able to blame *her* for it, either.

"You heard me."

"I don't think so." She folded her arms across her chest and jutted one hip out. "Rewind and hit play again."

He snorted. Damn, he'd missed her. "Fine. I'm willing to share custody of Emma. Plain enough."

She reached up to check his forehead with the backs of her fingers. "No fever."

There would be, if she touched him again.

"You're a funny woman, Sam."

"Not feeling the joke."

"Not joking."

"You're not, are you?" she asked, staring into his eyes as if looking for the pothole he wanted her to step into.

No, she didn't trust him.

And damned if that didn't hit him hard.

"No, I'm not joking about the custody thing," he said, since she seemed to need to hear it. "So are you interested or not?"

"Hell, yes. You don't have to say it again," she said, smiling. Then she stopped. Frowned. "Well, I guess you did. But you know what I mean."

"I'm beginning to think so."

"And that means . . ."

He took her arm in a firm grip. "I'll let you know when I figure it all out."

"That'll be a party."

She tried to pull free, but he only tightened his grip. "Hello? Where am I being dragged to?"

He looked at her and so was able to see the shock stamp itself on her features when he said, "To your lawyer. We'll just work this part out now."

She sputtered, but didn't speak.

As she stumbled along in his wake, Jeff smiled. Inwardly of course—he wasn't stupid enough to let her see his grin. But damned if it wasn't rewarding to know that he'd made Sam Marconi speechless.

Mike sat on the hood of her truck, crossed her feet at the ankles and leaned back against the windshield, folding her arms behind her head for a makeshift pillow.

Felt good to be away from the site for a while.

She'd picked up the new copper pipes for the second kitchen in Santa Cruz, but then she'd detoured before heading back to Grace's. Hell, even a Marconi needed a break from the hammers and saws every now and again.

And out here, she found the peace she always did.

A stand of trees encircled her. Just to the right was the eastern shore of the lake, where reeds dipped and swayed with the rippling water as if dancing to a tune only they could hear. At the northern edge of the lake, almost a half mile from where she sat, Nick Candellano's house hugged the shore. There was another house on the western side, but it was tucked behind the trees enough that all she ever really caught was a glimpse of sunlight glancing off windowpanes.

To her left—okay, *far* left—was the ocean, clean on the other side of Chandler. But even here, back in the trees, the sound of the waves reached her. Still, it was so soft, it was more a murmuring hush, like a soothing lullaby sung to a cranky baby.

The sun had to work hard to punch through the canopy of trees, so the dappled shade kept the temperature a good fifteen degrees cooler than anywhere else in town. A whisper of wind caressed her and she closed her eyes, the better to enjoy *her* spot.

No one else ever came here.

At least, Mike had never run into anyone.

And she came here as often as she could. She'd found this little piece of seclusion when she was a kid and had desperately needed a place all to herself. Scowling as memories rushed forward, pushing the present to the back of her mind, Mike remembered those quiet, moonlit nights when she was sixteen and finding out that parents didn't live forever.

Opening her eyes again, she stared up at the slivers of blue visible only when the leaves of the trees shifted with the wind.

"Mama."

God, just saying that word out loud brought comfort and pain and joy and misery and too many other emotions to try to put a name to. But her mother had really been on her mind a lot lately.

Not completely true, she thought. Thoughts of Mama were never really far away. But in the last week or so, they'd been so thick she could hardly think of anything else.

Had to be Emma's presence. Having the girl back in their lives was great. But at the same time, having her here was stirring up the memories of nine years ago. Making everything so close. So . . . hard to ignore.

"Not that I want to ignore you or anything, Mama," Mike said, accustomed to having one-sided conversations with her mother while she was here. "But thinking about you and about what an ass I was when you were so sick just makes me feel bad all over again."

Such language.

Mike smiled to herself, imagining Mama's response.

You were a child, Mike. You shouldn't be so angry at the girl you were.

"Hard not to be," she said.

"Is this a private conversation or can anybody join in?"

Mike shot straight up on the still-warm hood of her truck and looked around the clearing. What the hell? "Who's here?"

"I am."

"Yeah?" she asked, swinging her head around in the direction of the distinctly rough, male voice. "And who're you?"

He stepped out of the treeline and Mike's scowl deepened. Tall and scruffy-looking, he had dark brown hair that hung just past his collar. He swung his head to the right and his hair swished out of the way only to slide back down over his forehead. Probably would have blinded him if he hadn't been wearing glasses.

His features were sharp, as if carved by a hasty but talented sculptor. His jeans were threadbare at the knee and the hiking boots he wore were so beat-up, they made Mike's look brand-new. His black T-shirt was rumpled, as if he'd slept in it.

He shoved his hands into the front pockets of his jeans as he strolled—there was no other word for it—into the clearing. He walked right through the wild flowers growing in a scattershot of color amid the meadow grass and headed for the truck. And her.

"If you don't want to be eavesdropped on, you shouldn't talk so loud."

"Thanks for the advice," she said, sliding off the end of the hood to stand on her own two feet. The better to do some serious kicking—or make a run for it, whichever came first. "But that doesn't answer the whole 'Who're you' question."

"Lucas Gallagher."

"And why're you here?"

"That's two questions," he pointed out, still walking toward her with the air of a man who never hurried.

"There's a limit on questions?"

"We'll trade. Who're you?"

"Mike Marconi."

His eyebrows lifted slightly. "Never knew a woman named Mike."

"You still don't," she pointed out, inching closer to the door handle of her truck. He didn't look dangerous, but then, most criminals didn't walk around with signs proclaiming Danger around their necks.

"Don't be so skittish," he advised and came to a stop about ten feet from her.

"Who's skittish?" She stopped, too, embarrassed to

be caught trying to bolt. "And what kind of stupid word is that?"

"More questions." He shook his head, swinging his hair back from his face again. "Interesting woman."

"Gee, thanks."

"Now go away."

"Excuse me?"

"You're on private property," he said and turned his back on her to walk toward the lake. "Go away."

Something bubbled to life inside her. She was pretty sure it was the urge to throw something. "What do you mean, private property?"

"So many questions." He shot her an amused look over his shoulder. "Look it up."

"Just wait a damn minute," she shouted as he moved farther away. Only a second or two ago, she'd been thinking about getting the hell out of there. Now that he'd *told* her to, she wasn't in such a damn rush.

"Good-bye, Mike Marconi." He didn't look back, but he lifted one hand as if already waving her on her way.

She'd been dismissed.

Mike blinked, then looked around as if searching for someone she could say "Did you see that?" to. But she was alone and getting more so the farther he walked.

She thought about chasing him down and getting some answers out of him. But there was a cleaner way of doing that. She'd just head back to the job site and talk to Grace. As far as she knew, this land still belonged to the Van Horn family. And she made it her business to know, since she'd been saving every dime for years in the hope of one day having enough to buy it outright from Grace.

No way would this place have been sold without her knowing about it.

"Lucas Gallagher," she muttered, yanking the truck door open and wincing as the rusted metal screamed in protest. She climbed inside, turned the key, and cursed viciously, fluently, until the grumbling engine sputtered, coughed, and finally caught. "I'm not finished with you, yet."

Staring through the bug-splattered windshield, she watched the man as he wandered aimlessly around the edge of the lake. Maybe he'd trip and fall, hit his head on a rock and drown in the shallows.

"Nah," she whispered. "I'm just not that lucky."

Throwing the truck into reverse, she spun her wheels in the mud for a few interesting minutes, then backed up far enough to change gears. As she turned the truck around and headed for the road back to the highway, she checked her rearview mirror.

But he was already gone.

"Mommy says there's gonna be fireworks and rides and cotton candy and I can hold my own sparklers and write my name in the sky with 'em and everything," Emma said, words tumbling out of her mouth, one after the other, so close together they were almost impossible to separate. "And we get to have a picnic and see Mommy's friend Carla and her dog Abbey and Abbey's puppies maybe and maybe I could even get one and she said I could keep it here, 'cause I have my own room and everything and Isabel doesn't have a dog."

Jeff laughed as his daughter tried to bring him up to date on her life in five minutes or less. He'd only been gone two days and it felt like a hell of a lot longer. How the hell would he ever be able to stand being separated from her?

Just thinking about his condo back in the city and how quiet it would be without Emma running through the rooms, her shoes clacking on the bare wood floors, made him want to cringe. But he'd have to learn to deal with it, wouldn't he?

Glancing at Sam, he thought she looked more relaxed than she had since this whole thing started. And why shouldn't she? They'd already met with her lawyer and agreed to custody terms—at least temporarily—until they could work out a permanent solution.

It had been, he told himself as he listened with half an ear to Emma, more to give Sam peace of mind than anything else. Now she knew without a doubt that he wouldn't try to keep her from her daughter. Now, she at least knew that he was willing to work on the custody issue.

And maybe that would give them enough time to work out whatever the hell else was between them.

Dammit, he could still taste her.

All afternoon, she'd lingered on his lips, his tongue. He had her scent buried deep within him and couldn't seem to draw a breath without dragging her even deeper inside.

He wanted her.

Bad.

"Daddy, you're not listening."

He came up out of his thoughts like a deep-sea diver breaching the surface of the water and blinking stupidly at the sunlight. "What?"

"To me," Emma said, leaning in and capturing his face between her small palms. "You're not listening to me."

"Sorry, baby. What'd you say?"

She sighed. A deep, eloquent, dramatic sigh that women apparently were born knowing how to deliver. "I want you to see my room."

"Oh. Okay, show me." He stood up and took her hand. Then he shot a quick look at Sam, sitting curled up at the end of the red chenille sofa. "Maybe your mommy should come, too."

She gave him a wary smile. Not trusting yet, but not as openly hostile as she was a few days ago. That was something, wasn't it?

"I've seen it."

"No, Mommy, you have to come, too." Emma grabbed Sam's hand as she scooted out from between the sofa and the magazine-littered coffee table.

Sam's features softened and Jeff knew she wouldn't refuse Emma anything. He grinned as she got up and walked beside him. "Just the three of us," he murmured.

"And Cynthia makes four," Sam shot back.

Jeff winced a little. He kept forgetting about the fiancée he'd left in the city. And what did that say?

Emma pulled them determinedly down the long hall. Jeff looked around as they passed and caught a fleeting glimpse of what had to be Sam's room. Quilt-topped four-poster bed, flowers in a vase, postcards framed and hung on a wall. The second bedroom was empty save for a narrow bed, a chest of drawers, and a table with a globe-topped lamp on it. The bathroom was small and painted a deep sea green. Lighthouse prints hung on the walls and a white pedestal sink stood beneath an antique medicine cabinet and mirror.

Then Emma stopped in front of a third door and dropped their hands as she stepped inside and did a twirling spin. "Isn't it pretty, Daddy?"

He walked into the room, too, turning more slowly than his daughter, so he could see everything. Sam had turned the room into a little girl's fantasy. The walls were a summer-sky blue and one wall was covered with what looked like fluffy clouds. A canopied bed, with a Barbie bedspread. White wicker furniture and shelves filled with books and toys. There was even a tiny white wicker rocking chair in the corner, with a standing lamp alongside it, so Emma could curl up and read if she wanted to.

He shifted his gaze to Sam. "You really did a nice job in here."

She shrugged and leaned against the doorjamb. "I wanted her to be happy."

"I think you managed that," Jeff said as he walked toward her. Emma was talking a mile a minute, pulling out every book and holding it up for him to see. He smiled at her, but then turned back to Sam. "She loves it here."

Sam's eyes filled quickly, and she looked as surprised by it as he was. Damn, he'd always hated it when she cried. A man never felt so clumsy and useless as he did when faced with a woman's tears.

"Don't do that," he said and heard the whisper of blind panic in his own voice.

She laughed shortly and swiped her fingertips beneath her eyes. "It's just a little leak." She shifted a look at Emma, still happily pulling out book after book. "It just means something to me to hear you say that. That she loves being here."

"You're surprised?" He lifted one hand to smooth his fingertips along her cheek. God, she was still such a mystery to him. Her moods shifted and changed with nearly every breath. She could go from hard to soft, furious to sentimental, in the blink of an eye.

She'd touched something in him nine years ago and she was the only woman who ever had. Why should it even mildly surprise him to find that she could still reach him on levels he hadn't known he possessed?

"Sort of, I guess," she admitted, then straightened up to face him. "I know she doesn't have here what she has in the city and—"

"It's not about *what* she has," Jeff interrupted. "But about *who* she has." He tucked a strand of soft auburn hair behind her ear. "Now she has her father *and* her mother."

Sam sucked in air, then whooshed it out again. "Thanks. Not just for that," she added, "but for the custody thing."

Jeff smiled as he watched her. "Was it painful?"

"Thanking you, you mean?" She shrugged and her lips twitched just a little. "Only slightly. I'll take an aspirin."

"Daddy, will you read to me now?" Emma asked as she came up alongside him and tugged at his pants leg.

"I can't right now, honey," he said, pulling one of her thick braids. "I have to get back to the inn. See if they kept my room. But I'll come back and get you tomorrow, okay?"

Emma scowled up at him and it occurred to Jeff that she looked most like her mother when she got that disapproving expression on her face.

"You shouldn't go, Daddy. You should stay here. With Mommy and me."

"Oh . . ." Well, that caught him off guard. And judging by the poleaxed expression on Sam's face, she was right there with him. But now that Emma'd brought it up, the idea felt . . . *good* to him. Staying here? Right down a narrow hallway from Sam?

His blood boiled.

"Honey, I don't know—" Sam gave him a quick look, saw no help there at all, and refocused on Emma.

"Why not?" Emma demanded, turning to look up at her mother. "There's the other room. Daddy could stay there and then he could read to me at night, too. And you're the mommy and he's the daddy and I'm the little girl, so it would be good. Like Isabel says, mommies and daddies most times stay in the same house."

"Yes," Sam said. "Most of the time, that's true, but your daddy and I are—"

"Divorced, but you're friends, you said." Emma rushed in to finish Sam's sentence and leave her mother scrambling for an argument.

Jeff looked at Sam.

Sam looked at Jeff.

Emma looked at both of them.

"Not a good idea," Sam said.

"Scared?" Jeff asked.

"Oh please."

"Then why not?"

"Yes, Mommy, why not?"

Seconds ticked past. From down the hall and out in the kitchen, Jeff heard the refrigerator burp and hum.

Outside, someone was mowing their lawn. Inside, he waited.

Finally, Sam sighed and threw both hands wide.

Jeff grinned.

"Okay," she said. "I'm probably crazy, but okay."

Chapter Fifteen

"You *sold* it?" Mike couldn't believe it.

"Well, honey," Grace said softly, "I didn't really need the property, although Lucas says it's fine with him if the goats wander over, which I thought was just lovely of him, don't you think?"

"Sure," Mike said, nodding her head in a jerky motion that felt as if she were shaking the stones in her head. "Lovely."

"He's even thinking of buying the old vineyard property that runs behind the stand of woods." Grace pulled and tugged at the carded strands of cashmere, smoothing them into perfect alignment.

"The vineyard? He wants to make wine?" He hadn't looked like a winemaker to Mike. Serial killer, maybe.

"Oh no, dear." Grace set the wool aside, stood up and smoothed her hands down the front of her pale green slacks. "He said he didn't know a thing about it, but that he'd always liked grapes."

"Sure. Don't buy a bunch of grapes at the market," Mike muttered darkly, remembering the man with his dark brown eyes and lanky build. "Buy a vineyard so you can eat 'em right off the vine."

"Exactly." Grace reached out to pat Mike's cheek,

then stopped and stared at her. "I'm awfully sorry about the land, honey. I had no idea you might be interested in it."

"My fault," Mike admitted, her brain wheeling, looking for a way out of this situation. Trying to find some way she could still get her hands on the only piece of land she'd ever wanted. "I should have said something to you years ago, but—" She broke off and wagged her right foot, trying to shake off the goat determined to eat her bootlaces. "You just never seemed like you were in a hurry to sell and—"

"I wasn't. But that young man has a very . . . *persuasive* way of speaking," she said, smiling to herself.

"Oh yeah," Mike muttered darkly. "He's a real charmer."

"I thought so, too." Grace leaned in and smiled, then bent and pulled the goat off Mike's foot. "There now, Isabel, you go find something else to eat."

"Isabel?"

"Emma named her."

"Ah . . ."

Around them, the job site was bustling. The Gypsies had dinner cooking in several pots hung over fires, and the work crews were sidling close, looking for handouts.

Everything was normal, except for the boulder in the pit of Mike's stomach. She'd lost out on the property where she'd planned to build herself a house.

Unless . . .

"Maybe *he'll* sell it to me."

"Oh, I don't think so, dear," Grace said, reaching up to smooth her snow-white hair unnecessarily. "He seemed very determined to build there. He said he liked the quiet."

"Great." Well, this day couldn't get any better, could it?

"Is your father still here?" Grace asked.

"Somewhere," Mike muttered.

"I'll just go find him, then."

Grace moved off and Mike stood alone in the dappled shade of the maple tree. There had to be a way around Lucas Gallagher.

All she had to do was find it.

The next morning, Sam was still getting used to the fact that Jeff was living in her house. She'd heard him all night. Moving around in the guest room, settling in. And every moment, she was reliving that kiss.

She could almost feel the press of his mouth to hers. Feel the soft sigh of his breath dusting her cheek. Feel the shattering pounding of his heart against hers and the hard, implacable strength of his arms wrapped around her.

With that one kiss, he'd splintered her world.

He'd reminded her of what they'd had. What they'd lost. What she'd have given anything to have again.

Then she'd heard him taking a shower.

Oh, dear Lord, she'd listened to the splash and rush of the water and lain in her own bed, imagining that water pelting off his naked body, sluicing down his chest, across his abdomen and lower and lower.

By the time he'd turned the water off, she was exhausted. Drained. And headed for a long night of little sleep.

Bright and early this morning, she'd dragged herself to the kitchen, peeling her eyes open and propping them up through sheer force of will. It only pissed her off further to see that Jeff looked well rested and entirely too pleased with himself.

He was enjoying this.

Dammit.

"The carnival's tomorrow," Sam said, grabbing her cup and filling it to the brim with rich, dark coffee. She paused a moment, inhaled it slowly, deeply, letting the scent of caffeine jolt through her system. She sighed, took her first sip, and then paused again, relishing the near religious experience of that first morning shot of coffee.

"And . . ."

She looked over at Jeff as he picked up Emma's cereal bowl and walked with it to the sink.

"And," Sam said, scooting over a bit so that he could stand at the sink without actually brushing against her. It was too early, she was too sleep deprived, and dammit, she was just too . . . edgy to be able to stand it. "Emma's looking forward to it. We'll have a picnic and then watch the fireworks."

He set the bowl down in the sink, then turned, leaned a hip against the edge of the counter and stared down at her. He smiled as she inched farther away and that was enough to stop Sam in her tracks. She wouldn't let him know just how nervous he made her.

"Sounds like fun."

She nodded, saying good-bye to the faint notion that he might not want to attend. Of course he would. He'd want to spend the Fourth of July with Emma. "Okay, then. Tomorrow."

"What about today?"

Sam looked up at him and immediately wished she hadn't. He was just too good-looking this early in the morning. That had always been an irritation, as she remembered it. He rolled out of bed looking rumpled and sexy. She rolled out of bed, hair standing on end, eyes bleary.

More coffee, she told herself firmly. Taking a sip, she swallowed, then staring down at the inky black surface, she said, "Today, we're at Grace's. I have to finish the library walls, Jo's doing the floor in the study, and Mike's finishing up the kitchen."

"Sounds like fun, too."

"Huh?" She blinked up at him.

He put one finger on the bottom of her coffee cup and tipped it toward her mouth. "More coffee, Sam. It'll clear the cobwebs."

"They're clearing, thanks. What did you say about fun?"

He grinned at her. "I was just thinking about going to the job with you and Emma."

Her eyes narrowed. "Why?"

"Sam." He shook his head. "I thought we got past that whole trust thing yesterday."

"Not completely." What was he up to? Why was he being nice? And why was he so damn close?

He caged her, planting one hand on either side of her on the counter. "Then we'll have to work on that."

"Why?"

He laughed shortly. "You ask more questions than Emma."

"And get fewer answers."

He bent down, lowering his head to hers. When her eyes crossed as she tried to focus on him, Jeff smiled again. "You'll get your answers, Sam. We both will."

"What's that supposed to mean?" Dammit. She

could feel his breath on her face. She could smell him. All morning and shower and shampoo and *man*.

"Whatever you want it to mean."

She forced a laugh she didn't feel and tried to push past one of his arms. Sure. Like trying to move a steel rod. "You're doing the vague thing again."

"Let's see if I can get more clear."

He leaned in.

"What're you doing?" Did her voice really sound so breathy? Hungry?

"Not sure."

"You do remember that we're almost divorced?"

His mouth curved. "You know another word for almost divorced? 'Married.' "

Sam sucked in air. She knew she should have tried to dodge his move, but hey, it was early. She hadn't had nearly enough coffee yet. And truth to tell, she just plain didn't want to dodge it.

He kissed her again. Short. Sweet. Tantalizing.

And left Sam's knees wobbling like a pan of over-cooked pasta.

He pushed away from the counter, smiled at her again, and said, "I'll bring Emma to the site in a couple of hours."

Sam nodded.

At least, she was pretty sure she nodded.

Either that or every bone in her body was liquid and her head had simply fallen forward onto her chest.

When Jeff left the room, she heard him whistling as he walked off down the hallway. Lifting one hand, she rubbed her fingertips against her mouth and then turned to the coffeepot on the counter. She was either going to have to start drinking more of the stuff—or make it a lot stronger.

To deal with Jeff, she was going to need every brain cell she could muster.

"Are you *insane*?"

Sam's spine stiffened and her shoulders went soldier straight. Sure, she'd considered the fact that she might be leaning toward the "challenged" side of life. But it was one thing to accuse yourself of slipping out of your hammock. It was something else again when your family did it for you. "Excuse me?"

"You are," Jo said, answering her own question and nodding her head as if looking for reassurance from a nonexistent crowd. "You are nuts. It's the only explanation."

"I'm not nuts and it's no big deal."

"Said the fly, while watching the spider creep a little closer." Mike shook her head, clearly disgusted, then reached out and grabbed the pipe wrench off the floor beside her.

"Thanks. Always good to get the family's opinion."

"What opinion?" Papa stepped into the room and looked from one to the other of his daughters. "You want family opinion?"

Sam cringed. She already had a very good idea what Papa's opinion would be.

"Sam's letting Jeff move into her house."

"He's not moving in. He's just staying there for a while."

"He's moving in, girl," Mike warned, "in more ways than one."

She sent Mike a glare that should have curled her

hair. Mike just ducked under the kitchen sink and ignored her.

Papa frowned and as his face froze over, even his beard seemed to scowl. "Samantha, we need to talk. You girls go for a walk."

"Papa," Mike complained, already crawling back out, "I've almost got this piping finished and—"

"Finish later."

Jo and Mike wandered out slowly, as if reluctant to leave what looked like a promising conversation. But Hank Marconi was a patient man and he knew his daughters. They'd no doubt be hanging just by the doorway, hoping to eavesdrop. So when he finally did speak again, he kept his voice a whisper. "Samantha *mio cuore*, are you trying to be hurt again?"

My heart. He'd always called her that.

"No, Papa. I'm not." She sighed, walked across the room, and looked out the window at the yard, to where Emma and Jeff were getting a lesson in how to spin yarn from one of the Gypsies.

"Then what is this about?"

She leaned one shoulder against the wall and didn't tear her gaze from the window. "I'm not really sure anymore," she admitted. "It started out about Emma, but—"

Slowly, he walked across the floor until he was standing beside her. Laying one beefy hand on her shoulder, Hank thought about all the times he'd heard his middle daughter crying in the night. About the shadows he'd seen in her eyes and the brave front she'd plastered over a broken heart.

"Now it's about him, too, eh?" he asked quietly.

She turned, staring up at him with that tender heart

in her eyes, and Hank knew she was in for more pain and he wasn't sure what he could do about it. "You love him still."

"I didn't mean to," she said, shaking her head and gritting her teeth. "And I shouldn't. It's just stupid and I'm not stupid," she added quickly, "but I just can't seem to help it."

Wishing he could protect her as he had when she was a little girl, Hank did the only thing he could do. He opened his arms and held her close when she leaned into him. "Sam, you don't get to choose who you love," he said, staring over her head at the world beyond the glass panes—and the man his daughter loved. "It would be easier if we could. But maybe . . . not so exciting."

"I don't feel excited," she muttered against his chest and her voice was muffled and thick with tears she was too stubborn to shed.

He patted her back and rested his cheek against her head. "You feel worried."

"Yes."

"A little scared, too."

"Oh yeah."

"This is good."

"Good? How is this good, Papa?"

She pulled back and looked up at him. Hank cupped her cheeks with his palms. "It means you're careful. This is good, too. You're a grown woman, Sam. You have to make your own decisions. Go your own way."

She blew out a breath that ruffled his beard and made him smile.

"I wish I knew which way that was."

"You'll figure it out," he said. "And if Jeff is the one

for you . . ." He inhaled sharply and told himself he'd have to find a way to let go of old resentments. "Then we'll welcome him."

"You would?"

Hank shrugged. "He's Emma's papa, and as much as it kills me to admit it, he's a good one."

"He is, isn't he?" she asked, turning back to look at Jeff again.

"But he makes you cry again and I'm not going to be happy." His warning was a growl and made *her* smile, as he'd hoped it would. Hank worried. He would always worry about his girls. And at times like this, he really wished their mother were still here, to help him out. To find the right words. But since she wasn't, he had to trust his daughters to know what was in their hearts. Even if he thought they were wrong.

"Thank you, Papa."

He nodded, scrubbed one hand across his beard, then hmmphed and said, "Now go get Mike and tell her to finish the sink. Grace wants to talk about adding a whirlpool tub in the master bathroom."

Sam laughed shortly. "Well, that'll make Mike's day."

Hank watched her go and then shifted his gaze to the man who still owned Sam's heart. Maybe he'd just have a talk with Jeff.

The Fourth of July in Chandler was an event no one wanted to miss. Red, white, and blue bunting and streamers fluttered across every storefront, and American flags decorating every lamppost flapped in the breeze. Summer sizzled, but no one seemed to mind. There were Sno-Kone stands and kids selling lemonade from card table counters.

Jeff hadn't enjoyed anything so much in years.

Growing up, he had spent the Fourth at charity functions where even the children wore suits and ties and frilly dresses that precluded anything remotely resembling fun. Once it was dark enough, a few fireworks were tastefully displayed as a symphony played accompaniment.

Here, tinny circus music blared out of what looked like ancient speakers and kids waited for dusk so they could hold their own sparklers. Here, families gathered and argued and laughed and ate. A tawdry carnival squatted at the edge of town, beckoning the unwary to try their hands at the game booths or to climb aboard rides that looked as if they might fall down in a stiff wind. And it was all . . . great.

"Having fun?"

"Yeah," he said, glancing a little uneasily at Mike as she dropped onto the blanket beside him. "You?"

Her gaze swept the crowd, landed on Sam and Emma, preparing for a three-legged race. "I would be. If I knew what you were up to."

Jeff drew one knee up and rested his forearm atop it. He watched Sam too in her green tank top and denim shorts that displayed long, tanned limbs. "I'm not 'up to' anything, Mike."

"Thought you were here to get a divorce."

"So did I." When had that changed? *Had* it changed? It couldn't change. He was still engaged. Guilt gnawed at him, like a diet-conscious female eating a muffin one crumb at a time.

"And now?"

He shifted his gaze to look at her. "Now, I'm not sure of anything."

She looked at him, considering. Her long blond hair hung, as usual, in a thick braid down the middle of her back. When she tilted her head to look at him more closely, it fell over her shoulder. "You know, there may be hope for you."

He laughed shortly. "Thanks."

"If Papa doesn't kill you."

Jeff winced, remembering the little warning Hank had already delivered that morning. Hank was thirty years older and several inches shorter than Jeff, but that hadn't diminished the clear threat.

Hank stared up at Jeff and poked him in the chest with one thick index finger. "Make no mistake. Samantha cries one more tear over you and I will make your life a living hell."

"I don't want to hurt her, Hank."

"You love her?"

That had caught Jeff off balance. He hadn't even let himself think about love. All he'd been able to concentrate on was the amazing connection he and Sam still had together. His hesitation was all Hank had needed to bring the threat home.

"It's time you decide. Make up your mind what it is you want. Who it is you want."

"I'll keep that in mind," Jeff said tightly, shifting his gaze back to where Sam and Emma were laughing and hobbling across an open meadow. The sun was low enough in the sky that splashes of red and gold were already creeping across the horizon. And a slice of that late, dying sun fell across Sam, illuminating her, and Jeff felt a hard, solid jolt that rocked him right down to his bones.

Love?

Beside him, Mike snorted as she watched him. Then pushing herself to her feet, she looked down at him and shook her head. "Weasel-dog," she said thoughtfully, "you think too much."

Jeff didn't even notice when she wandered away.

Cynthia was furious.

Jeff should have been in the city with her. They had tickets to the symphony. Reservations at Jardinière, tickets to a show. And their wedding was in three short weeks.

She paced back and forth across her living room, counting the clicks of her heels as she stepped smartly on polished hardwood floors. Her mind raced even as her temper boiled. She'd never been so humiliated in her life.

That he would rather spend a national holiday in a poky little town with a grubby child and his homespun almost ex-wife instead of *her* just boggled the mind.

"And leaving me a *message* telling me he won't be back in town until Wednesday?" A message. He hadn't even had the decency to keep calling until he'd reached her personally. Oh no, he'd had his little office twit call and deliver his regrets that he couldn't be in the city for the Fourth.

"Regrets, my ass," she muttered and spun back around to pace off the twenty-seven steps to the white brick hearth. "This is *her* fault. Sam. What kind of name is that for a woman?"

When she reached the hearth, she grabbed hold of the cold brick mantel and stared at her own reflection in the gilt-framed mirror. She saw a beautiful woman with taste and elegance. She saw a woman who deserved the very best life had to offer. She saw a woman who *deserved* to be a Hendricks.

Thoughtfully, she took a deep breath, tried to count to ten, and gave it up at five. Scowling furiously, she hissed in a breath and muttered, "You've put in the time. You've played nice with the child. And dammit, you're not going to lose him *now.*"

She'd been *too* nice, that was the problem. Trying to be understanding and cooperative and compassionate. Definitely time to try another tack.

Cynthia snarled, slapped the mantel, and chipped a nail. In her frustration, she grabbed up the first thing she could reach—a Waterford candlestick—and hurled it into the cold fireplace. The satisfying crash and tinkle of fine crystal helped.

But not enough.

"None of this would be happening if not for the girl," she said. "You'd think she were the only child ever concei—"

A slow smile curved her mouth and she winked at her reflection.

She'd found the right button.

"Ferris wheel!" Emma crowed and jumped into the air, swinging her legs out ahead of her, clinging to her parents' hands, trusting them to hold on tight.

"You're way too big for this, kiddo," Jeff teased, even as he winked at Sam and gave the girl another swing.

"I'm still little, Daddy, swing!"

"How is she not tired?" Sam asked, amazed that her daughter seemed like the Energizer Bunny. Emma had been on full speed all day. She'd inhaled cotton candy, popcorn, Papa's special sausage sandwiches, Slurpees, Sno-Kones, and God knew what else. The kid had a cast-iron stomach and apparently boundless stores of energy.

"Ferris wheel, Mommy!"

Just hearing that word made Sam want to give the little girl anything in her power to deliver. Besides, she was having as much fun as Emma. Sam had always loved the celebration on the Fourth. But this year was special. Everything looked a little nicer, a little shinier. Even the tacky little carnival that showed up in Chandler every year had a special magic to it that she'd never noticed before.

She was hot and tired and had never felt better.

"You're loving this, aren't you?"

Sam turned and shot Jeff a quick look. "What's not to love?"

He stared at her for a long minute. "Good point."

How did he do that? How did he start a fire inside her with a look? And how could she avoid falling for the same man who'd broken her heart nine years before? Answer: She couldn't. She'd already admitted as much to Papa, so there was no point in lying to herself.

She still loved Jeff Hendricks.

Despite the fact that he was engaged to someone else.

Her grin faded as he continued to watch her and she felt the flames within licking at the core of her. To avoid thinking about it and certainly to avoid fanning those flames any hotter, Sam gave Emma's hand a squeeze and looked down at the little girl skipping between them. "Ferris wheel, you said?"

"Yes!"

"My favorite," Sam said and glanced at Jeff. "What do you think?"

"You lead, I'll follow."

Oh boy.

The sun slipped into the ocean and slashes of crimson and violet streaked across the sky in a wild abstract of color. A handful of stars blinked into existence and the lights on the Ferris wheel glistened brightly in the growing darkness.

They slipped into a bucket-like seat, with Emma between them, and the ride operator dropped the steel bar into place. Instantly, their car swung gently and as the giant wheel turned, the crowd fell far below them and the music floating toward them sounded hushed.

Emma laughed and squealed and as they picked up speed and the wheel moved faster and faster, the wind rushed past them, laughter faded in and out, and the world fell away.

And when she looked into Jeff's eyes, Sam felt the magic of the night rise up to surround them.

Chapter Sixteen

"I'll get a room at the inn for tonight if you'll be more comfortable."

Sam paused on the front porch and looked back at him. The glow of the porch light fell in a golden circle that extended just far enough to encompass Jeff, standing on the top step. His hair looked like black silk, the gold light danced in his eyes, and she felt a hard jolt of something hot and dangerous deep inside her.

Oh, she should take him up on that, she told herself sternly. It would be the smart thing to do. The *safe* thing to do.

With Emma spending the night with Papa, Sam and Jeff would be *way* too alone in the house.

But if she admitted that she was worried, wasn't that just making things worse? And why, she suddenly wondered, had Papa agreed when Emma'd asked to spend the night?

Wasn't *he* worried about leaving Sam and Jeff alone?

Apparently not.

So, if her father wasn't concerned, why should she be?

An excellent point.

"You don't have to do that," she said and hoped her

voice sounded stronger than she felt at the moment. "I'm very comfortable. Cozy, even." She blew out a breath. "We're two rational, mature adults, Jeff. I promise to restrain myself, so your virtue is safe."

He chuckled and the slow, deep roll of it rippled inside her like the slide of waves trickling onto shore at low tide.

Oh yeah. Mature. They'd be fine.

Sam tried to shove the key into the front door lock, missed and tried again.

"Want me to get that?"

"I can open my own door." Or could, if her hands weren't shaking, for God's sake. She finally got the key in and turned it. Then, pulling the key back out, she opened the door, tossed the key ring onto the closest table, and turned to face him as he came in behind her. *Smile. Make nice. No big deal.*

But there was something. She felt it. Had felt it all day. Maybe it was having Jeff there, with her family, almost as if he belonged with them. As if he were a part of them. Maybe it was that last ride on the Ferris wheel, feeling the world sliding past at a speed that had left her blinded to everything but him.

Oh boy.

"Want some coffee?" she blurted, grasping for straws.

"Yeah," he said, "why not?" He closed and locked the door behind him, then turned to her again. His eyes darkened and she wondered what he was thinking. No, forget that. She had a pretty good idea what he was thinking. What she'd like to know was what he was *feeling*.

But that had always been a mystery, even back when she'd had the right to wonder.

"Okay, good." She turned quickly and walked to the kitchen, kicking off her sandals as she went. They skittered across the wood floor and slammed up against the couch, but Sam hardly noticed. She just wanted to be doing something. Keeping her hands busy.

Besides. Coffee? Always good.

She bustled around the kitchen, getting the filter and grounds, and filling the pot with water. As she put it all together, she kept up a running stream of conversation.

"Fireworks were good tonight."

"Beautiful."

"And no one got sick this year, either."

"Sick?"

Sam shrugged, flipped the on button on the coffeepot, and stared at the little red light as if waiting for it to turn to green. "Um, Rachel Vickers usually brings some weird offering to the ptomaine gods, but this year she's so busy trying to get her husband reelected mayor, she didn't have time."

"Good for us."

"Boy howdy," Sam said. "You haven't lived until you've tasted her tuna and pineapple casserole."

"God."

"Come to think of it, not many live *after* they taste it."

"Suicide?"

Sam laughed, almost forgetting just how nervous she was. Why was she nervous? This was Jeff. The man she'd lost her virginity to. The man she'd once married and promised to love forever.

Oh yeah. *That's* why she was nervous.

"Of course, Carla's husband's running against the mayor this year and—"

"Carla Candellano's married?"

She shot him a quick look. Of course he knew Carla. He'd met all of Sam's friends nine years ago. He did have a connection to Chandler, albeit a shaky one. "Last year. Jackson Wyatt's her husband. Remember? My attorney?"

"Oh yeah."

Well, that's a good way to keep things light. Way to go.

"All of the Candellanos are campaigning for him. Saw the new flyer tonight." Flyers? Talking about flyers now? Pitiful. But she kept right on gabbing, because to an Italian, talking came as easy as breathing. Maybe easier. And when nerves were pushing the words out, they came in a torrent. "Mama's picture's on 'em and they say, 'Mama says, vote for Jackson.' They're really good. I think Paul did them up. He's amazing on a computer and—"

"You're babbling."

Had he moved closer?

She was just a little too wary to turn around and check.

"Where do you suppose the word 'babbling' comes from?" And who cares?

"I don't know."

"Yeah, me neither." God, this was fantastic conversation. Seriously. She should consider giving lessons in how to have a meaningless conversation. "So," Sam said, when the silence began to scream at her, "Emma seemed to have a great time today."

"Still is," he said from *way* too close behind her. "Your father said something about taking her back to Grace's house for dessert."

"Dessert?" Sam shook her head and listened to the hiss and whir of the coffeepot as if concentrating on a great piece of music. Come on, come on, she chanted silently. "The child did nothing but eat all day."

"She's having fun."

Sam nodded and shot him a quick glance. He *had* moved closer. Now she could smell him. Pure male. The tangy scent of his cologne. And the faint odor of cotton candy still clinging to him. God, was she drooling?

"Uh, yeah." Emma, she thought. They were talking about Emma. "She did have fun. That's the most important thing."

"I had fun, too."

"Did you?" Sam didn't look at him again. She could practically feel his breath on the back of her neck as it was. If she turned, they'd be nose to nose and then mouth to mouth and then . . . "I love the Fourth. Always a good time here."

"I had fun with you, Sam," he said and her hands stilled on the counter.

She drew in a long, deep breath and knew it wasn't going to do her any good since she couldn't seem to force it past the knot in her throat. Need coiled low in the pit of her stomach and sent long, snaking tentacles out to every corner of her body. She trembled with the force of the heat rising inside her. It was like the wildfires that burned through California nearly every summer, feeding on dried-out twigs and grasses. Combustible. Quick catching, long burning, and out of control in a heartbeat.

She swallowed hard and tried to get a grip. Tried to remind herself that there was no future here.

Only a past.

And at the moment . . . a present.

Nice goin', Sam. Oh, she couldn't just stand here

and wait all night for coffee. She pulled out the pot and shoved a cup under the stream of hot liquid, and managed to splash some over the back of her hand. "Ow!"

Instantly, Jeff was there. He shoved the pot back under the coffee, took the cup from her, and dragged her to the kitchen sink.

"I'm okay," she said, squirming in his grasp.

"You burned your hand."

"In no danger of dying." Although, she thought, there was a different kind of danger entirely swirling through the room.

Turning the cold tap on, Jeff ignored her attempts to get away, held her hand under the icy flow of water, and rubbed the red spot on the back of her hand with his fingertips.

"That's good," she said, her voice papery rough as ripples of awareness swam through her bloodstream. Had his touch always been so electric? So all-encompassing? "I'm fine, really."

"Uh-huh." He kept rubbing, as if she hadn't spoken, and the longer he kept it up, the more Sam figured she'd be unable to speak again.

She closed her eyes. Oh, big mistake. Now *all* she could concentrate on was the feel of his hands on hers. He snaked his fingers along her hand, her wrist, sliding up the length of her arm, and Sam had to lock her knees to keep from oozing down onto the floor.

"Jeff," she said as his fingers slid higher and higher, stroking, rubbing, caressing. The back of his hand brushed the side of her breast and her toes curled. "Jeff, do you really think—"

"Not thinking," he said and turned her toward him,

grabbing her close, pulling her tightly to him. "Feeling."

Her eyes popped open.

She met his gaze and read the same hunger and passion she knew were shining in her own.

He pressed her body along his, sliding his hands up and down her spine, to the curve of her behind and back up again. Her gaze locked with his and she watched his eyes as he touched, explored, discovered her anew.

Sam swallowed hard. Okay, this was way beyond dangerous. Creeping steadily toward hazardous. *Stop it*, she ordered. But she didn't hear anything, so she was pretty sure she didn't say it out loud. Because if she'd said it out loud, he would have stopped, and oh God, she didn't want him to stop.

His eyes glittered darkly. The muscle in his jaw twitched. His fingers dug into her back and held her to him until she felt his body, hard and tight against hers.

Fragments of memories stirred within her and the jagged pieces of the puzzle slowly came together to form an all-too-clear picture of other nights spent in Jeff's arms. God, she remembered it all. Everything. Good and bad. And she remembered just how passion could burst into furious bloom between them, goaded by something as simple—as all consuming—as a look.

"For days, Sam." He whispered brokenly as he touched her. "Days, I've wanted to do this. To touch you. To hold you." His hands swept up, his fingers speared through her hair, cupping the back of her head in his palms. "I need you, Sam. God, I need you."

She was lost.

As she'd known she would be.

His mouth took hers, claiming it in a frantic dance of desire, need. She felt his urgency and shared it. Her heartbeat pounded, thundering in her ears, and as she closed her eyes and gave herself up to the wonder of being in his arms again, Sam shut her brain down.

She didn't want to think, either.

Didn't want to second-guess this moment—the moment they'd been building toward since the day she'd opened her front door to find him stepping into her world again.

His tongue swept past her lips, tangling with hers in a breathless mating. Here was the fire. The magic she remembered. Her blood boiled and every nerve in her body stood straight up and begged for more. She held on, her fingers clawing at his shoulders, pulling him closer, closer.

It had been so long.

So very long.

She should stop him.

No, don't stop.

She groaned, a low moan of sound that shot from her soul, directly into his.

Jeff couldn't taste her enough. He needed to have the scent of her filling his mind, his heart, his soul. It seemed as though he'd been asleep, comatose, the last nine years of his life and now suddenly his blood was pumping, his heart racing. He caught her tight against him, desperate for her. His hands dropped to the hem of her shirt and slipped beneath, feeling that smooth, soft expanse of suntanned flesh beneath his fingertips, and he ached like a dying man.

Yes. Sam sucked in air through gritted teeth as Jeff dragged his hands up her bare skin. Her flesh sizzled and burned as though he were trailing lit matches along her nerve endings.

Her whole body felt *alive* as it hadn't since the last time he'd touched her. And she wanted to scream with the glory of having his hands on her again. Everything was moving so fast, so hurried, so frenzied. They fed off each other's hunger and lost themselves in the need to take and be taken.

Sam yanked at his shirt, pulling it free of his jeans. As it came up and over his head, she scraped her short nails across his broad chest, loving the hiss of his indrawn breath at her touch. He moved again, backing her up against the counter, shoving things out of the way as he made room.

"Sam, gotta have you. Need you. Need you now."

"Now," she demanded and wiggled as he pulled her shorts down her legs and then off. Cool night air kissed her skin and she shivered. "Now," she said again, kissing him, nibbling at his neck, his jaw, losing herself in the taste of him, in the soft sigh of his breath.

Her fingers fumbled with his belt buckle and zipper until he snatched her hands away and took care of it himself. *Good. Good. Now.*

Then she hopped when he grabbed her around the waist and plopped her onto the cold granite countertop. "Whoa! Cold."

"Not for long," he promised and moved closer. Holding her head with one hand, he took her mouth again as he moved between her legs and slid himself home.

Sam arched into him, holding his head to hers as she lifted her legs and locked them around his waist, pulling him tighter, deeper. So familiar, yet so new. He touched her core and she splintered. He sighed her name and she melted. He touched her breasts and she went up in flames.

His body rocked into hers, driving into her warmth, her depths, until she felt as though they were merging, becoming one. She took a breath, held it and scooted forward on the counter, trying to get closer, to take more of him inside.

Her body trembled as the first wave crested within her, so fast, so amazing, and then before she could mourn the loss of it, the wave rose again. She felt it grow, swell, carrying her higher and higher until she felt as though she could reach out and grab a star.

Then the skyrockets went off behind her eyes and she clamped her mouth shut, terrified she might just shout out her love for him in that one blinding moment. Her body was still trembling when he groaned and lost himself in her warmth.

Seconds, minutes, hell. Maybe *hours* passed as they stood there in the brightly lit kitchen, bodies still locked together. Her arms were draped over his shoulders, hands hanging limply against his back. She smiled against his skin and felt . . . okay, *great.*

He moved slightly and she hissed in a breath as warm, sparkler-like tingles dazzled her insides. She wanted to enjoy it. Wanted to luxuriate in the sensations coursing through her. But she couldn't. Already, that annoyingly sensible, logical little voice in the back of her mind was making itself heard.

Dammit.

She shivered, as the cool night air brushed her bare skin and quenched the last of the fires roaring through her. This wasn't supposed to happen, she thought sadly. Love him or not, he didn't belong to her anymore. He wasn't in her life, her world. He didn't *want* to be in her heart anymore.

So she forced a smile she didn't feel, dropped her head to his shoulder, sighed, and whispered, "Okay, I think we could use the term 'swept away' for this."

"Yeah, I guess we could." Jeff stroked one hand down the length of her spine and Sam shivered again, but not from the cold.

"We used to do that a lot, as I remember," Sam said, mentally drawing away even as she enjoyed the feel of his body, still locked with hers. "Get swept away, I mean."

He pulled his head back to look at her. An incredible sadness filled his eyes and his mouth curved into a hint of a smile. "I remember a lot of nights on the living room floor."

Oh, so did she. The nights when the need had been so big, so huge, the bed was too far away to worry about. She cupped his face in her palm and drew the pad of her thumb across his cheek. He sighed and caught her hand, planting a quick kiss on the palm.

Then slowly, reluctantly, he disentangled himself from her and took one cautious step back.

Distance. A little late, but still, no doubt, a good thing. She jumped off the counter and tried really hard not to think about having just had sex on her kitchen counter. But it was stamped in her memory forever now and she'd never be able to come into this room again without remembering. "Oh boy."

"That about covers it."

"I don't believe we just did that."

He scraped one hand across his jaw. "I can't believe I tossed you onto a counter."

"Yeah," she said, choking up a laugh. "I don't know whether to have it bronzed or disinfected."

A short, sharp laugh shot from his throat as he bent to snatch his clothes up off the floor. "Either way—I don't have an excuse for it."

"Who's asking for one?" Sam felt the first bubble of temper start to brew and tried to fight it. She didn't want him making excuses or, God help her, *apologizing* for what they'd just shared.

"You should be," he snapped as the last of their little "glow" disappeared. "Jesus, Sam!" He waved one hand at the room, at their clothes scattered across the floor, and shook his head. "I didn't even give you a choice."

Yep, there was the temper. Riding right along on the coattails of something glorious. Dammit. "Excuse me? Did you hear me beg you to stop?"

"No, but—"

"Then I made my choice, didn't I?" She stooped to pick up her clothes and bunched them in front of her like a shield. A little late, but better late than never. "For God's sake, Jeff. We *both* did this. You didn't take advantage of me."

"I didn't take any precautions, either."

Whoops. She glanced up at him, swinging her hair out of her eyes. He looked so torn between wanting to enjoy what had just happened and beating himself up over the whole thing that she took pity on him. "Don't worry about it. Lucky for you, I'm on the pill."

His breath whooshed out of him in a sigh of relief.

"That's good then. And I'm healthy," he said tightly. "You should know that."

"Ah, sex in the twenty-first century," Sam said, smirking. "Feel the romance." Then she paused, because she knew he was right. And they'd been stupid on a *lot* of levels. "I am too."

He nodded and grabbed up the rest of his clothes, then he just stood there, staring at her as if he weren't really sure what to say next.

Well, Sam knew just how he felt.

She clutched her clothes tightly to her. Sure, don't want him to see you naked or anything. *That* could be embarrassing. Oh God. She ignored the siren scent of coffee lingering in the air and started backing toward the doorway.

She had to say something. Had to at least *try* to make sense of this. Find a way to take them both off the hook for this one moment of craziness. "Look, this doesn't mean anything."

"You're right." Jeff nodded tightly, his mouth a grim slash, his eyes shadowed. "Just a quirk. Something we had to get out of our systems."

Disappointment flashed through her, but she pushed it away. She'd known going into this that he didn't love her. He loved someone else. A woman who was even now planning her wedding to the man standing naked in Sam's kitchen.

Could this get any sadder?

She wouldn't let him know how she felt. There were a *few* humiliations she'd rather pass on. So if he wanted to believe that nothing special had just happened, she'd play along.

"Right. Good." She held up one hand to point at him, realized she'd drawn her tank top off her breasts and slapped it back into place again. "And now that it's out of our systems, we can move on."

"That's good. That's what we'll do."

"Right. I'm just going to *move on*"—she laughed shortly—"to a shower now."

"You go ahead. I'll, uh . . ." He looked around, then shrugged. "I'll wait."

"Thanks." She inhaled sharply, blew it out, and then paused in the doorway. He looked . . . lost. And it was in her nature to try to help him be found. "Jeff, it's okay. I mean, we're okay. We'll be—"

"Fine."

"Right."

Oh God. Sam hustled down the hall and into the bathroom. Dumping her dirty clothes into the white wicker hamper, she leaned into the shower stall and turned on the water. Steam lifted as she pulled the glass door aside and stepped into the bath.

The hot water hit her body like a blessing and she dunked her head into the steady flow of it, hoping to wipe away the memory of what she'd just done. What *they'd* just done.

But she couldn't.

Worse, didn't *want* to.

If that was all she'd ever have of Jeff again, then why shouldn't she remember it? Cherish it?

She grabbed the bath gel, squirted some of the jasmine-scented lotion into her hand and smoothed it over her shoulders, her arms. Her body was humming nicely. She felt liquid, warm, delicious. And oh God, so miserable. She braced her hands on the shower wall and let the hot water pound relentlessly on her back.

She was going to lose him all over again. He was already gone—at least, mentally. He'd pulled so far away, she could barely see him. He was regretting what had happened. Probably feeling guilty as hell. As she should be, if it came down to it.

She'd slept with a man who was engaged to someone else. Okay, he was still married to her, but that didn't make this right. It only added yet one more layer to the craziness that was her life.

God, Jeff was probably packing. Trying to get the hell away from her before he had to face her again. Yes, he'd made the first move, but she'd been a close second, so he couldn't blame himself entirely. But oh God, it hurt to think that he felt guilty for touching her.

The shower door scraped open, and startled, she gasped, and turned, covered in floral-scented suds.

Jeff stood just outside the tub, watching her.

So. Not packing.

His eyes held her.

Her breath clogged in her throat. Her pulse did a wild two-step. Her blood rushed and her stomach flipped and other parts of her went even more warm. *Moving on?*

Not yet.

"Sam . . ."

She shook her head, swinging her wet hair back from her face. Mouth dry, she reached out for him and dragged him into the steamy bath with her. Going up on her toes, she leaned into him, her soapy skin sliding along his.

"Don't talk," she whispered.

His arms came around her and she slanted her mouth over his.

• • •

Morning sun poured through the window and lay across the bed like a spotlight. Outside, birds were singing, and a lawnmower growled in the distance.

Here in her bedroom, though, the silence was deafening.

Sam sat up, holding the sheet to her chest as she pushed her hair back out of her eyes and looked at the man beside her on the bed. Jeff was braced on one elbow, his dark hair tumbling across his forehead, the sheet draped low over his body.

Her mouth watered again.

Inhaling sharply, deeply, she then let the air slide from her lungs in a rush. "So," she said, trying to understand just what exactly had happened between them during the night. "We can call the first time being swept away. Maybe even stretch that to cover the second time."

"Yeah, we could," he said, reaching out to cover one of her hands with his own.

She looked at their joined hands because it was safer than looking into his eyes. Through the long night, she'd allowed herself to build foolish fantasy castles. But now morning was here, and with the sunlight came reality, crashing down on them.

"But by the fifth time, nobody was swept away."

"I know that, too," Jeff said and watched her avoid his gaze. Everything in him told him that what had happened during the night was right. Was what was supposed to be. But his heart was telling him it was wrong. And that he was the worst kind of bastard. He'd made promises to two different women in his life and he'd broken all of them.

He'd stumbled back into Sam's world, smashing and burning her everyday life around her. He had a woman waiting for him in San Francisco and a woman beside him here in a bed that was made for long, lazy mornings.

And both women deserved a hell of a lot better than they were getting from him.

"I don't know how to say this," she said softly, and pulled her hand from under his. "But I never planned to be the 'other woman.' And I don't like it."

Jeff sat up, reached out and brushed her hair back from her face. Letting his fingertips trail along her jaw, he smiled sadly and met her gaze. "I don't blame you. I never planned on being an asshole, either. And can't say I like it much."

He got off the bed and grabbed up his clothes. Stalking across the room, he stopped in the doorway and looked back at her. She hadn't moved. Sunlight played on her hair, her face, and he etched this picture of her into his mind. Because no matter what happened next, he would always have last night—and this morning.

"You're leaving."

"Yes, I am."

"Just like that." She clutched the pale lemon-yellow sheet to her chest and stared at him, clearly stunned.

He'd liked to have talked to her about the thoughts racing through his brain, but what the hell could he say? "I have to go to the city. Take care of a few things."

She flopped backward, landing on the stacked pile of pillows behind her. She looked rumpled and tempting and it took everything he had in him to keep from rushing back to that bed and grabbing her.

But that's exactly what had gotten them to this point, wasn't it? "Tell Emma I'll call her tonight."

Then he left.

While he still could.

Chapter Seventeen

Jo spotted her first. A gorgeous blonde in a designer suit, wearing three-inch pink high heels for God's sake, was hard to miss on a job site. Her stomach took a nosedive as she realized who Barbie in Pink had to be. "Psst! Mike!"

She kept her voice down, despite the clamor of electric tools rising from the yard below and waited until her younger sister turned to snarl at her.

"If you want help on this stinking roof, then let me lay the stupid paper so I can get back to my damn sinks."

Jo ignored the temper. Just part of Mike's charm. "Look," she said, pointing with the business end of her hammer.

"What?" Mike shot a glance at the yard, then whistled low and long. "Uh-oh."

"It's her, isn't it?"

"Oh yeah. Has to be. Weasel-dog's new babe." She shifted a look in the direction the blonde was walking. "And headed right for Sam."

"Think we should go down there?"

Mike's instinct was to do just that. But she didn't move. "No. This is Sam's shit. Besides, when has a Marconi needed help to do battle?"

"True," Jo said, watching as the cool blonde picked her way daintily across the yard. "But I don't think Sam's got the kind of weapons that chick uses."

Sam looked up as Cynthia approached and instantly felt heat rush up her neck to flood her face with color she hoped would pass as sunburn. Dear Lord. She *was* the other woman. And now she had to look Cynthia dead in the eye and pretend she *hadn't* had sex with Jeff the night before. Sure. No problem.

"Hello again." Cynthia smiled and held out a beautifully manicured hand.

Wincing slightly, Sam wiped her own paint-stained palm on her jeans, then took Cynthia's in a firm, fast shake. "Hi." She paused, then glanced at Grace, standing patiently in the shade. "Sorry. Grace Van Horn, Cynthia Fairwood. Cynthia, Grace."

"So nice to meet you." Cynthia smiled and her perfect, pearly-white teeth were displayed to, well . . . *perfection*.

"Hello. I've so enjoyed getting to know Jeff and Emma. She's a lovely child." Grace shifted a look from one woman to the other.

"Isn't she, though?" Cynthia agreed. "I can't tell you what she means to me. Well to *us,* Jeff and me."

Sam winced.

"Of course," Grace said smoothly, then turning to Sam, she said, "Why don't I go and keep Emma busy with her grandpa while you and Cynthia visit?"

Just what Sam wanted to do, she thought. Go have a nice long visit with her husband's fiancée. Good times.

"I can't imagine how you do this kind of work,"

Cynthia said with a quiet chuckle. "I would just be hopeless at it." She smiled. "I don't think I've ever even *held* a hammer."

Well, Sam thought, didn't she feel dainty.

Cynthia squeaked as one of the goats strolled up to touch the back of her knee with a whiskered snout.

"Sorry, sorry." Sam grabbed one of the goat's twisted horns and gave it a pull. "They won't hurt you."

Cynthia laughed shortly, uneasily, and kept a wary eye on the hairy beast still trying to snuffle at her hem. "If you say so," she said, clearly unconvinced. "But if you don't mind, could we take a walk away from it? I'd really like to talk to you. Woman to woman."

That couldn't be good. But Sam figured she owed it to the woman since she had spent most of the night before bouncing on her fiancé. Oh God.

"Sure, just head back the way you came, I'll catch up." She gave the goat a deliberate push in the opposite direction, then quickly followed in Cynthia's mincing footsteps.

"How do you stand the noise?" Cynthia asked with a careful shake of her head.

"You get used to it," Sam said, keeping her steps small, since Cynthia was tottering across the rocky ground on sky-high heels.

A few minutes later, they were out on the wide front lawn where the wind danced through the trees and ruffled Cynthia's perfectly cut hair before dropping it back into place.

Sam felt like the ugly stepsister in Cinderella's fairy tale. Cynthia's soft pink linen suit was spotless, and her matching bag and shoes screamed money and good taste. Alongside the blonde, Sam looked like a "before" picture in a magazine article about extreme makeovers. Torn jeans, paint-spattered T-shirt, and a ratty ponytail tucked through a baseball cap with a battered bill. All she really needed was a bright red letter *A* sewn to her chest and the picture would be complete.

Guilt, fresh and new, pumped through her and forced her to smile when she wanted to scream. "If you're looking for Jeff, he went back to the city this morning." *Right after he climbed out of my bed.*

"I know. He called me." Cynthia walked a little farther so that she could stand beneath one of the tall shade trees marching in formation around the perimeter of Grace's lawn. "That's why I'm here."

Uh-oh.

"I thought the two of us should have a chat—with Jeff out of the way."

Great. "Okay."

Cynthia smiled again and Sam couldn't help thinking that she'd be great in a toothpaste commercial.

"This is difficult for all of us," the blonde began. "Knowing what to do, how to act."

"Yeah, you're right," Sam said. She hadn't known last night, either. Not until Jeff had touched her, then she'd been certain of what to do. Although this morning, things were a little fuzzy again.

"I know what you're feeling."

Sam's gaze snapped up to hers. "You do?"

"Of course." Cynthia reached out and laid one hand on Sam's arm briefly. When she pulled her hand back, she rubbed her fingers, just in case she'd picked up some stray dirt. "This situation is difficult, at best. I understand how you feel about Emma. I love her, too. But

I think as adults, we have to decide what's in her best interests."

Irritation bristled inside Sam, but she fought it down. Temper wouldn't do any good, and besides, Cynthia was right. They *should* be thinking about Emma. Still, it stung to have someone else—*anyone* else—tell her what was best for *her* daughter. "I agree. And I think Jeff does, too."

"Of course he does. He's a wonderful father." Cynthia's teeth worried her bottom lip gently as if she were weighing her next words. "Samantha," she said finally, "I think, as women, we need to be honest with each other."

"Okay . . ." Guilt again. Sharp. Hot. Uncomfortable. It exploded inside Sam and made her shoulder blades twitch.

"Jeff and I are building a structured, safe environment for Emma. Until a couple of weeks ago, she was happy. Secure." Cynthia smiled again, softly, kindly. "She needs stability in her life, Samantha. And I believe I was giving her that. Until . . ."

Sam swallowed hard. "Until *me*."

"Frankly? Yes." Tucking her pink clutch bag beneath her left arm, Cynthia folded her hands at her waist. "Your . . . *reluctance* to let go of the past is making all of this more difficult than it has to be."

Was it? She turned and looked back over her shoulder to where she knew Emma was, playing with her aunts and her grandfather and the goats. Was Sam really making all of this worse? Harder on Emma?

"I'm sure you have some residual feelings for Jeff. He's a wonderful man, why wouldn't you?"

Residual. That put her neatly in her place, didn't it?

"Jeff's heritage, his business, his *world*, is in San Francisco. Yours is . . ." She waved a hand and looked worriedly at another goat as it wandered across the lawn. *"Here."*

True again. What had she been thinking? That Jeff would resign from his job, his career, and move to Chandler? Or could she really see herself giving up her life and becoming a corporate wife in San Francisco? God, no.

Sam breathed deeply and blew out the air on a sigh. Everything Cynthia said was absolutely true. Oh, she knew Emma was happy now. But she'd been happy before, too. And there was no doubt at all that Sam had thrown a monkey wrench into her daughter's life, messing things up until no one knew which side was up anymore.

She didn't want Emma to be unhappy. Torn between her father and mother. Hell, she didn't want *Jeff* to be unhappy either, if it came down to it.

But what about last night? What was that all about if he was thinking of her as an awkward intrusion from his past? Had last night been a courtesy fling? A fond farewell? A sort of "bon voyage" present to Sam?

Temper spurted to life inside her and began throttling all of the doubts and insecurities. Had Jeff just been looking for a way to get Sam out of his system? Or had it been more devious than that? Was he trying to soften her up so she'd sign the damn papers and get soft on the custody thing? Had he really hopped from Cynthia's bed to hers and then back again?

Was he really the weasel-dog Mike had always called him?

Dammit.

Thoughts, fears, suspicions, crashed noisily inside her mind, caroming off each other like scattered billiard balls on a pool table. Then Cynthia started talking again and Sam told herself to pay attention.

"Don't you see? You're a part of his past, Samantha, not his future." The woman's voice was a velvet-covered fist pounding at the foundations of everything she'd been feeling lately. "I know this is hard. Jeff and I have talked at great length about the *awkwardness* of the situation."

"Awkward?" He hadn't seemed awkward last night, she reminded herself, even as Cynthia's words chipped away at what was left of those fantasy castles she'd indulged in so briefly. Had she really been kidding herself? Had she really allowed herself to fall for him . . . *again*?

The blonde put one delicate hand to her abdomen and inhaled sharply.

"Are you okay?" Sam stepped forward instinctively, not sure if the other woman needed help or—

"Fine, thank you." Then taking another deep breath, Cynthia confided, "The morning sickness hasn't passed completely, that's all. I'm sure you remember how awful it was and—"

Morning sickness?

Sam's brain reeled and her heart took a direct hit. *Oh God.* Cynthia was *pregnant*?

She swayed on her feet, feeling the world tip and shake around her. Her stomach twisted and turned and she had to swallow hard to bite back the nausea roiling within. Cynthia was *pregnant*?

"You didn't know."

"No." Didn't know. Never considered it. Didn't know what to do about it. Pain splintered through Sam's body until it felt as though hundreds of thousands of tiny needles were jabbing at her and she wondered how she was able to stand under the assault.

"This is terrible," Cynthia muttered and looked around frantically, as if to reassure herself that no one was close enough to overhear. "I'm *so* sorry. I really am. I never should have—" She paused in her misery and gave Sam a halfhearted smile. "I thought Jeff would have told you by now, but I should have known he wouldn't." Her hand stayed atop her abdomen as if protecting the child within from hearing anything it shouldn't. "We wanted to wait until after the wedding to tell Emma, and—"

Cynthia's voice was a buzzing in Sam's ears. She knew the woman was talking, but she couldn't quite make out all the words over the hammering of her own heart. Pregnant. Jeff and Cynthia were going to have a child. Together.

She swayed again, then locked her knees to keep herself upright. Oh God. Images of the night before flashed in her brain and she resolutely wiped them out only to see them rise up vividly, over and over.

"I didn't mean to upset you with all of this, you must believe me." Cynthia took a hesitant step forward and looked deeply into Sam's eyes. "I know how hard this situation must be for you, really I do."

"I don't think you can," Sam said, and wondered if her voice sounded as distant to Cynthia as it did to her.

The blonde nodded slowly. "Maybe not," she admitted. "But as one mother to another," she confided, "I felt as though I had to tell you what Jeff's been too much of a gentleman to say." She paused, then continued. "He wants to put all of this behind him so the three of us—" she paused to smile again, "four now— can go on with our lives."

"Of course." How could there be more pain? she thought. How could it keep coming? Keep piling up inside her head, her heart?

"He feels very bad about his mother's machinations—and he doesn't want to hurt you again. But Sam." She paused and gently finished, "He's moved on. And he wants that for his daughter—his *children*— as well."

Children. Sam's stomach spun wildly. All she could think was that Jeff really had been bouncing between her bed and Cynthia's. How could he? How could he have made love to her, made her remember all the warmth and passion they'd once known—when all the time he *knew* Cynthia was pregnant with his child?

What had he been thinking?

What had he been planning?

Was he now going to walk away from Cynthia and *this* child as he had from Sam and Emma? Was he expecting to be able to keep Sam on the side for fun and games while he lived his life with Polly Perfection? Was he just using Sam before moving on?

Rage bubbled inside Sam, swamping the misery and nearly choking her.

Cynthia checked the slim gold watch on her left wrist and clucked her tongue. "I really have to be going. I'm meeting Jeff in the city for a late lunch." Conspiratorially, she leaned in close and added, "I'm hoping my tummy will have settled by then, since I'm absolutely *ravenous.* Eating for two does have its advantages, doesn't it? We get to eat just anything we like."

"Yeah." Sam choked the word out. "Sure."

The blonde shook her hair back from her face and smiled. "After lunch of course, we've got more meetings with the wedding planner and—then I'm going to have to see the dressmaker and get her to let the waist out just a tiny bit. Honestly, if the wedding wasn't coming so quickly now, I don't think I'd be able to keep my little 'surprise' from anyone—" She caught herself mid-sentence. "I'm sure you don't care about the last-minute details of our wedding."

"No," Sam said tightly, silently congratulating herself on her restraint. "I really don't."

Cynthia smiled again and Sam wanted to belt her one. But she didn't. Not only because she couldn't very well hit a *pregnant* woman, but because in reality, it wasn't the blonde screwing with her. It was Jeff. *Again.*

"There. I *have* upset you," Cynthia said sadly.

Sam shoved her hands into her jeans pockets and forced a smile she didn't feel. "Not at all. Ripping off a blindfold isn't always pretty. But you can see a lot clearer without one."

"Exactly," Cynthia cooed and risked patting Sam's forearm. "I'm so glad we understand each other."

"Oh, we're crystal clear," Sam said, and knew, without a doubt, that Cynthia had done this purposely. The woman had known Sam didn't have a clue about the baby—and she'd made sure Sam took the full hit. Couldn't really blame her, though, Sam thought. She was fighting for what was hers.

It was Jeff Hendricks Sam was going to ream the first chance she got.

"Good," Cynthia was saying. "I'm delighted that we have this resolved."

"Oh, it's resolved. Trust me. And I hope you and Jeff are very happy together," Sam said, forcing each word out of her mouth as though she were spitting out something foul. "I think you're made for each other."

"Aren't you sweet?" Cynthia's smile was a little hesitant this time, but not one to pass up a victory, she accepted Sam's surrender. "Well then, I'd better be going. Don't want to be late. Jeff worries so."

"I'm sure." She stood in the shade of the old trees and watched as Cynthia slid into her silver Mercedes coupe. She held her breath while the blonde fired up the expensive engine and blew it out as she finally pulled away from the curb and drove off down the narrow, tree-lined road.

So Jeff was worried about Cynthia, was he? Well, why wouldn't he be? She was pregnant. With his *child*, dammit.

A sick emptiness opened up inside Sam. And the only way to fill it was with anger. She let it pour through her, until her nerves danced and her hands shook. Worried about Cynthia? Well, Jeff had better spare some concern for Sam.

Things were about to get *real* bumpy.

"Why don't we just go into the city and break his legs?"

"Tempting, Mike," Sam said, shaking her head. "But no."

"Why the hell not?" Mike stormed around the interior of the second kitchen, instinctively stepping over the scattered debris. "He so deserves it."

"He *deserves* a hell of a lot more," Jo muttered, keeping her gaze fixed on Sam. "You slept with him, didn't you?"

Sam cringed. "Sleeping wasn't a big part of the night's festivities, but yeah."

"God, you're an idiot."

"Thanks, Mike. I love you, too."

"Shut up, Mike." Jo reached out and hugged Sam tightly, briefly, then let her go again. "You still love him, don't you?"

"Yes, but I'm thinking a lobotomy will take care of that." God, Mike was right. She *was* an idiot. Ever since Cynthia left, Sam had been mentally kicking herself. She'd done it again. Let herself be sucked into Jeff's orbit only to get splattered.

Sure, he'd agreed to a tentative custody agreement. He'd *needed* Sam on his side. He had a wedding, for God's sake, in three weeks. Not to mention, she thought with another mental kick, another *child* on the way—a fact she hadn't told her sisters about. After all, there was only so much humiliation she was willing to share.

Jeff had needed Sam to settle things between them. And the only way for him to get her signature on divorce papers had been to convince her that he'd be fair about the custody settlement. So what'd he do? Sign a paper agreeing to be fair—not an actual declaration of what that "fair" was going to be, mind you—and then bed her, so she'd stop thinking and just go with the heady rush of hormones. A little "understanding," a little sex, and *poof,* Sam was putty in his hands.

Oh, he was good.

He was very good.

And she'd been taken for another ride.

"How could I have been so stupid?" She slapped the heel of her hand against her forehead. "My God, if you could have heard Cynthia talking . . . how she and Jeff *discussed* me and just how *awkward* it was dealing with a woman who couldn't let go." *And how pregnant she is and how they want their little family together and settled, without Jeff's "ex" hanging around to muddle everything up.*

Adrenaline pumped through Sam's system until she couldn't stand still. She had to move or explode.

Stomping around the room, she ignored both of her sisters and kept up a steady stream of invective, aimed at the one person who'd let her down the most.

Her own damn self.

"I let myself get carried away." She shook her head, remembering Cynthia's pale, smooth hand pressed to her still flat—but *pregnant*—abdomen. Then she remembered Jeff and his touch, his kiss, his . . . "I let myself forget that we're from two different worlds."

"Don't be so hard on yourself," Mike said, then jumped out of the way as Sam stormed past, shaking her index finger at her.

"Hard? This isn't nearly hard enough. I should be kicked every minute for a solid hour. I should be strapped down in a health food store and force-fed carrot juice. I should be—" She stopped, threw her hands wide. "I can't even think of anything bad enough."

"I don't know," Mike said softly. "The carrot juice was pretty grim."

"Nothing's that grim," Jo said, then walked over to Sam. "Stop kicking yourself and go kick him. If he set you up, then you have to let him know you know."

"Huh?"

Jo smiled. "Go see the little prick. Tell him all about your chat with Cynthia. Tell him that you'll sign his divorce papers because you don't want him anywhere near you anymore. Then tell him you want joint custody or nothing."

"I should."

"Damn straight."

Sam nodded at Mike but Jo was still talking.

"He'll agree, Sam. He has to. He'll know that you're on to him and that the Marconis will make his life unlivable if he screws with you again."

"Good point." Okay, the pulsing, throbbing fury was easing up a little. Sam pulled in a deep breath. She could do this. She could look Jeff dead in the eye and tell him what she thought of his tactics. What she thought of his simpering fiancée and how she hoped he'd be *miserable* for the rest of his life. And she could tell him just what she thought of a man who left a *pregnant* fiancée home alone while he jumped into bed with his *wife*.

The bastard.

"Want us to go with you?" Mike asked.

"No. Thanks, but no." Sam shook her head and lifted her chin defiantly. Some of the things she had to say to Jeff couldn't be said with an audience. Even an audience of sisters who loved her. "This is something I need to do on my own."

"Then get out there and kick some Hendricks ass." Jo held out one hand. Mike laid hers atop Jo's. Sam reached out and laid her hand atop her sisters'.

And for a moment, they stood linked, blood to blood, and Sam knew she'd never really be alone.

Chapter Eighteen

Jeff had it all planned out.

Finally, and at last, he'd worked out what was important in his life and he was going to do whatever he had to do to get it. That one night with Sam had solidified everything inside him. He'd found his place in the world.

Beside Sam.

Guilt still crouched within when he thought about Cynthia. But breaking their engagement was the only decent thing to do. He wasn't looking forward to hurting Cynthia, but eventually she'd understand that this was the only solution. He couldn't marry someone else when he was still in love with his *wife*. He smiled to himself and thought about trying to hunt down the lazy county clerk who'd never bothered to file the divorce papers. Damned if he didn't want to buy the man a drink.

Or a car.

Or a house, maybe.

Without that lazy bastard, Jeff might never have discovered that he was still in love with Samantha Marconi. He would have gone through the rest of his life without her. Feeling only half-alive.

No doubt about it, he owed that clerk a huge debt.

He snatched a beer out of his refrigerator, then turned to look at the gleaming, spotless kitchen behind him. Not hard to be kept gleaming, since there was so rarely any life in it.

"Not like Sam's place," he thought aloud and his gaze slid to the wide swath of counter space. Just remembering taking Sam on her kitchen counter had him hungry and needy all over again. How had he ever convinced himself that marrying Cynthia was the right thing to do? When had he begun to believe that companionship, affection, were enough to build a life on?

Emma's face rose up in his mind and he smiled. His daughter. Sam's daughter. They'd be together. As they should have been from the very beginning. He wondered briefly what kind of family they'd have had by now if he hadn't been a moron and his mother hadn't interfered. If she hadn't stolen nine years of his and Sam's lives.

He took a long pull on the dark brown bottle, then lifted it in a toast. "Here's to me, Mother. I finally beat you. I'm finally going to have the woman I should have had all those years ago. And I hope you're spinning in whatever hell you landed in."

When the doorbell rang, he carried his beer with him as he walked through the too-quiet condo. Soon enough, this place would be sold. He already had a drooling real estate agent working on the details.

He'd have to commute at least a couple of days a week into the city to handle work. But his life, his *love*, would be in Chandler. He was happy, for the first time in nine years. And for the first time in way too long, he knew he was doing the right thing.

Sunlight streamed through the wall of windows

overlooking San Francisco. In the distance, the Golden Gate Bridge gleamed a dull orange against the backdrop of a cloud-studded sky. Far below, on the city streets, traffic hummed and surged like a growling beast.

Still smiling to himself, Jeff opened the door—and took a solid punch to his abdomen.

"Dammit, Sam!" Bent in half, he clutched one hand to his stomach and kicked the door shut as she stomped past him.

"You son of a bitch!"

"What the hell are you doing?" He stared at her in cautious amazement. Even from across the room, her pale blue eyes sparked with a dangerous temper he remembered way too well.

Was this really the woman he'd left a few hours ago, warm and naked in a bed?

She was pacing feverishly, her boots smacking rhythmically against the hardwood floors, then muffled as she hit the area rugs. Her jeans were worn and faded, her T-shirt splattered with flecks of yellow paint, and her mouth was set in a grim slash that worried him considerably. Jeff had been on the receiving end of Sam's temper too often to take it lightly.

Hell, she'd already hit him and was even now, he was sure, glancing around the room looking for something to throw at his head. "What's going on?"

"Like you don't know."

"Not a clue, babe."

"Don't call me babe."

"No problem." He lifted both hands, remembered his beer, and took a long swig.

"You son of a bitch."

"Huh?" he asked. "What the hell are you talking about?"

"You know damn well what I mean." Her eyes snapped and sizzled as she stalked toward him and stopped just a couple feet short of being within striking distance.

Small favors.

"Sam, I don't have a clue what's going on."

She glared at him, but he didn't back down. Hell, he didn't mind letting her take a shot or two at him when they were in the middle of an argument. But he'd be damned before he'd let himself be a punching bag without even knowing the reason *why*.

Damn, she looked good. Even in a fury, she was a woman who could stop a man's heart. Color flooded her face and the danger in her eyes only made her more exciting. More *amazing*.

How had he managed to live so long without her?

"*Cynthia* came to see me this morning."

"What? Why?" A prickle of warning slithered along his spine.

"*Worried?*" She snarled the question in a deceptively soft voice.

"Should I be?" Judging from the flash of pure, undiluted rage glittering in her eyes, he figured the answer was yes. Then he looked deeper and saw more than temper. Something deeper, more painful, and a kernel of panic rooted in his guts.

"You tell me." She folded her arms across her chest, tipped her head to one side, and studied him as if he were a less-than-interesting bug on a microscope slide.

Okay, clearly she was pissed and hurt and had decided he was her target, but before the flame war kicked in, he wanted to know exactly what he'd done.

"Why did she go to see you?" he asked tightly. And even as he asked it, his brain galloped, trying to find a reason for Cynthia to confront Sam. But he couldn't.

"Just what I wondered," Sam snapped and moved suddenly, stepping close enough to drill her index finger into his chest.

He snatched her hand and held it. Staring down at her, he watched emotions flicker across the surface of her eyes, each chasing the other, with pain the only constant. "What'd she say to you?"

"What *didn't* she say?" Sam pulled her hand free and bunched her fist. "Why don't I start out small and end with the *real* kicker?"

"Start anywhere you want," Jeff muttered, never taking his eyes off her. "Just start."

"Fine. She told me all about how you two have *discussed* the problem of *me.* She told me how 'awkward' it was for you to have me hanging around. To have to deal with me over Emma."

"She what?" Warning bells clanged in his brain again, but it was like hearing the hurricane-warning siren just as the wind snatched your house off the foundations. Way too late. Sam was on a tear and she was unstoppable.

"You heard me. What was last night, Jeff?" she demanded, getting right in his face. Tipping her head back, she glared up at him and Jeff felt her fury, her hurt, reach out to strangle him. "What was that? A mercy screw?"

"Sam—"

"A goodbye boink from the ex-husband?"

"Dammit, no." He set his beer bottle down on a glass-and-chrome table and turned back to her. "And we're *not* 'ex,' remember? Still married."

"Not for long," Sam muttered thickly and reached into the back pocket of her jeans. Whipping out the signed divorce papers, she threw them at him and snarled, "There. Signed, sealed, and delivered."

"I don't want them. I want you."

She choked out a laugh that scraped against her throat and brought unwelcome tears to her eyes. "Right. You want me. As much as you want Cynthia and the *baby* she's carrying?"

"Baby?" Jeff staggered a step or two, then caught himself. Fury hummed around Sam like a force field. And damned if he wasn't starting to feel it, too. "What baby?"

"See?" she snapped. "That was *my* question. When I got my voice back," she added.

"Cynthia told you she's pr—"

"Oh please, don't make this worse by trying to *deny* it. Cynthia told me how you wanted to keep it a secret from Emma. But you should have told *me*. You should have stayed *away* from me, dammit."

He heard the pain in her voice and it tore at him. Jeff didn't even know what to say to this. Hell, he'd never expected— Instantly, he drew up short and his brain kicked into high gear. *Pregnant?* Impossible. They were always too careful. And still, the threat of panic clawed at his chest.

"Did you think I wouldn't care?" Sam demanded, splintering his thoughts with the outrage coloring her voice. "Did you think I wouldn't remember what it was

like to be alone and pregnant? Do you think I'd want
that for *any* woman? Even *Cynthia*?"

Jeff reached for her, but Sam was too quick. She
jumped back and away, shaking her head and letting
her eyes spit fire at him.

"Don't you touch me," she muttered darkly.

Stung to the bone, Jeff dropped his hands to his sides,
then reached up and stabbed his fingers through his hair.
What the hell was he supposed to do? This would come
down to his word against Cynthia's, and why the hell
would Sam ever take his word for anything? They'd just
begun to feel their way back to each other and now *this*?

Reaching through the panicked desperation choking
him, he thought back, going over the last few weeks in
a blinding instant, trying to remember if Cynthia had
ever suggested, or hinted, or hell, come right out and
said she was pregnant.

But there was nothing.

And she *would* have told him.

So why did she claim to be *now*? And why go to
Sam with this news? Why wouldn't she come to *him*?

"I don't ever want to see you again," Sam said and
started past him.

He snapped her a look. "Dammit, don't walk away."

She looked at him and the pain in her eyes slashed at
him. He was going to lose her. She was going to walk out
of his life again, and this time there'd be no recovering.

"She's not pregnant," he blurted. "I know she's not."
His mind flashed back over the last several weeks, try-
ing to remember when Cynthia'd last had her period.
She always suffered with them. Cramps, migraines.
She usually took to her bed for days.

When the memory popped into Jeff's head, he wanted to shout. But Sam already was.

"You lying bastard—what were you going to do? Walk out on another pregnant wife? Waltz away to live with me and Emma like that baby never existed? Like you did to me?"

"I didn't know you were pregnant then."

"But you know about Cynthia now, don't you?"

"She's not pr—"

"Why would she lie?"

He laughed shortly, sharply. "Why *wouldn't* she?"

She shook her head as if she hadn't heard him.

"Think about it, Sam," he said, talking faster and faster, knowing their future rested on his ability to get through to her *now*. And the more he talked, the more things began to settle into place. Make sense. "She knows what happened between us. What better way to piss you off than to tell you that *she's* pregnant?"

She scraped both hands across her face and her breathing steadied a little. She shot him a suspicious glance.

The faster he talked, the more it made sense. If Cynthia was looking for a way to drive a wedge between him and Sam, she'd found the perfect way to do it. All he could hope was that Sam would be willing to listen to him. *Believe* him.

"There is no baby." He said it firmly, believing the words, trying to make Sam believe.

"What?"

"Sam, trust me. She just had her period a few weeks ago, and we haven't been together since then. Cynthia's not pregnant—and if she claims to be, then she's lying."

"No!" Her mouth worked, but no words came for a second or two. "She lied about a baby? Why would she do that? Why would she say that if it weren't true?" She shook her head fiercely and her fall of auburn hair whipped around her head. "What kind of woman does that?"

Jeff dragged a breath into heaving lungs. If she was willing to at least admit the possibilities, then he stood a chance. "I don't know," he admitted quietly. "A desperate one? A pissed-off one? All I know is, she *is* lying. I've hardly touched her since I saw you again."

"And I should believe you," Sam retorted, her voice just a tinny thread.

"*Yes.*"

"Because you've been so honest with me in the past, right?"

That kernel of panic was reasserting itself. There'd never been much "bend" in Sam. "Dammit, Sam, I wouldn't lie to you about this."

"Why would Cynthia lie about this?"

"How the hell do I know?" he blurted, throwing his hands wide. "Maybe so that *this* would happen. So you'd be so pissed, you'd walk out of my life forever." She was wavering, so he kept talking, words tumbling out, one after the other. "Dammit, Sam, she probably counted on us doing just what we did nine years ago. Stomping away from each other and never really confronting the issues. She *counted* on us not talking." It all made sense. A weird sort of logic. He sighed. "Don't you get it? She never thought you'd come here. Face me with this."

What was *wrong* with Sam that she desperately wanted to believe him, even *now*?

He bent, snatched up the papers, and gave them a quick look before shifting his gaze back to hers. How could she have trusted him again? How could she have allowed herself to fall right back into old patterns? One touch from Jeff and she was a steaming puddle of goo. One kiss and she was stripped and sitting on a kitchen counter.

That thought just infuriated her all over again and she had to draw a sharp breath before she could fire off every insult she'd spent the drive to the city thinking up.

"Whether she is or not, I'm done with this, Jeff. Cynthia can *have* you. As far as I'm concerned, you're no prize." God, she couldn't stand still. Needed to move. To hit. To throw.

"The red vase," he suggested. "Always hated it."

She shot a look at the table he pointed at and deliberately picked up a fragile *blue* bowl filled with mints instead.

"Sam . . ."

She threw it at the wall and winced in satisfaction as it exploded in a shower of sky-colored splinters.

"Listen to me," he said, his gaze moving over her features like a frantic caress. "I don't want Cynthia. I want you."

He stepped up close and Sam practically vibrated with the temper streaking through her. "Well, get over it, because you can't have me."

"This isn't over."

"Yeah, it is," she said.

"No way, Sam." He moved in on her again, but Sam was determined to keep a safe distance. "Cynthia's trying to split us up. She must have sensed that what I feel for you is too big and she fought back the only way she could think of."

"Even if I believe that, it doesn't mean anything," Sam said.

"How can it *not*?" he demanded.

"Jeff, it shouldn't be this *hard*. Don't you see? If we were meant to be together, it wouldn't be this *hard*."

He shook his head. "No way am I letting you out of my life again."

"You don't get a choice this time, Jeff. Nine years ago, you left me. Now it's my turn." She pulled a shuddering breath deep into her lungs. For God's sake, how had this all gone to shit so fast? How had it gotten even more complicated than it had been at the beginning? *Was* Cynthia lying? Was Jeff?

Did it *matter*?

No. Not anymore.

The ache inside her was all-encompassing now and she was willing to admit that it was done. Over.

She was a big believer in signs. Well, they couldn't be any clearer. This thing with Jeff? It was never going to work out. "Mike was right. You worked me."

"Mike's almost *never* right. And I wasn't *working* you, whatever the hell that means."

She ignored him and felt the first sputter of anger churning up in her gut, drowning the pain in a red haze. "It's my own damn fault."

"If you'll just listen to me—"

But she wasn't. Instead, Sam kept talking, more to herself than to him. "See, despite everything, I still loved you."

"You—"

"Loved," she repeated, meeting his gaze with a grim stare. "Past tense. Trust me, I'm getting over it."

"Christ, Sam, will you just let me—"

"Nine years," she snapped and rode the crest of the building fury within. "I loved you anyway. You left and I loved you. You divorced me and I loved you. You raised my baby and I *still* loved you." Whirling on him, she poked him in the chest with her finger again and wished it were a drill bit. "But I'm over you now, bud. I'm going to do whatever I have to do—*whoever* I have to do—to get over you this time. It's done. Past. Ended. Finito. Hasta la vista, baby."

"This isn't done. What's between us will *never* be done."

"You're wrong," Sam snapped. "Again."

"No I'm not. I didn't lie to you. Cynthia's not pregnant."

"Don't you get it?" she asked, shaking her head. "It doesn't matter. If she's not pregnant, she's still a part of you. Your fiancée." He took a long step toward her. "Come any closer and I swear I'll hit you again."

He advanced anyway. Grabbing her by the shoulders, he held on tight and loomed over her until she was forced to tilt her head back to look up at him. Then she kicked him.

"That hurt, dammit."

"Meant to."

"I didn't have any talks with Cynthia about you," he growled out. "And Cynthia's *not* pregnant."

"Sure, I believe you. You jumped from her bed into mine and then back again. A wonder you don't have whiplash."

"I didn't do that, either." His fingers tightened on her shoulders. "I haven't had sex with her in *weeks*."

She snorted.

"It's true. From the minute I first saw you again, I haven't even thought about another woman." He stared at her, as if willing her to believe him.

And maybe she did.

A little.

But it wasn't enough.

"That's your problem," she said and yanked herself free of his grip.

"And you love me."

"That's *my* problem."

"Sam, if you'd just calm down for a damn second—"

"I'm plenty calm. If I wasn't calm you'd be on the way to a hospital!" She paused, told herself to get a grip, and took a deep breath to help the effort. "We're divorced now, weasel-dog. And so help me God, if you try to cheat me out of joint custody of Emma, I'll sue you for every cent your mother ever had. And I'll fight it out in the courts for years. Even if I have to rob a bank to pay for the lawyers."

"I'm not trying to keep Emma from you. I want *us* to raise her together."

"There is no *us*." Four little words. And they had the power to sap what was left of the temper she'd been feeding for the last couple of hours. On the whole drive into the city, Sam had argued with herself, shouted and screamed her frustration, her hurt, her fury.

Now, it was over.

And she felt . . . empty.

Shaking her head, she walked past him to the door. Opening it, she turned back to look at him. Her heart ached and the bottom of her soul fell out so that misery could sweep in. "Stay away from me, Jeff. Just stay the hell away."

"Sam—"

She left. She didn't trust herself to keep the tears she felt welling up from the depths of her broken heart at bay. Didn't trust herself not to revert to the too-familiar puddle of goo if he touched her again.

Sniffling, she practically ran down the long, carpeted hall to the elevator and reached it, thank God, just as it opened.

And Cynthia stepped out.

Perfect.

She even had perfect timing.

The blonde stared at her as though she were a three-headed goat.

"What are you doing here?" she demanded.

Sam reached out and slapped one hand over the elevator door as it started to close. It opened again and she stepped inside. Turning around, she saw Jeff come up behind Cynthia and Sam forced a tight smile at the gorgeous picture they painted. "Don't worry about it. I'm leaving. Oh. And congratulations on the wedding *and* the baby. You win."

The doors slid closed.

An hour later, Emma jumped up onto the couch beside her mother. "Are we gonna watch a movie?"

"You bet, baby," Sam said and sniffed. "Any movie you want."

"The one with Ariel?"

Sam laughed. They'd already watched *The Little Mermaid* three times together. One more viewing and

Sam would know the dialogue by heart. But it didn't matter. Nothing mattered. She had the situation with Jeff settled. And she had her daughter in her arms.

So why did she want to cry?

"Sure, why not?"

"Are you sad, Mommy?"

"No, honey, I'm not sad." Miserable maybe, but not really sad.

"Papa says that sometimes you have to get sad before you get happy 'cause otherwise how would you know the difference?"

Sam looked down into Emma's serious face and felt her heart turn over. This one little girl was worth anything. Worth the nine years of loneliness, worth the pain of loving and losing Jeff for a second time.

"Papa's a smart man," Sam said, smoothing her daughter's silky hair back from her face. Then reaching out, she picked up the remote and hit the play button.

"I know and he's funny, too." Emma cuddled up next to Sam, snuggling under her arm and sighing as the credits began to roll and the music she loved swelled into the room. "He played games with me until I fell asleep and then he played more games with Grace all night."

"What?" The opening scenes of *The Little Mermaid* filled the screen, but Sam was staring at the top of her daughter's head. "All night?"

"Uh-huh. After the fireworks, we had a sleepover at Grace's house and I got to play with the goats, too. And then we played games, and when I fell asleep, they played more games."

"Games." Papa and Emma spent the night at Grace's house after the fireworks? Papa and Grace were playing "games" all night?

"Uh-huh. Grace says Papa knows *lots* of fun games."

Fun games?

"Oh God." Sam cringed and told herself not to think about it. There were just some images a daughter shouldn't have in her mind.

"Shh, Mommy." Emma leaned in farther. "The movie's starting. Can we have popcorn?"

Chapter Nineteen

Jeff took Cynthia's elbow and propelled her down the hall with more speed than grace. She was forced to take four steps for every one of his since she was wearing those ridiculously high heels that he almost never saw her out of.

Once inside his place, Jeff slammed the door and spun the woman he'd been about to marry around to face him. High color dusted her cheeks, her eyes sparkled with interest—and desire—and he wanted to pick her up and shake her.

She smiled up at him. "Jeff, I've never seen this caveman side of you." She licked her lips. "I like it."

"What the hell's your game, Cynthia?"

Her smile disappeared in a blink. "What are you talking about?" Her gaze shot past him to the closed door and the hallway beyond. "What did *she* say?"

He released her because he suddenly didn't trust himself to *not* give her that shake.

What an idiot he'd been.

As if watching his expression and planning her own actions accordingly, she smiled again. "Jeff, why don't we have a drink and sit down together to talk about . . ." Her voice trailed off as she turned and spotted the shattered remnants of the mint dish scattered across the floor. Whipping around, she said, "*She* did that, didn't she?"

"Sam?" He glanced at the bowl and found himself smiling grimly. Hell, even that nasty temper of hers was at least honest. "Yeah. She broke it."

"That woman is appalling."

"Excuse me?"

"Well, really, Jeff," Cynthia said, her voice smoothing over, her features relaxing. "I don't want to speak poorly of Emma's mother, but—"

Amazing, he thought with a weird sort of admiration. Even now, she was cool, controlled. "Cut the crap, Cynthia."

"What?" Her voice went as cold and sharp as an icicle.

"Sam told me what you said to her."

Cynthia smiled sadly. "You know, she's a woman on the edge, Jeff. She's liable to tell outrageous lies trying to defend her position."

"Funny," Jeff said thoughtfully. "Just what I was thinking about you."

"Excuse me?" One blond eyebrow lifted.

"Why'd you tell Sam you were pregnant?"

She blinked, and just for a second, stunned surprise lit her eyes, but she recovered quickly. "I didn't. I may have hinted that we're both hopeful, but—"

Even caught red-handed she was willing to play it out. He could admire her cool confidence even while asking himself why the hell he had never noticed just how duplicitous she could be. And the longer he watched her, the clearer things became to him. It was as if a blindfold were being lifted from his eyes a quarter inch at a time.

"You told Sam you were pregnant," he said thoughtfully, and continued before she could deny it again. "Knowing our history, you probably figured it was the one perfect thing to say that would get rid of her."

He shifted a look at her, but she was still calling his bluff. Not even by the flicker of an eyelash did she reveal what she was thinking, feeling. Or if she was feeling anything, which he was beginning to seriously doubt. "That's it, isn't it?"

She gave him an indulgent smile. "I don't know what you're talking about."

"Sure you do, Cyn."

She flinched at the shortened version of her name.

"It should have worked," he said, giving the devil her due even while a part of him wanted to kick her ass down the hallway. "You were counting on us repeating history, weren't you?"

She didn't answer. Instead, she walked quietly to the sofa and leaned one elegant hip against the high back.

"You thought Sam would be so pissed that she wouldn't talk to me about it. That we'd *never* talk about it. You figured," he went on, watching her eyes and seeing a flash of acknowledgment there, "she'd get mad, then I'd get mad, and we'd go our separate ways again without once comparing notes. Just like we did before."

Deliberately, she looked away from him, gazing down at her engagement ring, then checking her manicure.

"It was a pretty good plan, Cyn."

"Thank you."

Now it was his turn to be surprised. He hadn't actually expected her to admit anything. "Unfortunately for you, things were different this time. Sam and I were *both* different this time. And now we know the truth."

"Do you?"

Jeff sighed and let go of his last lingering bit of guilt about breaking his engagement to this woman. "Let's be honest, all right? You can keep the jewelry I've given you. The ring's yours. Everything else is, too. I just want the truth."

"Which truth would that be?" Cynthia wondered calmly. "The one where you're making a fool of yourself over another woman while you're engaged to *me*?"

"So that's it?" he asked idly, as temper spiked and dipped within. "Jealousy?"

"You must be kidding." Cynthia chuckled, shook her head gently, and looked at him. "You think *I'm* jealous of your construction worker?"

"What I want to know is why you did it."

"Excuse me?"

"Forget that," he said, waving his words away with one sweeping motion of his hand. "I figure I know why. You wanted to scare her off."

"I only told her what she had to know already." Cynthia stood up, adjusted the fall of her skirt. "That she was making a difficult situation untenable."

"I didn't ask you to do that."

"You didn't *have* to," she countered, just a little desperately. "I was only thinking of you. Of Emma. Of *us*."

"There is no *us*." Something dark and cold pinged inside him as he spoke the words Sam had said to him just a few minutes before. The difference was, he meant them. He only hoped to hell Sam hadn't.

"Of course there's an us," she said, walking toward him, giving him a gentle smile. "We're getting married in less than four weeks."

"You can't seriously still think that." When she lifted her arms to wrap them around his neck, he caught her wrists and took a step back. "The wedding's off."

Her jaw dropped, her eyes went wide with surprise. "You can't do that."

"I just did."

"Well, I won't allow it."

Jeff laughed and sheer fury erupted in the cool blonde's eyes, surprising him with the strength of it. He'd never seen Cynthia display so much raw emotion. He hadn't really believed her capable of it.

"Do you think I'm going to allow you to break this engagement?" Stunned, she opened and shut her mouth a few times, as if she couldn't quite think what to say next, and her breath hitched in her chest. "I won't let you embarrass me in front of my friends. *Our* friends."

"Our friends will get over the shock," he said. "In a couple of months, there'll be something else to talk about."

"You—"

"Besides, you don't have to be embarrassed in front of anyone, Cynthia. You can tell everyone *you* dumped *me*."

She stared at him as though he'd just been dropped onto earth from another planet. It was as if she didn't recognize him at all. And that let Jeff know without a doubt that he was doing the right thing.

God, he felt like he'd just been let out of prison.

"Don't think I won't," she countered, a flush of color rushing to her cheeks. Then she waited as if hoping her threat would make him see the light. Change his mind. When he only smiled at her, she still couldn't accept it. "You're seriously going to throw me over for that paint-spattered *bitch*?"

"Yeah," he said, and grinned. He felt life course back into his bloodstream just at the thought of having Sam as his own again. "I am."

"You bastard." The words came out flat, cold. But the heat in her slap had his head snapping back.

When she drew her hand back to hit him again though, he caught it at the wrist. "I give you that one, because I figure I owe you that much at least. But there's only one woman in this world who's allowed to hit me more than once. And it's not you."

"You son of a bitch."

He nodded. "That seems to be a popular theme today."

"I hate you."

"Probably," he agreed, and steered her toward the door. "Though once you get over your anger, I think you'll agree that we never would have worked out."

She pulled free of his grasp and marched smartly to the door. When she had it open and herself posed dramatically in the doorway, she stopped and looked him up and down in the most dismissive manner she could manage. "If you think I'm going to miss you—or that clumsy brat of a child, you're quite mistaken. I wish you misery with your little goat girl. May you get just what you deserve."

He shut the door so quickly behind her, he was

pretty sure it caught Cynthia on her fairly impressive ass. And he couldn't quite bring himself to care.

He had a wife to win back.

"We can find a hit man," Mike said the next morning, reaching for her coffee cup. "We're Italian. How hard can it be?"

"We don't need a hit man," Jo told her, and grabbed a cinnamon roll from the plate in the middle of the table. "We can break his legs and it won't cost us anything."

"You guys are the best," Sam said and wiped an imaginary tear from her eye. Picking up her latte, she lifted it in a toast to her sisters, took a sip, then set it down again. "Look, I really appreciate all the blood-thirsty support, but keep an eye out for Emma. I really don't want her to sneak up and hear her aunts plotting her father's death."

"Not death," Mike corrected. "Maiming."

"Right. Sorry." Still, Sam shot a look over her shoulder at the front door of the Leaf and Bean. Nope. Still no sign of Emma. Papa'd taken her to the library to get a book on mermaids and there was still no sign of them.

Outside the shop, the bright summer morning was already heating up. Sunlight bounced off storefronts and shimmered off the asphalt, and by noon, everyone in town would be looking for shade and something cold to drink. For now though, the Marconis had a rare Friday off and coffee was the order of the day.

The quiet ripple of conversation from the dozen or more people sprinkled around the room provided just enough background noise to keep the Marconi girls from being overheard.

"So it's over."

Sam looked at Jo. "Seems to be."

"You don't look happy."

"I'm not."

"If you love him that much, fight for him." Mike leaned her chair back onto two legs and rocked. "I don't understand it, but I'll back you."

"No. If he wants that blond bitch, then he can have her."

Jo shot Mike a look and the two of them turned interested gazes on Sam.

"What?" Sam demanded.

Mike shrugged. "It's just that Marconis don't give up that easy and this makes the second time you walked away instead of fighting."

Sam slapped herself upside the head. "Hello? Aren't you the one who was just offering to have him killed?"

"Maimed."

"Right. My mistake."

"Sam," Jo said, giving Mike a glare that should have worried her but instead had her snorting derisively. "You're not happy. What makes you think *he* is?"

"Cynthia said—"

"And you believed the bitch? Why?"

Sam kicked the legs of Mike's chair and smiled when her sister wobbled and had to fight to balance herself. "Because . . ." Her voice trailed off. Okay, there was a reason she'd believed Cynthia. It was . . .

"Uh-huh." More careful now, Mike eased her chair back onto four legs before continuing. "So now you're figuring out that Cynthia had more reason to lie than to tell you the truth?"

"Maybe—"

"And you gave Jeff every chance to explain, right?"
Mike said, laughing.

Sam winced. "He tried, but—"

"And when you gave him the divorce papers, did he
look happy?" Jo prompted.

No, he really hadn't. He'd looked . . . stunned. "Not
especially, but—"

"So then you let him talk and you heard him out
and—"

"Will you shut up? You know damn well I didn't listen to him." Sam shot first Mike, then Jo, furious
glances before she reached for her latte and chugged a
few swallows. The steaming hot milk lit up her throat
and brought tears to her eyes. But at least it was physical pain she could focus on. "I broke a bowl, slugged
him in the stomach, shouted at him, then left him
standing there with Polly Perfection."

"*She* was there?" Mike demanded.

"She got there as I was leaving."

"And you left him there alone with her," Jo said.

"He's *engaged* to her."

"And *married* to *you.*" Mike took a big bite of her
blueberry muffin and shook her head in disgust.

God, Sam's head hurt. She hadn't slept all night.
Every time she closed her eyes she thought about Jeff.
She remembered the stunned look on his face when
she'd told him that Cynthia claimed to be pregnant.
The desperation in his eyes when he'd tried to convince her that the blonde was lying. The hope that had
leaped up in his eyes and then died when she'd told
him she loved him but would get over it.

"God," she muttered, "this so sucks."

"Pretty much," Mike agreed.

Jo slapped the back of Mike's head.

"Hey."

"Well, for God's sake, give it a rest." Turning to face Sam, Jo leaned over and, meeting her gaze, said, "You told him you love him, right?"

"Yeah." Sam picked off a piece of cinnamon roll and tossed it into her mouth. "And I told him that I'd get over it."

Jo smiled. "The point is, you told him."

"Yeah, so?"

"So," she said, "ball's in his court now. Why don't you sit back and see what he does with it?"

Sam thought about it a minute, indulged herself in a few flights of fancy: Jeff storming onto the job site and carrying her off in his arms, or standing on a street corner, shouting his love for her, or even *crawling* back to her on two broken kneecaps to beg forgiveness. That last one she enjoyed the most, until she realized she wouldn't have much respect for a man who did that much crawling anyway.

But then reality crashed back down again and she reminded herself that this was Jeff. He was the calm, cool, rational half of this little duo. And he was no doubt already giving thanks that she'd signed the papers and walked out of his life.

Nope.

Ball in his court or not, nothing would change.

"Okay," Mike said into the silence, as if she knew Sam needed an emotional break. "If you've finished with the hearts and flowers portion of the program, let's talk about the home show."

Sam's eyes widened, she groaned, then leaned over

double and let her forehead smack the tabletop. "I forgot about the Home Show."

"Not surprising with everything else going on," Jo noted.

"It's tomorrow," Sam whined, her voice muffled as she still lay eyeball to glossy surface of table.

"Oh yeah."

She heard the amusement in Mike's voice. "I'm supposed to do a faux-finish painting seminar."

"Right again."

She lifted her head high enough to look at Mike. "You want to do it?"

Mike swung her long blond braid back over her shoulder. "I've got my own deal to worry about, remember? Plumbing for the amateur."

"And I'm explaining simple home repairs," Jo put in as she lifted her coffee cup, "so don't even ask me."

Sam groaned again and sat up.

"Papa's going over there today to finish setting up our booth." Mike pulled a piece of her muffin off and nibbled at it. "He said Grace is going along too. She wants a close look at the other booths to give her ideas, God help us, for her house."

"Grace is going with Papa?"

"Yeah, why?"

"No reason." Sam sighed inwardly and told herself that she had enough to think about. She was just going to stick her head in the proverbial sand over Papa and Grace. The less she knew, the happier she'd be. "Fine. I'll worry about it tomorrow. For now, we've got today off, so I think I'll take Emma to the beach."

"Good plan," Jo agreed. "Why don't we all go?"

"Ready for a refill?" Stevie asked as she walked up to the table carrying a tray loaded with three fresh lattes.

"You're a queen, Stevie," Mike said, reaching for one of the cups. "How'd you know we'd need more?"

"Are you kidding?" Stevie laughed and shifted the tray to a more comfortable position against her hip. "I know my customers. You guys are always good for at least two lattes each."

As she stacked the empty cups on the tray, she looked down at them and asked, "So why are the Marconi sisters going to the beach instead of the library?"

Mike gave her head a shake. "Why would we go to the library?"

Stevie just stared at them. "You guys have *got* to get out more. Haven't you heard?"

"What?" Jo scooted her chair around and looked up.

"People are finding *cash* in the books."

"Cash?" Mike repeated. "Money?"

"Yep," Stevie said, clearly enjoying the opportunity to tell some news. "Tens, twenties, even some fifties."

"I don't get it," Sam said.

"Nobody does," Stevie said. "But the library's been looking like the mall at Christmas for the last few days. Once word spread, the place has been packed. I hear Mrs. Rogan's been chasing people with her ruler."

Mrs. Rogan, who was, at last count, a hundred and ten, had been the town librarian since before God learned how to read. And she wielded her long yardstick like a broadsword in the hands of a knight. Every so often, one of Chandler's kids would get up the nerve to steal the damn thing, but Mrs. Rogan always replaced it.

"Who's putting the money there?" Jo wondered.

"Nobody knows," Stevie said, shrugging. Then as someone on the other side of the room called out for a refill, Stevie turned and lifted a hand in acknowledgment. "Gotta go. You guys want anything else, just call."

As she wandered off, Sam looked at her sisters. "Money in books? Doesn't make sense."

"Oh, I don't know," Mike said, easing her chair back onto two legs to rock again. "Papa always said that 'knowledge is the real wealth.' "

"Cute," Jo muttered.

Mike shrugged. "I try."

Jeff was a man possessed.

Sam's words kept ringing in his ears, driving him, pushing him. *She loves me.* He wouldn't believe it was past tense. Couldn't believe it. If he did, it would kill him. To find her again after all this time, to rediscover the magic of what they'd had, only to lose it again.

No.

He wouldn't let it happen.

Hell, since taking over the family bank, he'd handled hundreds of insurmountable situations. He'd doubled the bank's holdings, made their shareholders rich, and found that, like it or not, he *did* have an innate gift for the business end of things.

If he could do all of that and come out on top, then he could damn sure win Sam Marconi.

And he wouldn't quit until he pulled it off.

Reaching for the phone, he dialed.

When the phone rang, Sam turned and stared at it as though it were a writhing cobra preparing to strike. She set down the bottle of Lysol and tossed the dishcloth to the countertop she'd been busy cleaning, for the tenth time. It didn't matter how often she scrubbed it down, though, the memory of what she and Jeff had done there remained.

The phone rang again and it was as if he were in the room with her. She knew it was him calling. Felt it in her bones. And as the shrill ring bounced off the walls again, it was almost as if she could *hear* him, taunting her. *"Too scared to answer, Sam? Must mean you don't trust yourself to talk to me."*

"Scared, my ass," she muttered and stomped across the room to snatch up the receiver on the fifth ring. "What?"

"Is that the voice you use to frighten telemarketers?" Jeff asked.

"Don't call here." Her fingers tightened on the long, twisty cord, hanging from the old-fashioned blue wall phone.

"Have to if I want to talk to you. And Emma."

"You don't get to talk to me," Sam said, congratulating herself on her restraint. Her calmness. Her absolute indifference to hearing his voice rumble through her body. Until she looked at the cord, tight enough around her hand to cut off the circulation. "Dammit," she muttered and unwound the thing quickly.

"Sam, I—"

"Just a minute, I'll call Emma." She yanked the phone away from her ear, not quite trusting herself to remain strong. "Emma, your daddy's on the phone."

Footsteps, light and quick, sounded out and the little girl raced into the kitchen and crashed into her mother. Grinning her still gap-toothed smile, she reached up for the phone. "Hi, Daddy, do you miss me, I miss you. I went to the beach today and found some seashells and I met Jonas and he let me play with his dog Goliath and can I have a dog too and I'll name her Ariel and we'll play and—"

Sam tried to zone out while Emma chattered in a high-pitched voice filled with excitement. It had been a good day. She and her sisters and Emma had met up with Tasha Candellano and her son Jonas. Tasha was now officially past her baby's due date, and had headed to the beach to get away from her husband Nick's over-powering mother-henning. Sam smiled to herself over the amazing transformation of one of the most deter-minedly single men she'd ever known into a doting husband and frantic father-to-be.

"Mommy says I can have a dog and it can live here and I can visit it whenever I come to see Mommy," Emma was saying, as she shot her mother a quick smile. "But I don't wanna go back to San Francisco, Daddy. I wanna live here with my puppy and you and Mommy and then we can go to the beach all of us and—"

Little dreams, Sam thought as she picked up the bot-tle of Lysol and tucked it away under the sink. All Emma wanted were the things any kid wanted. A mom and dad to love each other. A puppy.

She turned on the hot water tap and washed her hands with a squirt of detergent.

"Okay," Emma said, lowering her voice to what she probably thought was a whisper. "I can. Okay. We're going to a house show tomorrow and Mommy said I can help, so you could too, and then we— *Okay.*"

Sam glanced at her, but Emma had wandered into

the doorway of the living room, where she continued to whisper. "I love you too, Daddy. Okay, I will. Bye."

Emma turned around and walked to Sam, handing her the phone receiver. Then she wrapped her arms around her mother's legs and squeezed.

"Thanks," Sam said, running her hand across Emma's baby-fine hair. "But what's the hug for?"

The little girl tipped her head back and looked up at her. "It's from Daddy," she said. "He wanted me to give you a hug. He said you needed one."

A twinge of something sharp and sweet tore at Sam's heart.

"Did you?" Emma asked.

Sam forced a smile. "I always need your hugs, mouse."

"I *love* you, Mommy."

One short sentence brought Sam to her knees. Wrapping her arms around her daughter, she held her close, inhaling the sweet, summery little-girl scent of her. No matter what else this summer had brought—no matter what pain she might be dealing with in the weeks to come—it had all been worth it.

She'd no doubt be lonely again, as she had been before. She would miss Jeff for the rest of her life and always wonder about what might have been. But there would never again be that soul-numbing emptiness, filled with haunting shadows and desperate cold.

Burying her face in the bend of her daughter's neck, Sam whispered, "Oh baby, I love you, too."

Chapter Twenty

The Home Show was a crowded, noisy, over-the-top showcase for local home-building talent. Every year, Marconi Construction took part in the festivities, and every year, they gleaned new customers and visited with old friends.

Booths lined the huge San Jose Convention Center and those manning the booths were like barkers at a carnival.

"Try this electric drill bit with a light embedded in the tip. No more drilling in the dark . . ."

"With this lamp, you'll only have to replace a bulb every two years, guaranteed, or your money back . . ."

"Why paint when you can *stucco*?"

"Aluminum siding is the 'green' way of building . . ."

"Wallpaper doesn't have to be a chore . . ."

Sam walked the narrow aisle between booths and shook her head at the chance to try out a new circular saw. The crowds were thick and the noise level higher than an elementary school at the start of summer vacation. Plus, over and above the roar of the mob and the shouts of the dealers, came an announcer's voice over a loudspeaker set at a level designed to shatter eardrums.

Ordinarily, Sam loved the Home Show. It was a chance to do the fun stuff and show off a little as she did it. She never failed to wow the crowd when she started demonstrating the varied kinds of faux-finish painting styles. She usually spent lots of time with bored kids being dragged around behind focused parents—and let those same kids vent a little frustration with a paintbrush.

But today, she just wanted to go home.

Hug her misery close.

Ever since leaving Jeff's condo the day before, she'd been going over and over everything. Her heart ached, but her head was clearer now, less fogged by fury, and she could admit that Cynthia'd had more reason to lie than tell the truth. And Jeff had probably been right when he said the woman had no doubt known exactly how Sam would react to such news. And it pissed her off to admit that she'd accommodated the perfect bitch even that much.

Sam shook her head at a man trying to hand her a flyer about roofing specials and remembered instead everything she'd said to Jeff the day before. Not that she regretted any of it or anything. But she kept remembering the look on his face when she'd told him she loved him.

Had it really been a spark of hope in his eyes? Or was she just finding new and unusual ways to torture herself? Safer, she told herself, to hang on to her anger and let the sorrow drain away. She'd be hurt less by temper than regret.

"'Bout time you got back," Mike shouted as Sam stepped up to the Marconi booth. "Jesus, did you go to Brazil and pick the coffee beans by hand?"

"Do you absolutely *have* to talk?" Sam handed her

the carrying tray filled with four cups of steaming hot coffee, courtesy of the Home Show's snack area, set up behind the hot tub and spa display. The coffee was probably poisonous, but any caffeine port in a storm.

Snatching one of the cups for herself, Sam glanced around for Emma.

"Yes, actually, I do." Mike took one of the cups and set the tray aside for Jo and Papa. "Jo's off drooling over the goodies at the True Touch tool booth. But if you're looking for Emma, she's wandering with Papa and Grace."

Sam winced. Papa and Grace. Even having them so close in the same sentence felt a little uncomfortable. But she so wasn't in the mood to think about that today. Besides, what the hell? *Somebody* should be happy.

"Excuse me," a huge woman in a garishly flowered dress said as she tapped Mike's arm. "Do you know where I can find those cute little lamps shaped like dogs?"

"God, no," Mike said, drawing her head back and staring at the woman with a horrified expression.

"They're down at the end of aisle three," Sam interrupted smoothly, shooting Mike a quelling look before smiling at the offended woman.

"Thank you."

As she moved off, Mike said in her own defense, "Well, do I *look* like I have dog lamps?"

Sam laughed and carried her coffee to the far end of the Marconi booth. Here, she had a sheet of primed plywood set up and awaiting her first painting demonstration. She'd brought a dozen of the plywood sheets so that she could keep up the demos for the entire two-day presentation.

She might not be in the mood for it, but she was determined to do a good job. Marconi Construction was always looking for new clients. Even though they'd be tied up with Grace's place for the next two months, there was no harm in having future jobs lined up. And with the hundreds of people wandering through the show, they were bound to pick up their fair share.

Getting busy, she knelt beside the row of neatly stacked paint cans, brushes, sponges, and rollers. She shoved Jeff to the back of her mind, where no doubt he'd still be lingering in ten years. But if her heart was aching, no one else would ever know about it.

Jeff walked into what looked to him like an Arabian bazaar. But he was willing to bet this place was a lot louder. Shouted conversations rose and fell like ocean waves and there was a background hum of machinery whining at the various booths. Thousands of people were crammed into a warehouse nowhere near big enough to hold all of them, and he guessed the fire marshals were going nuts trying to keep a lid on the place.

Trying to find Sam was going to be like searching the shore for a particular grain of sand. But he was a man on a mission.

She loves me.

All he had to do was keep reminding himself of that and he'd find a way back into her heart. Her life. And that was more important than anything.

Stepping into the chaos, he bumped into a big man in overalls, then steered around him, squeezing between kids and parents, darting into gaps in the crowd, and scanning the booths as he passed. The urge to hurry dogged him. Seconds ticked into minutes and the minutes flew.

He felt the urgency pounding inside him and went with it. Nine years gone. Nine years when they could have been happy, making more babies, loving each other crazy. They'd lost too much time together already and he wasn't willing to wait even one more day.

Thanks to talking to Emma last night, he'd known about the Home Show and hadn't wasted precious time going to Chandler first. Maybe this wasn't the best place to be hunting Sam down.

But dammit, he was through waiting.

Jeff's gaze swept the crowd, searching for a familiar face. At this stage of the game, he'd even be willing to catch a glimpse of Mike or Jo. At least then he'd know he was on the right road. "Too many damn people," he muttered.

"Ain't that the truth?" A man beside him grinned and shook his head helplessly as the crowd carried him away, like a feather buffeted by the wind.

Jeff laughed and waved as if saying good-bye to an old friend. Then he ducked his head, hunched his shoulders, and hit the crowd like a three-hundred-pound linebacker sacking a quarterback.

"Can I paint now, Mommy?"

"Sure, baby," Sam said, grinning at her daughter. "You can show these nice people how easy it is to sponge-paint."

A half-dozen people stood around her in a semicircle and watched as Sam tugged a rubber glove onto

Emma's small hand. Then she helped her dip the sea sponge into a paint tray of dark green paint and scrape off the excess against the edge.

"As you'll see," Sam said, addressing the interested faces turned toward her, "sponge painting is so easy, your kids can help you decorate."

"I don't know if that's a plus," someone muttered.

Sam laughed. "Up to you, but my daughter Emma will show you just how creative children can be." Then to Emma, she said, "Go ahead, baby, show these nice people how easy it is."

Eagerly, Emma practically launched herself at the plywood sheet. Since the little girl had already been helping Sam on the job site, she was confident and raring to go. This was her second demonstration of the morning and she was already handling it like a pro.

Carefully, she reached out and pressed the sponge to the flat white surface, then pulled it back. The imprint of the sponge left a delicate, lacy pattern of green paint. As everyone watched, Emma repeated the process two or three times, overlapping and turning the sponge so that the pattern never really repeated, but left the sheet of plywood looking as though it had been wallpapered.

"Well, I'm impressed," one woman said and stepped forward to take one of Sam's business cards. "And you, little one," she added, smiling down at Emma, "are a very talented painter."

"Just like her mother."

Sam froze.

Her smile fell away like a stone dropped into a well.

Turning slowly, she faced Jeff with what she hoped, for the sake of prospective customers, was a civilized expression.

"Daddy!" Emma ran at him, still clutching her paint sponge. Before he could dodge out of the way, Jeff's jeans were decorated nicely.

Small satisfaction, but Sam would take it.

He stepped into the booth as the customers left.

Her stomach jittered and her blood pumped in a frantic rush. "Go away."

"Not until we talk."

"We talked yesterday." Sam bent down, snapped the lid on the paint can, then turned to take the sponge and the rubber glove from Emma.

"No, *you* talked," Jeff muttered, grabbing up a handful of snack bar napkins emblazoned with the words "Hot Dogs and Beer—a Marriage Made in Heaven," and rubbed them across his paint-smeared jeans. Finally, he gave it up and looked at her. "Now it's my turn."

"There's nothing left to be said," Sam said, standing up to look him dead in the eye.

"Well, you won't know that until I try, will you?"

All around them, the crowds shifted and moved, surging through the building like lemmings rushing toward a cliff's edge. They moved as one, winding and meandering up and down the aisles, their voices ever rising to compensate for the noise level.

"Mommy?" Emma took Sam's hand. "Are you mad at Daddy?"

"No, honey," she lied smoothly and gave that small hand a squeeze. "I'm just too busy to talk right now."

Jeff snorted. "You don't look busy."

"Trouble?" Mike strolled up, thumbs tucked in the front pockets of her jeans.

"Not yet," Jeff said, sliding her a glance and hoping

to hell she wouldn't start in on him. A wise man only tried to handle one Marconi woman at a time. "Mike," he said, "I just have a few things I need to say to Sam."

Mike met his gaze for a long minute, then shifted a look at her sister. Sam stood with one hip hitched higher than the other and her arms folded across her chest. She tapped the toe of one boot against the concrete floor in a staccato beat that belied the serene expression on her face.

"Aunt Mike, my daddy came!"

"Yeah," Mike said, clearly making a decision. "I can see that. Why don't you and me go find Papa and Aunt Jo and tell them? I think your mommy and daddy want to talk."

Sam lurched forward, making a grab for her sister and missing. "Mike, don't you leave here."

"Thanks, Mike," Jeff said.

"Don't make me sorry, weasel-dog."

Emma laughed. "Aunt Mike really thinks you're *great,* Daddy."

"Oh man." Mike winced, but kept moving, dragging Emma in her wake. This love business was really way too complicated, she thought and wondered when in the hell she'd gone soft enough to cut the weasel-dog a break.

Sam thought about chasing Mike down to kill her, but there'd be time later. Instead, she faced down the man from her past. "Do we really have to put each other through more of what happened yesterday?"

"There's that warm Italian welcome I've missed so much."

She smirked at him. "I can show you a warm Italian good-bye."

"I've had one of those. I never want another one."

Sam inhaled sharply, deeply, and it didn't help. Her insides jumped and her mouth went dry. Dammit, where were all the customers? Most of the morning, she'd been tortured by people asking inane questions. She'd given demonstrations, pointed out directions to the restrooms, and even turned down a dinner invitation.

Now, all of a sudden, when she most needed a distraction, there was *no one*?

What was up with that?

"I broke it off with Cynthia."

Her head snapped up and she pinned him.

"She admitted that she lied to break us up."

Sam sucked in a shaky breath. "Well, she did a good job of it."

"Don't let her win," Jeff said softly.

His voice, his very nearness, touched something deep inside her and made her want to forget all the pain. Forget being careful. But clearly, her body didn't know enough to protect itself, so it would be up to her brain to handle it. "Don't you get it, Jeff? *Nobody* wins here."

"Doesn't have to be that way."

Her stomach did a quick somersault, then nose-dived to her knees. "It's too late for us. Go back to your girlfriend."

"I don't want a girlfriend," he said. "I *want* my wife."

Too late. Too late. The words echoed over and over inside her, bouncing to the beat of her thundering pulse. Her blood bubbled and boiled in her veins and she could almost feel each one of her cells exploding with want and need. But she couldn't do this. Not again. Couldn't let herself love him only to be slapped down for it. Do it once, it's bad luck. Twice, you're an idiot. Three times, and the guys in white coats would come looking for her.

"I'm not your wife," she reminded him. "Not anymore. I signed your stupid papers, remember?"

"I tore them up."

Oh God. He tore them up. What was she supposed to do now? "I—" She stopped and looked around wildly. She needed something to do with her hands. Needed something to hold. To throw. To twist.

Deep within her, fury warred with misery and strangled the tiny bud of hope that sprouted in the bottom of her soul. She couldn't risk this. Couldn't love him and lose him. Not again. "I can't do this, Jeff. Not again."

A woman stepped up out of the crowd. "Excuse me, but are you going to be giving another demonstration of the faux-suede look?"

"I can show you right now." Eagerly, Sam grabbed the woman and dragged her bodily into the booth. Concentrating solely on the short brunette, she ignored Jeff, ignored her every instinct, and turned to the one thing that had never let her down. Her work.

Jeff quietly simmered for about ten seconds. He had half a mind to grab her, toss her over his shoulder, and race out of the building. But they'd never make it through the crowds.

"Sam," he growled, and paid no attention as the customer gave him a wary look. "Why do you have to be so damn stubborn?"

"It's not stubbornness," she said, without even turning to glance at him. "It's self-preservation."

"Excuse me," the confused-looking woman asked, "but am I interrupting something?"

"Yes," Jeff said.

"No," Sam insisted.

The woman winced, but stood her ground. Clearly, she was siding with Sam on this one. Didn't surprise him. Women, of course, would stick together.

"This isn't finished," he grumbled, glaring at the back of Sam's rock-hard head. Couldn't she see that they belonged together? That fate had smiled on them for a change and had presented them with a shot at what they should have had nine years ago? "Dammit, Sam . . ."

She completely ignored him and that just fired off what was left of his self-control. For God's sake, he'd told her he wanted her. That he'd called it off with Cynthia. That he loved her.

Hadn't he?

Jeff straightened up, frowning.

No.

He hadn't mentioned that one little detail.

Stupid.

He watched her studiously avoiding noticing his existence and knew that making her listen was going to take more than a quiet chat in a dark corner. She was scared—and that shook him. *Nothing* had ever scared Sam Marconi. But he'd seen it in her eyes just a minute ago. He'd watched as she'd fought an internal battle over whether or not to believe. To trust. To take another chance on him.

He couldn't blame her.

He'd let her down before. Sure, they'd both made

mistakes, but he was only in a position to do something about the ones *he'd* made. Jeff wouldn't lose what he'd just found again.

He'd have to find a way to make her listen. Make her hear him.

His gaze frantic, he scanned the crowd, and got an idea. Jumping into the sea of people, he let them carry him toward his goal.

Sam took a deep breath and let it slide from her lungs on a sad sigh. He was gone. It was better that way, she knew it. But dammit, if he wanted her so badly, why hadn't he tried harder?

And just how contrary could she be? she wondered as she set up a private demonstration area. She tells him she doesn't want him, but then is pissed off when he doesn't try harder to do what she told him not to do?

God. Her head was going to explode.

"Honey," the short brunette standing beside her said, "none of my business, but are you out of your mind?"

"What?" She looked up to see the woman smiling at her.

"The guy's clearly nuts about you," she said. "Why not cut him a break?"

"Wish I could," Sam said, and shifted her gaze to the crowd, amazed at just how quickly Jeff had managed to disappear. "But we had our chance."

"Maybe," the woman said, "but if he'd been looking at *me* like that, I wouldn't have let him go."

Sam sighed again. "I didn't *let* him go," she reminded the woman. "He *left*."

"If you say so . . ."

Getting back to business, Sam concentrated on

work. She painted a small section of the plywood board with black glaze. Then she ripped off a big piece of Saran Wrap and laid it over the glaze. Laying her palms over the plastic wrap, she gathered the thin film and pushed out the air bubbles. When she was finished, she peeled off the plastic wrap and left behind a section of paint that looked as if it were actually suede fabric wallpaper.

"Wonderful. Just what I'm looking for in my family room," the woman cooed. "You may not know jack about men, but you're great on the painting end of things."

Sam absently handed over one of their business cards as she thanked the woman and said good-bye. The instant she was alone again, though, Sam's mind returned to Jeff. She looked across the crowd, and told herself she was an idiot to think he'd hang around. She'd sent him on his way. Told him thanks but no thanks. Of course he'd leave. Jeff had never been a man to make a scene. He wouldn't want to have it out with her here.

Hell, she was surprised he'd even shown up at the Home Show. Too many people. Too much risk of embarrassment. Too *public* for a Hendricks.

"Excuse me!"

A deep, familiar voice shouted over the loudspeaker and Sam's heart leaped up to lodge in her throat.

"Hello?" Jeff's voice came again, even louder this time, and the crowd began to quiet instinctively. Low murmurs of conversation rippled, but mostly the sounds of "Shhhh . . ." could be heard.

"Thanks," he called out as the silence deepened.

"Oh God," Sam whispered, moving out of her booth

to stand at the end of the aisle, where, over the heads of the people in front of her, she could see him standing center stage. His dark blue shirt looked a little rumpled, his jeans carried Emma's green paint like a badge of honor, and his gaze swept the crowd, searching, she knew, for *her*.

"Hate to interrupt everything," Jeff was saying, clutching the microphone and stalking back and forth across the front of the stage like a demented emcee, "but I need to talk to my wife and this is the only way I can think of to make her listen."

"Hey," a man from the crowd shouted, "if it works for you, I'll give it a try!"

His wife slapped his arm and laughed along with everyone else.

Sam just shook her head and tried to disappear into the throng. But suddenly, her family was standing right behind her and she had nowhere to go.

"No use hiding," Jeff shouted, as he spotted her. Pointing one finger at her, he said, "Sam Marconi, I *love* you."

She sucked in a gulp of air and ducked her head. Eagles soared in her stomach and her knees wobbled hard enough to make her reach out and grab hold of a display table bearing samples of lawn mulch.

"Yeah," Jeff said, keeping his gaze locked on the only woman who'd ever mattered in his life. "I love you, Sam. Always have. Should have told you before—"

"Yes," a woman in the crowd called out. "You should have!"

Everyone laughed again and the sound rolled back

and across the sea of people like a tidal wave, picking up speed and power as it moved.

"But I'm saying it now," Jeff went on, words racing out of his mouth in his effort to make her hear. Make her believe. "And if you'll let me, I'll say it every day for the rest of our lives."

"Atta boy," someone shouted.

"Gotta give it to the weasel-dog," Mike murmured. She let go of Emma's hand and the little girl scampered through the crowd toward the stage. "He gets an A for effort on this one."

Jo said, "Looks like he means it."

"Maybe," Sam whispered, not paying any attention at all to the faces turned toward her. All she could see was Jeff. His eyes. The love on his face. Oh, she wanted to believe. But still, stubbornness kept her in place. A wary sense of disbelief glued her feet to the floor.

"Sam," Jeff said, his voice deepening into a rough whisper that bounced off the walls and reverberated deep inside her. "I was wrong." He paused and let that last word sink in. "I was wrong about everything."

Sam's breath hitched.

His gaze locked with hers. "Wrong not to trust you. Not to believe in us. I was wrong to walk away. And I've *paid*. For nine years, I've lived without you—and I don't want to go another day without seeing you, holding you, loving you."

"Oh God." Sam's voice came on a sigh.

"Wow," Mike said. "Color me impressed."

"He loves you." Papa's voice. Right behind her. Gently, he pushed her forward, and as she started walking, she heard Grace say, "It's about time."

Sam's heart felt full enough to break through the wall of her chest. Every step was slow, tentative, but she was drawn on by the sound of Jeff's voice.

"I can't stand to wake up one more morning without you, Sam," he said, his voice thick, rough with emotion. "I can't live without you."

Tears blurred her vision, but she kept walking as the crowd parted to let her pass. Her gaze locked with Jeff's, she watched him smile.

Still holding the microphone tightly, and speaking only to her, he said, "I love Emma more than anything in the world, Sam. But even if we'd never had her, I would still want to be with you." He looked deeply into her eyes. "Still *need* to be with you."

Sam believed.

She really believed. Tears erupted in her eyes just as the crowd's muttered approval began to swell and grow.

When she reached the edge of the stage, Jeff dropped the mike and jumped down to stand beside her. Cupping her face in his hands, he whispered, "Marry me again. Love me. Let me love you. God, I love you so much, Sam. Only you. *Always* you."

"What'd he say?" someone in the back of the crowd shouted.

Sam laughed through her tears and smiled up at him.

Jeff wiped those tears away gently. "You never cry."

"Happy crying," she assured him.

"So I can take this as a yes?"

She reached up and cupped his cheek in the palm of her hand. Finally, she was sure. No more doubts. No more worries. No more haunted memories or lonely dreams. Here was everything she'd ever wanted.

Here was love.

And so much more.

Nodding, she stared at him through teary eyes and said, "I love *you*, Jeff. Always have. Always will."

He grinned and her heart jumped into life.

"Just what I wanted to hear." Drawing her close, he wrapped his arms around her and kissed her hard and long.

Over the cheers of the crowd, someone shouted, "What'd she say?"

Emma grinned at her parents, picked up the microphone and said softly, "She said *yes*."

Watch for

Mike's Story: A Crazy Kind of Love

Coming in January 2005 from St. Martin's Paperbacks

Watch for

Lost In
Sensation

by
Maureen Child

Coming from Silhouette Desire in October 2004

LIS 03/04

#1 BESTSELLING AUTHOR
MAUREEN CHILD

FINDING YOU

Carla Candellano has faced a tragedy she'd like to put behind her, but no one has been able to penetrate the wall she has built around herself—until she meets six-year-old Reese Wyatt. Reese hasn't spoken since her mother died last year, and it's friendship at first sight for Carla and little Reese. But it's the girl's worried father, Jackson, who arouses Carla's curiosity, and passion, in ways she never imagined…

"An absolutely wonderful contemporary romance. A delightful blend of humor and emotion, this sexy love story will definitely keep readers turning the pages."
—Kristin Hannah, author of *Distant Shores*

"Heartwarming, sexy, and impossible to put down… Maureen Child always writes a guaranteed winner, and this is no exception."
—Susan Mallery, author of *Married for a Month*

ISBN: 0-312-98920-2

**AVAILABLE WHEREVER BOOKS ARE SOLD FROM
ST. MARTIN'S PAPERBACKS**

FY 2/03

#1 BESTSELLING AUTHOR
MAUREEN CHILD

KNOWING YOU

Ever since Stevie Ryan was a young girl, she was in love with her best friend Carla's older brother Nick Candellano. But Nick had to complicate things by growing up gorgeous—and breaking Stevie's heart. Now she's convinced that forgetting him is the way to go. And it's working out fine…until she and Nick's brother, Paul, spend one sultry night together. Has the right brother been under Stevie's nose all along?

"Maureen Child infuses her writing with the perfect blend of laughter, tears and romance. Her well-crafted characters, humor, and understanding of what it means to be part of a family makes each of her novels a treat to be savored."

—Jill Marie Landis, author of *Magnolia Creek*

ISBN: 0-312-98920-2

**AVAILABLE WHEREVER BOOKS ARE SOLD FROM
ST. MARTIN'S PAPERBACKS**